Also by Ian Hopkins

Skelp the Aged (with John Duignan), Pegasus 2016

Stage Plays:
Citizen Singh (with Gurmeet Mattu); *Every Bloody Sunday* (with Gurmeet Mattu); *Albatross Soup* (with John Duignan).

Radio:
Naked Radio;
Six of the Best

Television:
Not the Nine o' Clock News;
Three of a Kind; Naked Video;
Spitting Image

Writing in progress:
A Glutton-Free Diet – a satirical novel set at the time of the Scottish 1979 referendum. A screenplay about Thomas Muir, the 'father of Scottish democracy. The final part in the Mungo Laird trilogy after Skelp and Buick – working title 'It Hurts But We Need the Money' (with John Duignan)

Also by John Duignan

Fiction:
Skelp the Aged (with Ian Hopkins) Pegasus 2016
Saving the Last Dance (Kindle)
Katherine Black Doesn't Dance (Cider Apple Press/Kindle)
Things To Do When The Music Stops (Cider Apple Press/Kindle)

Non-fiction:
Quantitative Methods for Business Research (Cengage, 2014);
Dictionary of Research Methods for Business (Oxford University Press, 2016)

Stage play:
Albatross Soup (with Ian Hopkins)

Radio:
(with Ian Hopkins) Naked Radio;
Six of the Best

Television:
(with Ian Hopkins) Not the Nine o' Clock News

The Buick Stops Here

John Duignan & Ian Hopkins

The Buick Stops Here

Pegasus

PEGASUS PAPERBACK

© Copyright 2017
John Duignan and Ian Hopkins

The right of John Duignan and Ian Hopkins to be identified as
author of
this work has been asserted by them in accordance with the
Copyright, Designs and Patents Act 1988

A CIP catalogue record for this title is
available from the British Library

ISBN-978 1 910903 09 4

*Pegasus is an imprint of
Pegasus Elliot MacKenzie Publishers
Ltd.* www.pegasuspublishers.com

First Published in 2017

**Pegasus
Sheraton House Castle Park
Cambridge CB3 0AX England**

Printed & Bound in Great Britain

Acknowledgments

Gordon Kirk, Jean Kirk, Alec Gardiner, Graeme Hyslop, Michael Duignan and Margaret Duignan read an early draft and commented both critically and extensively. Their contribution is gratefully acknowledged by Ian and John. They are in no way responsible for any remaining weaknesses in the content.

We should also like to thank all the staff at Pegasus who helped us but particularly Claire-Rose Charlton in both marketing *and* production and Suzanne Mulvey our commissioning editor for her strong belief in us from her word go for both our novels. (Also the *high heid yins* at Pegasus who sanctioned the generous 'entertainment allowance' (for wine and one soft drink) for our first novel's initial launch at Waterstone's Sauchiehall St. Glasgow – an audience of 100 plus again eagerly awaits a similar munificence second time around…)

Dedication

To Gordon Kirk, for invaluable advice and encouragement (not for the first time), and to our families.

Prolegemnon Preloggemanon: An introductory wee word about The Buick Stops Here 23

The Buick Stops Here 25

Part 1: The homecoming 27

Chapter 1: Touchdown (and lift off)....................29

Chapter 2: Déjà vu for the second time...........................34

Chapter 3: Lang may your rum leak...............................40

Chapter 4: Indeed: it's no' fair so it's no' – it's *The System* 44

Chapter 5: The start of the Walk – A Long Day's Journey and a half...48

Chapter 6: Goodbye to Gdansk – and dropped quote marks 52

Chapter 7: Assignation in a sick nation 55

Chapter 8: Ahead of the curve or round the bend...........59

Chapter 9: Frenchie...63

Chapter 10: Mungo finally does the (first) business with Meg...68

Chapter 11: Visiting time – not yet: nae rush 72

Chapter 12: Intolerance and *Skelp the Aged* 80

Chapter 13:The Turnip Prize 86

Chapter 14: At last, Mungo makes for the Queen Mary and Ethel (no relation) 89

Chapter 15: Doppelganger on my shoulder and nae big bright moon above..99

Chapter 16: Later: Home is the sailor... getting closer to the hospital 101

Chapter 17: Mungo meets Albie...................................104

Chapter 18: The hospital at last – reflections in glass double doors..112

Chapter 19: Reveille for the reviled.............................117

Chapter 20: Carnival relations.....................................120

Chapter 21: Another chapter in the same recovery space 126

Chapter 22: A forgotten project, *pro tem*......................130

Chapter 23: Good news: Bad news: Worse news?.......132

Chapter 24: Some days in the life of a turf accountant.139

Chapter 25: Joint enterprise (see Supreme Court's recent ruling on this: Feb, 2016; what a farce, milud). 144

Chapter 26: Emissions complaint – not compliant........148

Chapter 27: My old friend, the booze. 153

Chapter 28: Reflections in a golden puddle (or on the back of a shiny coat 156

Chapter 29: Men and manopause................................162

Chapter 30: Philosophy versus Common Sense 164

Part 2: The not so gentle touch 171

Chapter 31: The whims of the father. 173

Chapter 32: Then she went to open the shoap and lo, it stood agape. 179

Chapter 33:*'L'enfer, c'est les autres'*... family members particularly 183

Chapter 34: Here comes the son 185

Chapter 35: Applied arithmetic and delegation 200

Chapter 36: And they're off! 203

Chapter 37: Three wise punters: well, one and Nearly, one other..211

Chapter 38: Mungo's muddled mingling.......................215

Chapter 39: Poleaxed..221

Chapter 40: Polish entry – pre-Brexit. 223

Chapter 41:More work in progress … 225

Chapter 42: Pontificating punters 231

Chapter 43: Short commoners 236

Chapter 44: A wish called Fonda 241

Chapter 45: Roll up, up (not for smoking) 245

Chapter 46: The evening of reckoning. 247

Chapter 47: Coma toes. 249

Chapter 48: How Mungo met Mourinho. 253

Chapter 48(B): A vow of atoning silence.....................257

Chapter 49: The heavy squad 259

Chapter 50: Uncle Richard and Great Aunty Binty and the great big hickory-shafted sledgehammer 263

Epilogue 1: The explanation explained 269

Epilogue 2: Idris Redux: with one limp they were free ..275

APPENDICES 278

[A NOTE ON THE TREATMENT OF SQUARE BRACKETS []: Generally, text within square brackets may be treated as *optional* as the content will not appear in the final examination]

Prolegemnon Preloggemanon: an introductory wee word about *The Buick Stops Here*

In the prequel Skelp the Aged, the septuagenarians Mungo and Ethel Laird were last seen happily ensconced and invariably suffused with the afterglow attendant upon the consumption of Buckie-coladas – very nice with the local sardines – in their new abode in the Algarve. Their escape from the clutches of various financial predators resulted in nine Portuguese months of near bliss.

However, for reasons beyond the ken of the Lairds' medical knowledge, Ethel has become poorly, with a painfully tender gut, side and lower back. Despite her not having a single prejudiced bone in her body (not even that wee stapes thing in her ear – for she will not hear a word against furriners) – yes, despite this, no foreign hand will be laid on her unless that hand is propping up the good old NHS.

Mungo, sees this as a timeous diversion from the little matter of being well behind in paying back the last sharks (Atlantic Ocean Finance) to bail them out, tide them over, keep them afloat, whatever… Something will turn up back in Alba (he refused to use the term 'Blighty' out of sheer patriotism or being unsure how to pronounce words with 'gh' in them). History has shown that he has form with financial affairs. Yes, the more he ignores the problem, the more certain he is that something will turn up. It always has in the past. And so to Borrfoot!

Vamos!

Gravitational waves and the chronology of the buik – an explanation

It is common to assert that Einstein first predicted gravitational waves – 'ripples in the fabric of spacetime'[1]. But more accurately they are a consequence of his *field equation* (e.g. Penrose, 2004). When we first started out writing the sequel to *Skelp the Aged*, gravitational waves had not been detected – they existed only in theory. For much of his adult life – and before – Mungo Laird had experienced disorienting 'events', that we now understand could have been explained by 'ripples in the fabric of his spacetime'; but man of science that he is, he would have realised that these would not have constituted sufficient proof of their existence to lead to a Nobel Prize. And so we set out to capture the next period in his life with some confidence that the time-line of the key events in this life would follow a more or less linear form, in which, for any given week, Tuesday comes after Monday and before Wednesday. But then a strange thing happened, that at first we could not explain: one of the chapters moved itself on the table of contents; what is now Chapter 29 – for the moment anyway. **(No need to seek it out: we dumped it... eventually!)** This happened sometime in September of a previous year. Then all became clear; in February of this year (2016 atow), scientists announced that they had detected gravitational waves. But here's the killer: *they had actually been detected in September 2015, which coincided with what was, but is no longer, Chapter 29, moving on the Table of Contents!* If only we had thought about it at the time. Anyway, this is an elliptical way of saying that if when reading this work, you get the occasional sense that there is a right good ripple in your spacetime continuum, well you now know the reason. Or not.

---

[1] *Effectively the stretching and contracting of Space and Time from the collision of super-massive bodies such as black holes.*

The Buick Stops Here

Being Volume Two: the sometimes reliable memoirs of Mungo Ballantyne Usher Laird - gentleman boulevardier (or, *A history of psychiatry in several pairts*).

Part One

The homecoming

Chapter 1

Touchdown (and lift off)

So. When the emergency arose – running short of walking-about cash and the little matter of Ethel's medical something-or-other – and it was determined that we would need to return to Glasgow from the Algarve, it was by the goodwill and enterprise of my factotum, Mourinho, that we secured a pair of airline tickets at rates that were so low, that even we, having spent our winter-fuel allowance (a new parasol for the terrace), could afford them. And without further ado, we found ourselves in premium class and looking forward to the eleven-hour journey from Faro to Glasgow. The only other passengers were a group of males in full Special Forces night gear, one of them having a hood over his head and tied at the neck. Probably a stag party heading for Polski, with the diffident groom in the hood.

To say that we had never heard of Legion Air, would be to dwell on the inessentials in modern transport. Anyway, where else for fifty-seven zlotys (for two, returns) would you get to see Srebrenica, Kosovo, Tirana, Rzeszow and Bodrum on one trip? It was a night flight, we were strongly advised (some would say, physically restrained) against exiting the plane (top-of-the-range неломающийся), the cabin lights were off (the bulbs had been removed on an earlier mission it seems) and we were asked to keep quiet (gags available on request).

On one occasion we were parked (if that is the correct aeronautical term) in what appeared to be a field of beetroots, while the white goods that took up most of the cabin space were 'dis-loaded', the term used by Jason our purser. There was a brief sortie into what we assumed was crop-spraying over an unidentified country with lots of sand, illuminated by

29

the spotlights of many Toyota 4x4 gun-carriers (emissions compliant).

The only brief moment of doubt came when, just before take-off – actually we were trundling down the tarmac at close to V1 (aeronautical term for speed at which it's now or never!) – there was a tannoy announcement asking if anyone had an old school atlas on them, or even an AA guide to Europe or even – at a push and a last resort – a working Satnav with a male voice.

That was resolved, and we were good-to-go, though once in the air Ethel asked, 'Mungo, shouldn't they have taken us through the emergency drill that everyone ignores?' I pointed out that it would be quite difficult for the crew, given the biohazard suits they all wore (with the exception of Jason); at that she nodded her great head sagely and cracked open our first duty-free Buckie of the day.

As for Jason, when he came around with the cheese toasties – he apologised that the barbecue wouldn't light – at first I found it a bit off-putting that he wore a string vest above very fetching seersucker pantaloons. To a lesser degree, I was discomfited by the fact that his arms from fingertip to shoulder were covered in a gentian-violet solution. I naturally assumed the worst: that he had impetigo at worst or gingivitis at best. Who among us of our generation has not had an upper-lip encrusted with those suppurating turpi scabie (scabs) that scream for attention; and which caused mothers everywhere to keep their children from playing near me for the next few years? Whether that damaged forever one's social skills, not to mention the deep psychological scar imprinted on one's soul, is for each one of you to determine in the solitude of some darkened room. On a brighter note, I should point out that ours was non-bullous impetigo – I fear that Jason's was the other sort, or indeed, the unmentionable, some would say, unforgiveable, gingivitis.

ANYWAY, within minutes of engaging Jason in conversation, I felt myself blush for thinking the worst of the dear young man and his gentian limbs, for he was quick to ease my fears: before becoming 'air-crew' (technical term for stewardess), Jason had worked in a circus where he tended the elephants, among which duties was included administering enemas when the great pachyderms were irregular in their bowel movements. At one moment I thought I caught him measuring up Ethel, but that could have been a trick of the light coming from the ack-ack as it burst harmlessly outside our craft. Unfortunately, Jason's skin reacted to this (not the ack-ack, the elephant business), and so it was with great sorrow that he had to give up show business.

With which explanation – which also neatly accounted for the seersucker pantaloons and the string vest – I was then happy to accept the toastie, which I washed down with a free glass of a paraffin-based spirit, that took the edge off my hunger (and the roof off my palate).

[A fuller account of this trip is currently being considered by a moderator on TripAdvisor. But to give a hint of my review of Legion Air, it got ***** stars, as did the cabin crew – including the driver who eventually found Glasgow by literally flying under the radar. How we escaped the public health officials and the SWAT team is for another time].

'Hell's teeth!' Mungo expostulated as he woke with a start. Phew that was a bit near the suspension of disbelief line, he thought, wiping his brow with Ethel's sleeve – she was sleeping soundly despite having participated in the background to the dream. Then, 'Oh Sweet Jesus save us,' he offered in prayer and in panic, as the lovely flight attendant in the navy blue uniform bent to inquire solicitously if she could flog him something. *Ryanair!* Mungo strove to get back to his dream before they landed and were charged for having to get off the plane and for use of the steps they would need unless they fancied the drop (*dreep*, Sc.).

Mungo (and Ethel – without whom he'd be an innocent abroad) had had a recent scare on their travels. For reasons that need not concern us, whilst on a jaunt to Lisbon from their Algarve bolt-hole, they'd taken a 'taster cruise' of a few days. What a nightmare: first they discovered within an hour of casting-off (nautical term) that the buggers did not offer Buckie. After a long disquisition with the *sommelier* (Francis from Goa), it was decided that Wolf Blass was the nearest

31

equivalent to their drink of choice (no need to add Benylin for that subtle flavour), BUT AT $35 PER BOTTLE!

To which they expressed their opinion rather forcefully and they were put ashore. In the days and nights following that, Mungo and Ethel had nightmares in which the image of Géricault's daub, *The Raft of the Medusa* featured large. For copyright reasons we have not reproduced Géricault, instead we have commissioned an artist's reconstruction of that infamous episode on the high seas of the Western Med on the next page.

THE WOLF BLASS NAVAL ENGAGEMENT (ARTIST'S IMPRESSION)
↳ (NOT TO SCALE)

Chapter 2

Déjà vu for the second time

So. Back in Borrfoot, the cradle of Mungo Laird's soul, the fountain well of his wisdom, the footbath of his polymathimism. At the airport, Ethel and Mungo were greeted by Tim and Idris Waters[2] (the Wattersessess), their only indigenous friends, who were now the owners of what had once been Villa Laird. Idris – she was working her second taxi shift – took Ethel directly to the hospital as she, Ethel, was eager to offer a critique of the service that awaited her. Tim took Mungo back to Villa Idris, by bus (McGills – good service, Big Sandy) where he needed a hand with the buckets in the roof space.

For a moment, Mungo did feel a bit ill at ease within himself, that he had not gone with Ethel to the hospital. But by the force of his steel-trap brain, he quickly forgot about it; a ploy that had served him well in the past for abnegating any vestiges of what some 'experts' term guilt. Ho-hum, he said, and that was enough. Conscience clear.

To see what they are up to and what they are thinking and saying about world events, we will join Mungo and Tim in the loft, where, as well as the smell of burnt toast, starling-crottes-miasma and little fluttering creatures of indeterminate phylogeny, there was tension in the air between them.

The tension between Mungo and Tim lay like a thick cloud of fog on the Tyne; like a damp cat's blanket over a hen coop; like when a million wildebeest on the Serengeti first detect among them the musk of a lion (which is a wee bit like toasted cheese without a pickle). The tension, we say, was like a billion-volt (10^9 v) cable stretched across the Beauly Firth

---

[2] *Actually their name was Walters, but they were so peed-off at people slurring their name they just went along with it.*

when the tide is out and those killer whales from Iceland don't know what awaits them (wait till the Japs get them on the slab, chortle, chortle). This palpable tension, Mungo didn't notice and he set about his task with his usual admixture of enthusiasm, incompetence as well as a soupçon of insouciance – which never goes wrong when there's tension around.

When he set his mind to a task such as this today – they were emptying the buckets that gave a veneer of water-tightness to the property – Mungo was relentless (for a wee while at least); and like one of those funny people on a wee island next to Arran (good golf, by the way), who all seem to be called Sammy Ling, he entered a state of auskörpererfahrung (dwam in Scots; effete inefficacious condition in English): his mantra was simple: the buckets are all. The buckets are all; I am the bucket; the bucket is within me; I am the bucket; peace be the bucket; I am the bucket. I feel like a bucket; I shall have a bucket starting with a Buckie and turning it and its successors into a RIGHT GOOD BUCKET.

Mungo at this stage in his developmental self-awareness, believed that if he really got going there was a chance that he would achieve transcendental bliss, oneness with the One, serenity, even Nirvana or at worst an Ethel-free Zone or Zen.

It drove Tim pure mental.

But Tim, being husband and bedfellow (most nights) of Idris, chatelaine of ex-Villa Laird, concentrated on the task in hand which was to empty buckets and, if need be, place recruits under suspected future leaks based upon the BBC weather forecast – in which latter respect, it shows that Tim was still in a state of innocence. [We disdain to even comment on those posturing weather people – with the exception of Carol Kirkwood, who, though the Doris Day of climatology, is in danger of falling into the trap of hubris. But these issues, and more will be addressed by a submission Mungo is preparing for the renewal of the BBC Charter. They will not know what hit them.]

ANYHOW:

Mungo, his face beatific as he chanted his mantra, reached for the overflowing bucket (number twelve and the day was still young) and tied it to the rope before carefully lowering it towards the troubled countenance of Tim. The rainwater lapped, and slurped, mocking Mungo's pain – both physical aches and mental anguish – well sometimes the mantra is not quite tuned-in (imagine BT Broadband).

'Sorry aboot this, Mungo. It's this knee. Ah never know when it'll go...'

Mungo assumed that it *could well be* the weather, more specifically the rain that caused the increase in the severity of the *possible* pain in Tim's wonky patella. So now Tim was *apparently* unable to climb the Ramsay-ladder to the attic to empty the overflowing fifteen buckets. Three left. Still Tim did assist in the four bedrooms the floor below, emptying them into the top bathroom sink and returning the buckets up to a puffing, aching Mungo, trying very hard to be sympathetic and understanding.

Mungo, who was totally *au courant* (*up to scratch*) with the immigration debate, thought that there must surely be a Polish plumber somewhere that could rig up a system to do away with the labour of the buckets... but his name would probably turn out to be Artur Sisyphus.

[Although the name *Mungo* does not seem to appear in the Greek Classics, in many respects his life could be seen as an endless cycle of pushing a big lump of a boulder up a hill only for it to roll away from him. It has even been suggested (by somebody) that *Mungo*, like Sisyphus, 'personifies humanity and its disastrous pursuit of perfection by any means necessary, in which the great rock repeatedly rushing down the mount symbolises the accelerating pace of unsustainable civilisation toward cataclysmic collapse and cultural oblivion that ends each historical age and restarts the Sisyphean cycle'. (James Clement van Pelt, cited in Wikipedia. Would you want to be featured on so-called Wikipedia?) Ho hum.]

The problem with the roof at Villa Laird had predated Idris and Tim's assumption of the deeds, and indeed had been a legacy of Mungo and Ethel's tenure when they failed to pay heed to the banal homilies of some politician going on about mending the roof when the sun is shining. (To which we say: in Scotland? Awa ya plonker!) In more recent times, it had been exacerbated by the fact that the last 'roofer' had taken slates from the roof. This had been done in the absence of Idris and Tim and they had been suffering ever since. The 'roofer' had appeared, and between Tim's Clydebank vernacular and the *mittel-european* of the 'roofer', an agreement had been reached. But when the job had been completed during an exceptionally dry spell, Tim began to suspect that something had gone wrong in the translation; for the 'roofer' had handed *him*, (Tim), three hundred and forty-three pounds. It was only when the first shower of rain came in – not forecast by those posturing peacocks at the Beeb weather centre; (anyone surprised?) – that Tim began to have a really bad feeling. He climbed up to the back of the garden – which apart from doing his other knee in, was level with the roof – and there he saw the large bare patch of slates. Or a patch of no-slates. Thus the buckets.

But all of that was in the past [*and in the past it must...*].

As we noted above there was tension in the air between Tim and Mungo that stretched like a TV cooking series of series of repeats...skip that... but the important thing is this tension between them (unnoticed by Mungo, recall, because he was nearly in that state of bliss we mentioned earlier) had nothing at all to do with the roof...SO,

Tim climbed the Ramsay-ladder (despite what was claimed earlier in the context of his gammy knee by us and he) and joined Mungo among the old suitcases, the prams – one of which it was believed was used at the christening of Edward VII – the moth-eaten carpets, the underfelt, the over-felt, the Christmas trees (real, surreal, not so real, no' real, empyreal and downright pagan); the boxes of decorations (food for the moths); the decorative lights – the bulbs mostly blown; the boxes of cutlery (real Sheffield steel: to wield these you needed the arms of an tattooed dinner-lady/person or a stoker on an iron-ore carrier docked at Klang Port, Malaysia); and brown paper parcels tied up with *twine* (that last word gets round another plagiarism charge).

Yes, Tim joined Mungo among all that useless junk – the detritus of generations of joyful/joyless (delete as appropriate) festivities; what stories they could tell if they could speak (they'd be worth a few bob if they *could* speak). Tension was in the air that stretched between them like … the similes we badly used before… if you can think up a better one, email us… or John Lloyd when he (please God) makes another splendid *Blackadder*.

'You got Bupa then, Mungo?' Tim said, interrupting the internal, inconsequential, sesquipedalian rant of the narrators.

Mungo looked at the back of his hands – they all (well all two) looked mottled, but that was because of the little holes in the roof through which sunlight (the rain had gone) entered in charming little rays. (The *chiaroscuro*[3] effect resonant of in the left hand of the guy second on the left, in *Supper at Emmaus (Wieczerza w Emmaus*, for the benefit of the Polish plumber.)

All of these artistic allusions and less raced through Mungo's brain at a speed[4] incalculable by modern science as he replied:

'Bupa? Don't think so, Tim. Had a spot of it back in Malaya.'

[Note in another chapter Mungo makes an allusion to *Malaysia*. This is of course an unfortunate anachronism, given the dates he was 'serving' there; and more 'trivial' than 'unfortunate' given Mungo's memory.]

'*Quinine*,' he added, 'added to gin,' he added again. 'All gone,' he added. And a moment later, he added, 'Mind you, whatsisname, the little fellow, me son, he had something treacherous in that last book. Along with the little gal. Sister person. Could have been your whatchercallit? Public health

---

[3] *Great word to use at a party of posers (poseurs) if you can manage to insert Caravaggio (if you can spell it) into the craic.*

[4] *299,792,458 m/s (in a vacuum, of course), For example Weyl fermions – 'could be used to solve the traffic jams that you get with electrons in electronics – they can move in a much more efficient, ordered way than electrons.' (M. Zahid Hasan, 2015, IBTimes. We still think the 'wee elbows on the neurons giving it laldy' model says it all. See Skelp the Aged. Although the Edinburgh tram system might be a contender.*

bods took a keen interest in it – stayed away they did, after first visit,' he added.

Tim was by now dizzy with the parabolic, diabolic and shambolic nature of Mungo's thought processes, so decided to cut through all the crottes:

'Mungo. You've got private health insurance. Admit it.'

Chapter 3

Lang may your rum leak

Tim was by now dizzy with the parabolic, diabolic and shambolic nature of Mungo's thought processes, so decided to cut through all the crottes.

'Mungo. You've got private health insurance. Admit it,' he said with a hollow echoing effect.

Tim was an old school socialist who had bitterly accepted that the Berlin wall had tumbled, and there was now no chance of tanks ever being parked again on George Square (though in this we do not concur: tanks there would brighten and liven it up). It was not the only edifice close to his heart that had been torn down in homage to the new barbarians: his old school had been burned down and in its place now stood a Turkish barbers. What had been the playground alternated between being a permanent Gypsy encampment (full mod. cons; en suite (with footbath), air con., valet parking) and a site for Europe's largest car boot sale. There is no irrefutable evidence that any money laundering takes place, though one can find the odd bottle of Kaolin and Morphine[5].

Mungo on the other hand was a tory with a small and larger tee (tT). He was also old school – no less than St Kentigern's'; where the apostrophe should go has been a matter of debate within the debating society for aeons (a fair stretch of time, bags of eras). Basically, the old school network has fractured

---

[5] *Note for travellers – not of the Romany/gypsy/new age/whateverthedevil-they-want-to-be-called this week variety – Kaolin and Morphine is simply the best for all variants of Delhi Belly (no offence intended, Delhi; largest output of law graduates in the world so you can't be too careful what you say), but do not try and take it into Malaysia or Indonesia. We warned you first. No postal orders, please.*

into two competing factions: bifurcated and fractured into those who stick the apostrophe in the conventional place and those who say you can stick the apostrophe in a less conventional place i.e. where the sun wouldn't be seen dead shining unless you paid it.

How this is germane to our tale is that Mungo is counted by both factions as being 'one of us'. So, wherever he goes and needs a little shove-up or a jump-up a queue, then the Old Kentigernian thing kicks in. Not that there are many of the buggers in important positions – there are probably more of them in Castle Huntley.[6]

'Mungo, you've got private health insurance!' Tim accused, dragging us back to the present (an' no' afore time!).

'Have I?' Mungo said brightly, coming out of his serene state of bucket-bliss. With the speed of the aforementioned something-fermions, Mungo wished he had something wrong with himself that he could get seen-to by those posh consultants down at Ross Hall (not one of the buggers an old Kentigernian; which gave him some confidence in their competence). But drat it all: he was perfect in mind and body. So what use was this news imparted by Tim that he had private health insurance?

The problem with Mungo was that at an age when he should have been having problems with his *waterworks* (medicalese), he was as in control of that department as if he was superintendent of the Boulder Dam where at the press of a button water flows or does not; power is generated or is not. How many of you out there of a septuagenarian tendency can say the same (be honest, no one's listening)? WELL HERE IS THE SECRET WHICH WE DISPENSE FREE: (money back if not satisfied):

---

[6] *Castle Huntly is Scotland's only open prison accommodating a capacity of 285 low supervision adult male offenders from any Local Authority area [...] the emphasis is on careful preparation for release. Activity focuses on enhanced personal responsibility, job readiness and positive citizenship with the aim of reducing the risk of re-offending and contributing to safer communities. So there! Rest easy – we can all sleep at peace in our beds.*

MUNGO'S WATERWORKS: How this came about was as a result of one of the unintended consequences of his untrammelled devotion (sometimes) to the Zoroastrian *one-legged dance of Yü* (about which less later). He had adopted this practice when bored out of his skull at cocktail parties. He would see how long he could stand on one leg before the other one cramped up. This led to him being avoided for purposes of conversation, thus reducing the overwhelming sense of *ennui* engendered by listening to civilians prattle on.

Unwittingly, in engaging in this activity, the participant (*dancer*, to give it a technical name) is at the same time likely to go through all the muscular contractions of what medical types (*doctors*) call, *pelvic-floor[7]exercises*. The result of which, Mungo did not leak or have to rush to go to the lavvy every time he went into the kitchen to do the dishes. For a moment, as these thoughts and more rushed through his brain at yon high speed, Mungo considered penning an article that would postulate that the pelvic-floor muscles of practicing Zoroastrians will be found to be stronger than those of normal people. (Which of course, while we cannot print it, means they get e*******s easier than some of you; they leak less than some of you; and are less prone to premature you-know-what.) HOWEVER, he had misplaced his bookies pen and the article would need to wait.

AND ANYWAY,

---

[7] *Note the hyphen – astute readers, unlike one of the authors, will realise that this means the exercises do not need to be done on the floor, prostrate (prostate?) or supine. This will improve your bladder or bowel control, and improve/stop any leakage. Strong pelvic-floor muscles help to achieve erection and may prevent premature ejaculation. Basically you are trying to have your willie twitch up (no hands please) and you're anus contract, while not raising your eyebrows or those of bystanders. These are available for women, but without the erection business, with modifications to what should or should not be twitched.*

*https://www.nhs.uk/Planners/pregnancycareplanner/.../BandBF_* **pelvic_floor***_women* there was a loud rapping sound that brought Mungo out of his state of despondency about having (according to Tim) private medical insurance but nothing to blow it on.

'No offence meant, Mungo, but I've had this,' Tim rapped his knee, 'and this...' he made to tap his heart then remembered on time what the doc had said, '...this heart business for months, years wi' the knee. And Ethel... well she swans in and gets taken in right away. For whit? A gall bladder? That's whit ah call real bladdy gall ... It's jeest no fair, so it's no.'

Chapter 4

Indeed: it's no' fair so it's no' – it's *The System*

And indeed it is 'no fair'. It's the way it works. Queue-jumping[8] in the NHS.

THIS IS EASILY DEMONSTRATED: Best place to see it at work is Friday nights down at your A&E. You've accidentally (no, *sincerely*) cut off your big toe with the Flymo [this in no way is meant to impugn Husqvarna AB – a Swedish ~~mob~~ company who, being Swedish, have taken all reasonable precautions to make their machines idiot-proof; in so doing they are only guilty of underestimating the crass stupidity of mankind when given a machine, any machine. All right, the size of the print in the safety instructions is best read with the Hubble telescope, but there you go. And anyway it's another, albeit minor, contribution to the solution to the Rev TE ('Tam') Malthus's nagging worries about world population].

ANYWAY: Friday nights at A&E: you've cut a bit of your big toe off and only the Asda *Bag for Life* wrapped around your size nine (now 8.5), is preventing a total loss of nearly one-and-one-quarter gallons of the red stuff. And you've been *triaged*; and you're patiently waiting your turn; and you're not drunk (A Friday night?! Come-on!); and you're not abusive. And lo: two be-tattooed, shaven-headed, drunken louts in string vests materialise and just because their actual wrist bones are jutting through the skin and in danger of causing serious damage to passers-by, and they're being abusive and wanting to fight, they are taken ahead of you. *S'nofairsoit'sno*! (Later their husbands will come looking for them and they fight each other and then they too get ahead of you. Bastards!)

---

[8] *Researchers say baboons form orderly queues. http://www.bbc.co.uk/news/science-environment-36086332; has anybody thought of telling the French and the Dutch?*

ANYWAY: that is the gist of Tim's complaint against Ethel, though not couched in such intemperate and inflammatory and probably racist and/or discriminatory language against the be-tattooed fighting community – we celebrate diversity, remember? (you huv tae these days...or else). Ethel jumped the queue according to the narrative offered by Tim.

BUT WAIT! Those of you who number Glasgow University among your almae matres, will recall your Foucault[9] (aye, that yin again): for every narrative, there's an alternative point of view that is equally valid. Tim was right; Ethel was *queue-jumping*; but from Ethel's perspective she was *not queue jumping*: she was taking advantage of a little known (fortunately, for if it gets oot, the NHS will be *swamped*, pardon for that word), WE SAY, she was taking advantage of reciprocal arrangements between Iberia and the (at time of writing) United Kingdom that had been arranged by their faithful houseboy and myrmidon, Mourinho who was safely in the Algarve discharging his duties. (To clarify things: Ethel was not one of the two be-tattooed women mentioned in the paragraph above.)

Having duly taken account of Tim's utterance re private health insurance, and having forgotten it, sometime later Mungo casually looked up and over his spectacles and last Sunday's *Sunday Mail* (*The Sunday Mail;* NOT *'The Mail on Sunday'*) at Tim whose head was nearly lost in *The Sun's* racing section (excellent value and sometimes in colour for the BIG events all thrown in for much less than a third of today's price-colluding, monopsonistic, *soi-disant* 'quality' dailies). They were in what used to be Mungo's favourite hidey-hole (from Ethel), the kitchen. What used to be *his* kitchen. (Actually the tiny lavatory under the stairs was his last or often first resort come emergency hidey-hole from Ethel when they owned the house but strictly speaking – and we do sometimes – the kitchen was a close second favourite.) ·

'Tim, your opinion on some little matter would be appreciated by my good self.'

---

[9] *This is the last time we will say this: it's **Michel** Foucault; no the wan wi' the pendulum (Leon, no relation) for demonstrating that the earth spins (allegedly).*

Tim shifted uncomfortably in his chair and looked about. In the past this kind of opening gambit among his many 'freens' usually presaged 'a tap'… or, in the precise vernacular, 'Could you see your way clear to sub me a tenner or even eighty pence if the first number is a bit excessive?'

Over the decades or year he had known Mungo, the old guy didn't come across to him as a tapper. Sure he was totally incompetent in most of the little things that normal folk find easy to *navigate*[10]– like making toast without dropping it in the sink; like remembering to put water in the kettle before switching it on; like making sure there was toilet paper at hand before locking the lavvy door and sitting down to the daily business of 'expurgation and equine selection'. And although Mungo had made an arse of his financial dealings up to the point at which Idris had taken over Villa Laird, he had escaped that one unscathed – okay there was the small point of Ethel discharging a shotgun and causing a bent cop to experience *syncope* (medical jargon: *to faint*); but who among us has not done that at some juncture, and justifiably so?

The point being, Tim acknowledged, Mungo did not try and tap money from Idris or himself – all these thoughts and many more raced through Tim's cerebral matter in less time than it took to (type) process the above (words), which was admittedly quite a long time given one of us had an accident with a Flymo just prior – no blame attached to the manufacturer, we hasten to add, and will sign a disclaimer or even a waiver, post hoc, as soon as one can grasp a writing implement.

At which point Tim realised that since Mungo had made the utterance that occasioned that train of thought, he, Mungo, had gone and made toast for both of them – and yes, it was a bit damp at the edges; but the sink into which it had probably fallen was clean. And now Mungo awaited Tim's response which was forthcoming as set out faithfully below:

---

[10] *Navigate = sociological jargon for getting out of your pit, having had something to eat and drink, for having got across the road without being knocked on your arse by a passing marketing-director of some uni, etc., etc. and having made it home in one piece. Nothing to do with boats.*

'Whit?' Tim expostulated.

'Thing is, Tim, I need to visit my good lady Ethel and before doing so I need to come up with something she terms 'a project'. Any ideas?'

FLASHBACK: What had happened was that Idris whisked Ethel straight to the hospital from the aerodrome while Mungo went straight to Villa Laird to set up bivouac, with Tim. Idris on her return had passed on the information – *instruction* – that to occupy himself during her indisposition, Mungo needed *A Project.*

'Whit?' Tim counter-proposed.

'I agree entirely Tim. But I also agreed with Idris. The thing is, Ethel gets all of her ideas from the telly, the word, *project*! Everyone is looking for a *project*: place in the sun; location, location, location, etc. and all these chaps and chapettes with hundreds of thousands are looking for a *project*. So, anyway I agreed with Idris – *in loco* Ethel.'

'Whit?'

'The thing is I don't have a scooby as to what it or she means. Or they for that matter. Those folks on the telly. What say you?'

In the time it took to wring out the water from the edge of his toast and eat the little, almost dry bit that was left – it weighed in at 4cm x 6cm – Tim had got to the nub, the very heart, the core, the kernel, the centre of gravity of Ethel's lemma (not to be confused with dilemma for Mungo had no choice; nor with analemma, which as every schoolboy knows is the curve traced out by a celestial body, which almost brings us to the *one-legged dance of Yü.* But not quite yet).

And so Tim said he would give it some thought. And with that he made his excuses and left.

Chapter 5

The start of the walk – a long day's journey and a half

So. Meantime. Idris fed and watered him and exhorted Mungo to visit his beloved Ethel in the hospital; and in truth, to be separate from her for more than an hour was far too much for him to encapsulate in two words or less. And so he set out with glad heart and he was sorely tempted to take a diversion such was his state of well-being – all of this occasioned by the cards at Worcester and Chepstow. But being a man of great determination he was not to be diverted from his mission. Not if he had anything to do with it. (What the Gods decided, well that was another matter, old sport.)

BUT STILL, as he walked the lanes and leafy byways of Borrfoot, this thought flashed through his mind: where did all these trees come from? However, it went too quickly for it to leave a lasting impression. If form was anything to go on, Mungo would have bet that he would awaken at 3.14 a.m. with some inchoate concern prompted by the dissonance occasioned by the surfeit of greenery, the sound of the birds in the trees, and the high-powered scooshing racket from the bus depot wherein the previous night's half-digested curries of uncertain provenance,[11] all the curried-crap from Big Sandy's

---

[11] *We remark without prejudice or further comment, but since that non-occidental curryshop opened there has been a dearth of canine companions among all classes in the town, with concomittant absence of dog-shit, which, unlike the curries, is welcomed. Further, this is in no way a sleight or slander or even slight slander on those who cook and eat below the 38th parallel on a certain peninsula– and most certainly not aimed at those good people who live above it: we love your barber, Dear Brother Leader, and a puppy is not just for Christmas; it's for whatever way you want to cook it (we eschew the cheap laugh about wokking the dog – or pup).*

buses were being sluiced away into the stygian depths of the River Bevvy (see photo below):

The mighty River Bevvy, sweetly flowing

These sweet thoughts, like The Bevvy, flowed through the steeltrap mind of our hero, causing him to pause and reflect on an earlier time. A time more than ten minutes ago, for what had happened in the previous ten minutes – any previous ten minutes – was a mystery to Mungo. But take him back, ten months, ten years, three-score-years-and-ten, and he thought he knew what he was talking about. We will for a moment accompany him in his reflection, for it will provide a yardstick or metre-stick by which the new, vibrant, cosmopolitan Borrfoot can be judged.

Borrfoot revisited – with abject apologies to yon Brideshead writer wi' the teddy bear fixation

Borrfoot, in those days – that is more than ten minutes ago – would have been a city of aquatint (smudgy, grey, dull – you're all familiar with Goya's *The Sleep of Reason Produces Monsters*; well it would have been like that, except that someone had nicked the copper and zinc necessary for that process; and in doing so, did us all a favour since it is easier just to use chalk; and it looks more convincing and can be rubbed away with a sleeve, and sometimes that sleeve has a leather patch about the elbow – in which case there is a decent chance that the arm within that sleeve is Mungo Laird. Or not).

In her spacious and quiet streets men stalked and boaked as they had done in Newman's day; her autumnal mists, her autumnal springtime, and the rare glory of autumnal summer days – such as that day with the melancholic stench of the woollie works, and the multi-coloured River Bevvy in which the young punted and did other unmentionable things in the water, evoking another time – a time when the chestnut was in flower and the bells, had they not gone the way of the copper and zinc (nicked, alas), would have rung-out high and clear over her gables and cupolas; the cupolas are next to go – lead and more copper. Yes, all of these exhaled the soft airs of centuries of yoof. It was this cloistral hush which gave our laughter its resonance, and carried it still, joyously, over the intervening racket (the bus wash again).

But those days are over now and in the past they must … oops, that was close: another three words and the plagiarism polis would have been flat-footing around to our howf.

ANYWAY, reflecting upon the Borrfoot of his youth, Mungo Laird could declare that while he had never been unhappy in his life today he was as unhappy as he ever could remember being in all of his seventy-seven years. Which made it a pretty normal[12] sort of day in the life of Mungo; and he was happy at that for he did not like surprises.

On foot, in Borrfoot but not quite barefoot, he was on his way to the Queen Margaret hospital to visit his wife Ethel, but realising that all this reflection had taken longer than anticipated, he decided to skip the walking bit and take a hackney.

---

[12] *Discrimination early-warning: on the unlikely chance that our use of the term 'normal' (as in 'normal men') may offend some of our readers, we serve notice that we use it in the Gaussian sense. Vide, Duignan, OUP, 2016, Dictionary of Business Research Methods; Duignan, Quantitative Analysis for Business Research (Cengage, 2014)*

The first two taxi drivers in the long idle rank outside Borrfoot's *Waitrose* [about which one of us had not been informed in advance; otherwise it would have been mentioned in the same sentence as Asda along with the newly constructed Outreach of the National Theatre of Scotland – about which the other one of us had not been informed] ANYWAY THE TAXI DRIVERS listened politely to Mungo and one said,

'Gdzie chcesz iść, sir?'

To which Mungo riposted, *„Dudek i Boruc, państwu także'*

and left with his honour intact. For Mungo there was never a need for l'esprit d'escaliers – he shot from the hip (the left one, for the right one was well shot) when it came to dealing with troublesome foreigners.

Whether it was the speed with which he delivered his rejoinder that caused the quote marks to drop down or not, he was not the kind of man who would let fallen quote marks stand in his way. He sped on his way, for when he left the house that morning he was given a quest by the lovely Idris. But dash it, she had forgotten to give him a little piece of paper with the nature of that errand set out in simple terms. He still sped on for he had faith in his powers of recall and at some stage in his day, he would call to mind what the devil he was supposed to be doing. (WE KNOW: He was meant to be going to the hospital to visit Ethel, but we'll let him find his own way, as there has been quite enough authorial intrusion thus far.)

Chapter 6

Goodbye to Gdansk – and dropped quote marks

With the sounds of the Gdansk shipyards receding, he took pause and sat on a bench and read the little brass plaque attached to it, and was astounded by what he saw. What it said did not matter – it was the fact that the little rectangle measuring 4" x 8" (10cm x 20cm) made of brass[13] was still attached to the bench! For a moment, Mungo considered taking it into protective custody, but then thought: whoa! This is the new Borrfoot! They've even got a blessed Waitrose! Just as he parked his bottom on the bench for a rest, who came along but Idris, his current landlady – as we have remarked more than once.

„Mungo,' she said, at the same time wondering why the quote marks were upside down, not realising this was a hangover from Mungo's encounter with the taxi drivers of furrin provenance, „where are you going?'

„Was just going to ask you that, Idris.'

„I'm going for dog food, then to the hairdressers, and then the...' she replied, now ignoring the problem with the quote marks.

„Sorry, Idris, I meant: I was going to ask you where I was going.'

Idris seemed relieved at this, „To the hospital, Mungo. To visit Ethel. Are you having mild cognitive impairment (MCI), beyond what is expected in normal aging? No need to worry as it's usually associated with *hippocampal atrophy*. It'll get

---

[13]*For the record the plaque was dedicated to the memory of a cooncilor who was loved and reviled in equal measure, and often by the same people – a nice touch that reflects how well our elected representatives are in touch with the common people, causing a right big daud of ambivalence, inter alia.*

better – and even if it gets worse you'll no remember tae worry aboot it,' she said reaching into her large shopping sack of Santanian proportions.

„Not at all, Idris. It's not a memory thing. It's an attention thing. I simply don't pay enough attention to what people tell me. That's the problem with people of age, like myself: there's nothing wrong with our brains, no question of hippocampal atrophy. It's just that we've lived so long that we've come to not give a bugger about the things that seem so important to others. If we paid attention, we would remember everything. But we've taken a decision – consciously or sub-consciously – not to take things too seriously.'

Idris was not to know it, but for more than forty-years, Mungo had employed a memory-training exercise that he had not publicised, and which he used every single day that he was conscious. First thing in the morning, he would repeat *Sam Clemens* twenty times. Sam Clemens (as you don't need us to tell you) being the real name of Mark Twain. And in over forty years of saying *Sam Clemens* he never forgot Sam Clemens. One morning he woke up – about five months into this mental-regime – remembered to say Sam Clemens, but had forgotten what the bugger's pen name was. And to this day, he still remembers Sam Clemens and means to get round to looking him up some day.

[Parenthetically, in that brief disquisition to... whatsername above... on memory and retention, Mungo had disquisited the essence of a paper he had been intending to send off to various publications, among them: the soi-disant British Medical Journal (huh!), The International Journal of Geriatric Psychiatry, Acta Psychiatrica Scandinavica (pretentious, quoi?!), The Night Soil Association Journal, The Angling Times, and as a backstop to avoid confusion, The Anglian Times and The Anglican Times. However he had forgotten to get stamps and those learned instruments for the dissemination of knowledge would just have to get on with the dross they tended to recycle (the honourable exceptions being The Anglian Times, The Angling Times and The Anglican Times).]

After a delightful lunch with Idris on the park bench – she shared a Polo mint of uncertain vintage found in the stairwell of her canvas shopping bag, and one third of a Toffee Crisp, about which she assured Mungo, when he cavilled about accepting it, that it was good for toothache. And true to her word, on his first bite he felt a shaft of pain pass through his upper-left bicuspids and where his wisdom teeth should appear some day. He wished now he had brought a hip flask of his favourite nostrum: two parts Buckie to one part Kaolin and Morphine (hereafter K&M).

MEANTIME, Idris has sallied forth to get her dog food and other delicacies; Mungo – still on the bench remember, now has a mission: to get to hospital to see his wife... whatsername... Ethel. He stood and as he went past the fountain, he looked in the basin and reflected and reflected and his mind went back to the golden days – about nine months previously according to an earlier report about how long ago he had left for Portugal.

In those roseate tinted days, he reflected (he was still looking at his fizzug in the puddle) if he had approached a taxi rank in the old sullen Borrfoot, they would have told him to f*ck off unless he was promising a fare to Inverness with the guarantee of a fare on the way back, plus extras for luggage and a booking fee for the return journey. But all that had changed.

In the same way they had impacted upon goalkeeping, these Poles had so much more to answer for – not just the vodka distilled from fermenting pigeon crotte (*odchody gołębi*), but also the sense of a willingness to provide services (not excluding goalies), and ancillary bus services (not excluding picking up white-goods at Asda and delivering to the door included in the price of a day ticket). For this alone Big Sandy Easdale, of McGills Buses, deserves that knighthood which has been lost in the post at the time of writing (8.25 a.m.).

Chapter 7

Assignation in a sick nation

And so, happy with life but disturbed by the brave new world that was skelping him on the napper each new day, Mungo pressed on regardless. Given that Borrfoot had once exported lavvy pans throughout the Empire (in return for Empire wines and spices to spice the wines), it was apposite that Mungo should eschew taking a cab to his next appointment which was with a delightful young financier – he has not forgotten about Ethel: he can only do one quest at a time.

This delightful young *woman* (it's apparently sexist to use the term *young lady*, and we would hate to offend the feminists – which can be worse than offending the M*****s –*not* Mormons). WE Say, this delightful young woman no longer used the term Financial Advisor on the grounds that it had been tainted by a motley crew of be-knighted and benighted arrivistes.

[In this respect it is an interesting commentary on our universities, to peruse the lists of those in receipt of 'honorary degrees': among the innocent and sometimes deserving, you will find parcels of rogues, the usual suspects. Is it time the so-called NUS did something useful and put a stop to these practices? Just asking like.]

And so Mungo anticipated with some relish (it was a French restaurant after all and you need something to disguise the overweening taste of pats of *beurre* and cloven garlic) his assignation with Meg Dalgliesh; for, although some parts of his memory were a touch faulty, those dealing with the visual delights of womanhood were pretty sound-to-vivid, and he recalled uber-vividly and with scorching acuity that Meg turned a pretty ankle or two.

And at that thought he stood and put his foot down a drain and turned his ankle. *Ouch*! But one of the advantages of his model of the neural system[14] is that if you can trick those little neurons – *the cells with the elbows that nudge each other and pass the message (or not) on to the brain* – then you don't always feel the pain. And did this not happen in Mungo's case because just at that moment,

'Dirty auld baistairt.' A woman passing by snapped at him – she was wearing probably the last paisley-pattern headscarf worn by a freeborn, spinster Borrdookian, that would have been well-received at the Grand Mosque of Cairo – but that's another story.

'I beg your pardon, madame?' he said as she glared at him. He thought she had pretty ankles and…

'There you go again aboot ma ankles! F*ckin' pervert.' And with that she spun on her heels (Primark, £11.69) and clicked off (one of the heels was loose – no fault of Primark, we hasten to add), looking for a pair of community police officers or brave Jehovah's Witnesses as witnesses (leaving aside whether they would swear on the *guid buik*, or *affirm* – if the latter, it always gets up the Sheriff's nose, even if he's the biggest atheist in the Lodge).

Mungo realised that he was still afflicted with what he had termed *cognitive-vocalisation syndrome*, but since he did not carry his copy of the DSM-5[15] this bright morning, he could not recall the cure.

---

[14] *Mungo has demonstrated that all neurological science can be explained in one sentence: neurons are cells that have elbows attached to each side; one cell is excited by something, such as a Victoria's Secret Ad (normal males and all females) then it elbows the cells on either side of it and says: what about that then? Eh?! These cells become excited; eventually the message gets to the brain and the bit dealing with emotions or whatever. See also* **Toward a Model of Functional Brain Processes I: Central Nervous System Functional Micro-architecture**, *Mark H. Bickhard, Axiomathes, September 2015, Volume 25, Issue 3 pp 217-238: it's just saying what Mungo said, but in over-complicated chat.*

[15] *Diagnostic and Statistical Manual of Mental Disorders, 5th edition, of the American Psychiatric Association. If you think you have some mental illness (syndrome in psychobabble) and it does not appear in this work, there's nothing wrong with you, so you need to*

As he dwelt on this condition, he took heart from the fact that many years ago, he had become convinced that he had acquired *late-onset-Tourette's syndrome*. This came to him as he wandered about the corridors of Villa Laird – in a sloff[16] of despond – he was speaking aloud without thinking: at first he thought it must be one of the ghosts (a family of ghosts had moved in decades before when the old asylum was closed down, and some of his ancestors had to find a new abode). Suddenly he recognised *The Voice* – yes, it was his own. What he was saying was nothing remarkable: he was repeating over and over phrases like: *ph*cqu'em; the bastards; they can all ph*cque off.*

But then a cure was at hand – he was not alone, for when he walked down into the old town to get his *Mail Racing Section* – nicked from PackiePower the turf accountant, all about him did he not hear: *f*ck'em; the bastards; they can all f*ckoff*? One day he asked one of his fellow Tourette's-townsmen what it was all about: *cooncillors. The f*ckin' cooncil*. And with that the scales were lifted from his eyes (he had been to the fish van). He did not have Tourette's of any vintage. There is a lesson here: men (it's almost always men) of a certain age – those from mid-forties and upwards – all come to behave like that. We have even heard it in the hallowed corridors of our finest university (okay, a bit of poetic licence involved).

[On discovering this truth, Mungo realised something: Tourette's syndrome is best understood as a condition whereby young men act as if they were in their mid-forties and beyond. This is probably a genetic mis-step that can be corrected by altering the time-clock of the DNA and RNA. To this end, Mungo thought he would share his knowledge, and so penned a paper and sent it off to the usual publications.

---

buck up. If you can recall what DSM stands for, there is nothing wrong with your memory.

[16] *We have taken the liberty of simplifying for the reader the spelling of 'slough' to make it easier to pronounce. Now if only John Bunyan had done that in the first place, we would not need to have done so. (We're still not sure how to pronounce 'slough' though. Or should that be 'thuff'?)*

Although he heard little by return – the usual letter from the solicitors representing the BMA – he took pleasure in the knowledge that the recipients, on reading his treatise, would have responded instinctively with *f*ck him! the mad old bastard.*]

CHAPTER 8

Ahead of the curve or round the bend

So. His appointment with Meg: to discuss his options for re-capitalisation or leveraging or loan acquisition – he was in desperate straits, though this could not have been discerned from his demeanour. His meeting was for one o'clock, but not at his favourite French restaurant – Fat Eddy's in another town, the very one where he had sealed his first *coup de financement* (a loan or, in Borrfoot vernacular, a *sub*). Instead it was at a new eatery of the French persuasion, of which more later as Mungo gets close to it.

As he approached his rendezvous, he thought it wise to check with passers-by if he still was exhibiting signs of *cognitive-vocalisation*. One elegant youngish man, was wearing a particularly attractive tie – pink teddies on an iris background in shot-silk, over a phthalo-green[17] Andy-Pandy suit. In the breeze, as he passed the young man, the tie caught Mungo's eye and it started watering again. The young man stopped and said, 'Why thank you.' At which he seemed to suffer a facial tick that involved strange convolutions of an exposed tongue and counter-convolutions of his (rather too-finely plucked) eyebrows. Mungo wondered if he was having a fit (*stroke* in medical jargon) and whether he should get some help for both of them.

The youngish man seemed suddenly angryish (but *not* Ireish) and in retort to Mungo's thoughts, said, 'Who's having

---

[17] Phthalocyanine *for the pedantic. Best thought of as 'an intensely blue-green-coloured aromatic macrocyclic compound that is widely used in dyeing'. (Wikipedia: we definitely do not endorse this 'reference' resource, though if in a hurry we might resort to it out of desperation. It boils down to this: would you trust a 'dictionary' that allowed you to insert entries?) Nice colour though.*

a fit? Oh, bugger off, you old tease, you. You're all the same, so you are. If you can't do the dirt, don't do the flirt.' At which he turned and strode off on a pair of fine ankles above tan Sperry Top-Siders (yes, the gold cup perforated ones: Mr Porter, £150; cash accepted and a belt round the back thrown in).

After that little piece of unpleasantness, Mungo was in a sweat – if he was still saying aloud what he was thinking internally, then it could be a problem with Fat Freddie (brother of Fat Eddy), who ran the restaurant; not to mention the cloakroom girl with the nice… white blouse. At which thought a man of a certain age, who looked like he sold payment protection insurance, said, 'Oh her! *Phowarrrhh*!' with associated slavering sounds and arm gestures of a laddish bent. (Upwards.)

'*Non-capisco*,' Mungo said, with a Gallic and Gaelic gesture – a garlic one would come after he had dined – a gesture that involved temporarily dislocating one collarbone and the opposite eyebrow, on completion of which Mungo moved on. As for Meg Dalgliesh, he dared not even think what he would think about her if she was wearing sussies… oh my god, he gasped and fell to the ground with foam coming from his mouth.

For a moment he was sure he had something not recognised by DSM-5, and that next he would be renting (not *leasing*) his gown and pulling his hair (he would have had a job getting a grip on it, unless it was the nasal, aural or anal variants). But then it all became clear to him: he had tripped over a scabby wee dug on a leash two miles long; and since he had just started to eat the double-nougat ice cream we forgot to mention a couple of lines above, this was now presenting a curious sight to the alarmed elderly lady-woman on the other end of the leash. For a moment she was transported back to biblical times (*Old Testament*), when it was common for wayfarers to fall and writhe about and foam at the mouth and rent their gowns (pre-Primark) and pull at their cranium hair.

'That you, Mungo Laird?!' the ancient personage screeched, while her wee dug lapped at the foam coming from his mouth. 'Drunk again. Hell mend you for all the people you sold that vile pish to – *Laird's Lager* indeed,' she ended somewhat censoriously, before sauntering off, happy with her contribution to inter-gender relations that bright morning.

Five minutes later, when she was about six hundred metres away (she moved quite smartly for her age), she tugged at the leash and her wee dug was jerked away from Mungo, but not before it took the remnants of the double-nougat[18] wafers. Mungo had consoled himself with the knowledge that the recently arrived 38th Parallel kebab shop would have its day with that wee dug.

But Meg Dalgliesh – for the moment forget about the suspenders issue – had her own concerns, which was worrying for someone who had adopted a persona untainted by any sign of human frailty. It will be recalled from Volume One, that Ms Dalgliesh was in part the architect of Mungo's (most recent) fall from grace into ignominy; but who, by one of those literary caprices, in the end helped spirit Mungo and Ethel away to the better part of Iberia, while at the same time ensuring that a pair of crooks who played the Discrimination Act clumsily, ended up at HM Pleasure, (and possibly at the pleasure of a few others over and above and below).

Her concerns now were of a more immediately compelling sort: the company had been taken over by a bunch of furriners[19] who had indicated their intentions of pursuing *ethical policies* – seriously! While at the same time they were putting all existing employees on notice that they would be judged by their results. Each employee had been given three months to come up with *the killer deal*.

Meg had only her existing client base, and while these had been her milch cows of the recent past, *those days were gone now and in the past they must...* ANYWAY Meg did a quick

---

[18] *Pronunciation note: nougat should not be pronounced in the effete French style; it is pronounced nugget – as if it was a dod of gold or a shitty piece of 'chicken' sold in a take-away of dubious provenance – remember the dearth of dogs mentioned above apart from the wee yapper that licked the foam from Mungo's fizzug? Well for legal reasons, we're not suggesting any connection.*

[19] *Fellow Europeans – we celebrate diversity. Allegedly.*

scope (where did she get that word? At Edinburgh uni of course – where they had dumbed-down not just the courses but also the language). YES, a quick *scope* had told her what she knew all too well: she was dealing with the 'dregs' (no offence intended) of those desperate for loans. And symptomatic of her state of desperation, today she had agreed to meet that crazy old coot Mungo Laird.

'*Whitfur*?'[20] she might have asked herself, as we ask ourselves.

---

[20] *Glesga dialect, literally 'what for?' In this context she could have expressed it as 'why the f*ck did I agree to meet the old coot when I don't have my troubles to seek?' 'Whitfur' is more efficient.*

Chapter 9

Frenchie

So. There was a time (ten months before) when Fat Eddy's was the only French restaurant (as the name suggests) in another small town that could have been twinned with Borrfoot and had at that time been chosen by Meg to inconvenience Mungo. But given all the changes that had taken place – and not all of them for the better in Mungo's view: the Waitrose (who needs it when you've got Lidl?! – not a paid endorsement though we would consider a consideration); the Guggenheim annex; the National Theatre Outreach 'Interaction Space' (a wee tiny theatre without seats, where the audience would be encouraged to 'mingle' with the luvvies, and would be given immunity from prosecution under the Sexual Offences Against the Person Act); not to mention the projected V&A – well dash it: if *Dundee* can get one, why no Borrfoot?!)

BUT GIVEN ALL THE CHANGES... Fat Eddy's had opened a branch in Borrfoot and was only one of many French[21] restaurants that had sprung up during Mungo's absence, and was hosted by Fat Eddy's brother (frère) Fat Freddy. (And actually he was even Fatter, but we'll leave it at Fat as we also celebrate obesity.)

While on another day Mungo might have been *nonplussed* (standard English usage) by finding Fat Eddy's outreach restaurant in the town, this day he was *nonplussed* (American usage), and so it was with delight that he set his eyes on Meg Dalgliesh who had done so much for him in the past.

[VOICE-OVER: Today Meg is wearing Dolce & Gabbana Satin-trimmed stretch wool-and-silk blend blazer with

---

[21] *We think, on the balance of probabilities, that it is possible that it is a 'coincidence' that the number of horses in the surrounding countryside has taken a nose-dive.*

matching skirt (£1600 for the jaiket alone!) Unlike the men's two piece, this does not 'scream centre of attention'; but still makes a nice alternative to an evening dress, in our opinion: 89% wool, 10% silk, 1% elastane; lining: 94% silk, 6% elastane – Dry Clean at Gas mark 7; not suitable for microwaving].

So. On this day, nothing could upset his equilibrium, his sense of purpose and control. (He often had days like these and was usually wrong on all three counts, but hey-ho, if the jar was more than half-full, well he could soon fix that, provided he could get the lid off.)

After Mungo's futile attempts at air-kissing Meg (he ended up making contact with a pair of mock-velvet curtains that framed the window – quite a pleasing experience, and was tempted to give them some tongue, but his business sense took over), and they had hardly sat down when Mungo's mobile went *dring-dring*.

'I just have to take this call, my dear,' he said, reaching into his pocket and stepping outside (they had a window seat and the window was open, and the sill was low-enough for Mungo to step over it without doing too much damage to his undercarriage or his dignity).

Outside, in the bright sunshine and the warm, balmy air (not just the town had changed), Mungo took his hand out of his pocket and remembered he no longer had a mobie – he had received one as a going away present or something from his son… whatsisname, but when it ran out of credit Mungo couldn't find where to insert the money, so he binned it.

But he had most definitely heard a clear *dring-dring*. Ho-hum, he said with an *insouciance* he neither felt nor understood the meaning of, and stepped back inside where he found Meg on her mobie and looking very distraught. He felt a stab of sympathy for the divine creature and, realising that the poor thing was vulnerable, decided to drop a fork and have a look up her skirt to test his theory that she always wore sussies.

[Mungo's fascination with – some might say, *obsession* – with that article of woman's allure, can be traced all the way back to Ethel who, in an experimental phase (brief) of their married life, tried out a set of deep red sussies. In transports of delight, Mungo got entangled in the gear with the eventual outcome being a smart trebuchet effect – if the bedroom wall had been missing, Mungo might have encompassed Borrfoot from the air. Still, never put him off, did it?]

BACK TO THE PRESENT AND MEG'S VULNERABLE MOMENT: Hardly had Mungo got down on his knees – half-way down the thought struck him that he might never get back on his feet, so creaky were his knees; but ever the pioneer, he made it onto the carpet. (General George off-cut, £5.70 per sq.yd.) WE SAY, hardly had Mungo got down on his knees to 'scope' Meg's legs, when that ~~French scoundrel~~ genial restaurateur Fat Freddy chose to bring the menu. There was nothing for it but to get back onto his chair and behave with another dose of yon insouciance stuff that the French think they have invented.

While he pretended to consult the menu, he scoped the little bistrette and had a strong feeling of déja-vu, not for the second time, *for there was only about ten covers in the place and at each, the diners were talking into mobiles. It looked as if they were phoning each other across the crockery and silverware and glass and the polka-dot paper table covers. It's good to talk.* He felt that he might have been a character in another book, one that had been written not too long before this one. And sure as blazes, when that thought had been articulated in his steel-trap brain, why sure as the same blazes...

Mungo ordered some drinks, but nothing for Meg – still vulnerable on that phone call – nothing for Meg, not because he was skint – though he was, and the thought of paying the bill was not at that point allowed to intrude into that steel-trap brain – nothing ordered for Meg as he was from the old school that never presumed to tell a lady what to drink. He settled down content to wait and watched the young waitresses go about their business efficiently but with an hauteur that suggested they were indeed French – the kind from around Île-de-France – or from Kelvinside and doing politics at Glasgow Uni and had been trained in the Ubiquitous Chip.

At some point, Meg ended her call and her head dropped to the table – not literally, even though it is a French place; but even they draw the line at the chop... nowadays. Speaking of which, Mungo ordered les côtelettes d'agneau (he had been assured by Fat Freddy, that they were almost as good as lamb chops, but better). When asked how he would like them done, after great thought, Mungo said, 'Oh, dash it, just fry them in lard until the sparks fly.' This made an impression on the restaurateur as lard was making a comeback in the kitchens of the great and the good and that in many ways he, Mungo, was – wait for the American cliché – 'ahead of the curve'.

[Later we will have things coming out of *left field* (a disorienting surprise); *curve-ball* (a ball that sets out in one direction and ends up in another – like a Scottish football player's attempt at a simple shot, the tosser!... never realising he was on *the back foot*... woof! It's over the bar.]

Meg for her part, was obviously upset by the call she had taken, for she ordered steak-and-ale pie, which was not on the menu until she gave Fat Freddy *the stare* that had stood her in good stead when at uni if a tutor dared to consider giving her a mark less than a First. (Edinburgh, by the way: all two-and-a-half Glasgow ones rejected her).

For drinks, Mungo ordered a Buckie-special, but had to settle for an inferior Malbec.[22] In many ways, the upsurge in the consumption of Argentinean Malbec can be seen as revenge for the Falklands. In other ways, more innocent ways, it should be seen as the Argies getting rid of their surplus pish.

Meg had a dry-smoked Manhattan, which Mungo thought was some sort of fish-based cocktail, until he stole a slug of it while Meg was taking another phone call.

---

[22] *It has been demonstrated elsewhere – Skelp the Aged – that Fat Eddy knew the nuances of booze and boozers, for when Mungo had first asked for a Buckie at the original Fat Eddy's (in another town), Eddy, with great perspicacity had suggested that the Argentinian Malbecs that were becoming so popular with those who didn't have a scooby about wine, had some of the qualities of the Buckie. And so it had come to pass. But the test ultimately would be when on ordering a Malbec in Buenos Aires one was offered a Buckie. Until then, the jury is out.*

[His taste buds told him that the T2R receptors had activated the G-protein causing activation of phospholipase C, although he did not think in these terms – *bitter, damned bitter,* he judged. However, since ninety per cent of what gustationists call *taste* is actually *smell* – which means that olfactorialists do nine times more work than gustationists – Mungo, not bothering with this piece of information, took another slug of Meg's drink and decided it was indeed fish-based. Probably mackerel – though it could simply have been that the spirit had been filtered through some toilet door made out of fish boxes somewhere to the east of the Hebrides. And anyway, what we taste and smell all comes down ultimately to those little neurons giving their elbows laldy and passing on the message to the brain. Or not.]

MEANTIME, Meg wanted to get down to business as she scoffed her hastily produced steak-and-ale pie with chips and peas (and a wee sprig of something that looked as if it had been deposited by a pigeon in a gutter where it had borne many, unhygienic offspring). When she saw her glass was empty, she beckoned Freddy who had been hovering and hoovering the curtains (some white stuff seemed to have attached itself to these – and there was no evidence that it was of a smegmatic nature, so we'll draw a cheese-cloth over that question).

Mungo was in a pensive mood, concerned by Meg's lack of menace, so he ordered a refill. Being the sort of gentleman he was, Mungo could not let the lady sip alone and he ordered a double schooner of the Malbec to compensate for the fact that Freddy had no Benylin (original recipe) to hand to soften the juice of the pampas.

'Mungo, if I appear a bit distracted it's because I'm a bit distracted,' Meg said, not with her customary hint of menace or steel. 'Now what was it you wanted?'

Chapter 10

Mungo finally does the (first) business with Meg

'Mungo, if I appear a bit distracted it's because I'm a bit distracted,' Meg said, not with her customary hint of menace or steel. 'Now what was it you wanted?'

Mungo wiped his mouth with a corner of the table cover, as was his habit – he always made a point of saving his napkin for later; a pity about the curtains – he should have brought a carrier bag he mused.

He took Meg's hand across the table, 'My dear Meg, my purpose was... well I am in a little bit of a dilemma, but you, my dear? Why I've never seen you like this before: so distracted. So vulnerable.' A thought flashed through his mind to drop his fork, but he would need to scrabble around in his pocket for it. 'Is there something you would like to share with me?'

Although normally and always a sincere man, Mungo was thinking feverishly about how he might get some sense of whether she was in sussies today, and so like the poet with his muse, the silver-tongued devil let slip those words that many men have uttered and have lived (or not) to regret, 'Tell me what's wrong, dear.'

And it was if a damned dam had burst – it all came gushing out in a cataract that almost cleared one of his cataracts. And of course, great listener that he was – trained by Ethel to switch-off those little neurons that worked their elbows in the sound-part of the neural networks – he could not get her to stop yapping on about the job, the new owners, the targets, the ethical policies... yada, yadda, yaddda, yadddda... During which time, she's blubing and blubbing and blubbbing and the state of her eyes and face...?

If women (no offence intended) could see their fizzugs at such times there would be a lot less waterworks. (And a stack more close-quarter coupling). Of course her eyes have swollen up like the last rope-a-dope to act as punch bag for yon big Ukrainian geezer or his brother; her skin is all blotchy as if she has bathed with poison-ivy (not *the* Poison Ivy by Uma Thurman in Batman Umpteen); and all the time Mungo has finished his fifth Malbec – which is beginning to improve; probably aged due to the length of time they had been at table and has slugged off Meg's third dry-roasted Manhattan or whatever, as she was in no emotional state to savour its nuanced whatever.

And then it came to him – there was no alternative: ~~that French git~~ their genial host Fat Freddy had refused to bring him any more drink. And whyfur?! All because he had made to wipe his mouth on the curtains, the table cover being sopping (Sc. *souming*) wet. WE SAY, and then it came to him – a way out… for both of them. A way of calming Meg down and getting what he wanted. (Not the question of the sussies for now.)

Just when Meg paused for breath, Mungo pitched his pitch (not a curve ball and not from left field nor ahead of the curve but near enough off the front foot). He thought that he might be able to help Meg. He had proved to be a good bet before, so he pitched his pitch (from right field?): he needed 'walking-about money' until his ship came in.

Meg laughed bitterly (that was the dry-smoked Manhattan probably) then, almost hysterical, exclaimed, 'that kind of sub I can give you from my purse, Mungo,' (that slip of the tongue, the class betrayal – *sub* – probably due to the Arbroath-smoked Manhattan, perhaps). She continued, 'my employers need me to get A BIG PROJECT,' she said raising her voice and the font size. A capital investment that will make their eyes water. Do you have that? Anything in mind? A subway system for Edinburgh? Tram system for Glasgow? Road system for Dundee? No, I thought not. Thanks for trying Mungo.' Upon which she fell into a reverie, (Mungo had fallen into a plant pot during this, but covered it nicely by plucking a sprig of something which he placed in his glass.)

Now, fully composed, Mungo sat back and through narrow-slitted eyes (Malbec/lust-effect) gazed with a contained compassion and barely contained passion at Meg. For a time, he toyed with his glass then was shocked to find it was empty

– apart from the sprig of something someone had placed in it. He made what was intended as an imperious gesture to Fat Freddy and fell off his chair. Not for the first time.

AND THERE IT WAS: THE FACE OF HEAVEN. Sussies! And he hadn't even been thinking about them for all of the previous few minutes.

Restored from the recumbent position (TU speak for 'sleeping on the job and getting caught'), by Freddy and a couple of very charming waitresses, as well as getting a good hold on one of the curtains, Mungo gibbered intelligently (to his ears) how this would do both of them good.

Meg was still somewhat emotional – helped by Mungo saying loudly for all in the restaurant to hear, 'You should see your face, Meg. No offence my dear, but it's a mess.' He turned and invited all the other diners to pass comment, which they were only too happy to do: is there a more pleasing sight for a woman than a pretty one looking godawful? And of course there was a queue of them wanting to have selfies with Meg, and the click of all those mobies was like a cash register to O2, TalkTalk, Orange, T-Mobile and the rest (BT was down at that moment. No change there).

Regaining consciousness – Meg might be emotional, but she still packed a wallop for a petite woman – Mungo called for the bill and was most gratified when Meg brushed his offer aside and settled with a smile on a face that reminded him of a gigantic strawberry he had seen somewhere, and which had half of it torn away by a chough[23] – it must have been on Islay or somewhere for you don't get them on the mainland, he reasoned. He thought then of asking if she could see her way clear to include a cairry-oot (he of course did not use that vulgar phrase – we have provided it as a guide to what he had in mind), but decided against. Meg leaned across and said to him,

'Mungo, I feel so much better having got it all out in the open.'

---

[23] *Pronounced 'chuff'. A timely clue on how to pronounce 'slough' as in 'slough of despond'. Or is it? Latin name, by the way, Pyrrhocorax-pyrrhocorax. If you can say that you should be well chuffed.*

'So do I,' Mungo said, but only to himself as he adjusted himself under the table, for he remembered the view from the carpet.

'Yes my dear – it's good to talk.' (He thinks he said, though he was still half-to-entirely-cut and gibbering frantically).

'And I like your proposition. The Project. Let me do the sums and get back to you.'

'Proposition?' Mungo said to himself – he thought. What have I proposed? But before he could seriously worry about what he might have let himself in for, his mental training kicked-in and he cast any dark thoughts to the deepest recesses of his steel-trap brain, where they would lie until the time came to really worry[24] about them.

Yes, it had turned out a good day after all. And the day had not ended, and so he determined to sally forth to visit his beloved Ethel. Which was, after all, the point of getting out his scratcher that bless'd morn, that … Henry V Part Deux… the bit round about St Crispin's or Pork Scratching's Day.

---

[24] *If more people took this approach, there would be less need for all those counsellors and psychiatrists that the NHS feels compelled to employ instead of nurses and sawbones and porters for getting us to and from the trolley.*

Chapter 11

Visiting time – NOT YET: nae rush

So. Although things had gone passably well since Idris had left him parked on the bench, albeit with his non-baggie troosers stuck to the wet paint (we forgot to mention that first time round), and although that wee yelp of a scabby dug had stolen his double-nougat (nugget!), and although that strange woman from his past had indicated that he might be once more in the grip of that condition whereby he vocalises for all and sundry his innermost thoughts – many of which would pass over the head of even the most educated, or under that of the most uneducated citizen – and although he had an inter-cultural exchange with cabbies of diverse origin ('we celebrate diversity', just in case like), things, or 'events, dear boy, events', had begun to look just a ba' hair off from the moment he had bounded (well, limped) into the taxi of unknown provenance.

But what made the whole day worth the effort was of course the view of heaven had he only remembered.[25] Alas, he recalled nothing of the view up Meg's skirt, though paradoxically, he recalled the business end of that meeting. (Later he would have reason to recall les côtelettes d'agneau, and regret not having a hip flask of the elixir of his life, K&M).

And although we say he took a taxi, we interject that prior to that, who should he bump into, but his co-landlord, Tim Waters. Tim speculated that according to Idris, Mungo should have by this time been to the Queen Margaret to see how Ethel was faring. But with more of that *insouciance* stuff than he

---

[25] *Had Mungo only known it, there is on record examples of brain surgery being carried out while the patient is conscious and which (allegedly) recovered memories that had been lost: e.g. that by Sir Victor Horsley before WW1. See Appendix 3*

knew what to do with, Mungo brushed this aside and remarked that there was plenty of time – these dashed modern visiting hours would be the death of visitors as there were no restrictions and so no good excuses for cutting the visits completely. When will the NHS begin to treat visitors like the germ-ridden nuisances that they are?

The two friends grasped the opportunity to take their (first ever) daily constitutional during which Mungo regaled Tim with the awe he felt for the wondrous transformation of the old town.

As they skirted the harbour, Mungo remarked that in his yoof (he had a caramel in his mouth at the time and did not want to slevver over his waistcoat (British Heart Foundation, Byres Rd, zł 25 or £4.50 at current exchange rate)), there had never to his knowledge been any ocean-going liner (Big Boat) anchoring in the middle of the town. And indeed that is the case even to this day, for Borrfoot has no harbour in the conventional sense. However, one of the most popular pastimes of the Borrdookians is to take a walk down to the Harbour of an evening. (If Wigan can have a Pier…and a Road…and a seminal novel using both for a Title…who is to deny Borrfoot?))

Below we present an artist's impression of Borrfoot Harbour (some details may differ from finished job).

Borrfoot Harbour (Artist's Impression)

The construction of the Harbour arose serendipitously and is one of the few things the Irn-Bru flaunting former MP and equally otiose MSP counter-part do not feel compelled to take credit for. Situated at a strategic point on the mighty River Bevvy which flows through Borrfoot, after merging with the Cart it flows into the Clyde near where the jobbie boat used to sail from – so all you good people of Erskine (Erskinites – biblical sounding almost), if you're still wondering thirty years later what is that pungent whiff…?

ANYWAY to the harbour – it's construction we say rose ~~serendipittissoul~~ eh… by chance – that was lucky (or lucky chance if you prefer).

As has been established in another work, the source of The Bevvy, had never knowingly been pinpointed. Archie McIndoe-Woodrow (now Sir Archie McIndoe-Woodrow of that ilk), spent seven years following it. At one point Archie had thought he might need to hack his foot off to escape entanglement with a Tesco trolley; but in a moment of geniusistical inspiration, he resorted to dragging the trolley with him, and after some other adventures not worth considering, (Sir) Archie demonstrated irrefutably that the source of The Bevvy was an overflow pipe in a decrepit mansion to the east of the Ayrshire village of Dunlop, whose ballcock had ceased to function correctly because of an exceptionally warm summer circa 1932. He proved this by a series of maps, historical records of the Met Office and with diagrams from the *Plumbers' Mate Handbook* – a volume that, despite the questionable apostrophe, is in its own way on par with the *Diagnostic and Statistical Manual of Mental Disorders* (for who has not gone at least temporarily insane over a toilet that will not flush?).

In the event, Sir Archie M-W, on being given the freedom of the town, showed his undying gratitude by building a global empire based on shopping-trolley-recovery-and-recycling, and moved away to some tax haven just west of Liverpool.

But what is germane to our account – recall: the serendipitous construction of Borrfoot Harbour ('water-space') is that in clearing the upper reaches of The Bevvy of the shopping trolleys, Sir Archie inadvertently changed the flow-rate and a build-up of non-Tesco trolleys happened in the lower reaches, that just happened to be the old town square (known locally and colloquially, as The Old Town Square). This was rapidly inundated and before long a wily entrepreneur (James T Wyllie) quickly brought little boat things from Rouken Glen Boating Pond – which had coincidently dried up at this time – and hired them out to passing Borrdookians who are known globally for their affinity with the sea.

Before you could say 'Mutiny on the Bounty' [pub quiz question: name the boat in the film of that name – you would be surprised how many people say 'Mayflower'; correct answer in Appendix 7]. ANYWAY, the boats took off – not literally: they're boats after all; next came a candy floss stall, then a burger stall, followed by an arcade with all sorts of gaming machines; and very quickly the seagulls moved down or up from Saltcoats and up or down from the Broomielaw.

By the logic of the circumstances it was only a matter of time before in October of each and every year, landladies from Blackpool arrived in their hordes for the *Oktoberfest*. Well it was only a matter of time before Royal Caribbean explored the possibility of one of their really big boats calling in should Cannes or Monaco be closed due to the weather, ***and a chance to charge \$35 for a bottle of Wolf Blass!*** [Watch them – they'll *accidentally* charge you for a bottle of water from the mini-bar: apart from WC Fields dictum about never drinking water, the water in the bottle you wouldn't use to dilute windscreen-wash, never mind drink. You've been warned – it's on the record and in the public domain and all the lawyers in the world will not get one of us to retract. (The baistarts!) (Well… we'll see later, once one of us has cooled down over that episode in the Western Med wi' The Pirates o' the Caribbean.]

[In case you have forgotten, we reproduce an artist's reconstruction of that infamous naval engagement below]

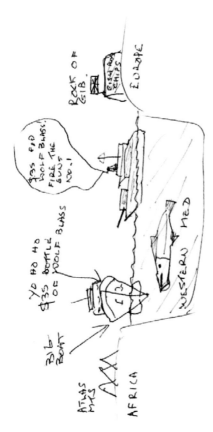

THE CONSTRUCTION OF BORRFOOT HARBOUR: Anyway, The Cooncil hired a couple of waspish architects from Barcelona as well as a *cordon bleu* chef – and why not? Waspish Catalan architects have to eat like the rest of us. Why two Catalan architects of an *hymenopteran* disposition? Well for one, the two of them were very 'social with narrow waists'; and secondly, have a look at the mess yon Catalans made of Holyrood – after that they could only get better, you would think. And by jingo, they did. See the proof below.

BORRFOOT HARBOUR ANTE-DELUVIAN

Post-deluvian Borrfoot Harbour (artist's impression: Final appearance may differ in some minor details).

Chapter 12

Intolerance and Skelp the Aged

After their circuit of the harbour, and having passed over the Rialto twice – Mungo remarked, 'That new, Tim?' The said Tim demurring an opinion, the two friends took a table at one of the many waterside restaurants that had sprung up in anticipation of the new development. All about them the air was replete with café culture, and just to sample a smattering of the topics one could pluck at random words and phrases such as…

'It may or may not be art, but I know what I like, Hermione…'

'Well you must be in the un-saveable throws of coprophilia, Fanny, because this etching is excremental…'

The only sour note for Mungo was that the outreach-Nardini's had a queue that went round the block, and he would not have a chance to inspect and compare the young ladies of Borrfoot and environs who, he presumed, would be serving those delicious Senior's Choice Traditional Fish Tea, (£7.50, 'For the over 60s only please!', Fish and Chips, Tea, Bread and Butter, yum, yum,) with the divine young ladies of Largs, the home of the original Nardini's.

Once comfortable, Tim ordered in French (of a sort) a *Caffè latte suprème* (dubious accents included in price), with the lightest dusting of finely ground chocolate (free range, fair trade, emissions compliant). Mungo was disappointed to find that Buckie was not yet on the wine list (it being mid-morning too!), and settled for something awful.

So. The conversation covered such diverse topics as having failed to deal with the issue of what the devil did Ethel mean by A PROJECT for Mungo. Tim said, 'We've failed to deal with the issue of what the devil Ethel meant by a Project, Mungo.'

When Idris got back from installing Ethel in the hospital, she said that Ethel had mentioned that Mungo needed something to keep him occupied while she, Ethel, wife and mistress of many years, was confined to bed. '*A project*' Idris reported Ethel had said. To make matters worse, that very morning while they were on buckets-duty, Tim had raised the matter as well. Does the man not take a hint for here he was bringing it up once more?

'A Project? What does that mean, Tim?' Mungo mused. This was the third time that day that the word had cropped up. His self-preservation instincts kicked in and he banished that word from his mind. But Tim, being the husband (or *mari*, since we are in a pavement café of a French bent or *penchant*) of Idris, had instructions to gee-up Mungo and get him a Project.

So. Now they had not faced up to that conundrum. At which point Tim had said the aforementioned words, which might be worth repeating, or not – 'Mungo, we've failed to deal with the issue of what the devil Ethel meant by a Project, Mungo.' Much in the same manner that Mungo had adopted Tim's dodgy-knee gait, so too had Tim begun to adopt certain speech patterns of his older friend – though that could have come from moving into Villa Laird, as it then was. Probably a matter that could only be settled by a complete psychiatric examination for which we do not have the time, nor Tim the money.

ANYWAY, Mungo expostulated, 'By Jove, so we have, Tim. Let's let it rest for a bit, I suggest. Sort of germinating much in the same way that so-called sparks of genius are no such thing.' He said as if he had an idea of what he was talking. He continued in a similar vein, 'Let's talk of other things, or better yet, let's feast our eyes on the Human Comedy[26] that streams past us.'

After some time, Tim it was who raised and propounded, expounded and banged on yet again upon the question of what the devil was meant by 'a project'. While Mungo listened with one side of his brain (and his opposite ear), Tim explained it was a social disease that was contracted by watching too much afternoon television (*telly*).

---

[26] *La Comedie Humaine, Balzac. Supposedly ninety odd novels. Did he never take a brek? Requests for reading order, have led us to conclude you should start at the back – the sports pages.*

'You take two people – the man person is invariably a tosser, though the woman sometimes is one as well (if a woman can be a tosser – tossess?). Sometimes it's two men.'

'Brothers, then.' Mungo contributed, and briefly his thoughts turned to his own brother whose name he forgot, before he caught Tim's blushing reply,

'No really, Mungo,' ripostes Tim, looking about in case someone else is listening.

'Ah, cousins.' Mungo liked that idea – after all it has been hinted more than once, that he and Ethel are cousins of the more-than-kissing variety.

'No really, Mungo,' Tim expostulates quietly, his blush transformed from salmon pink to the deepest *Rinstead Pastel*-hue, and very fetching too.

'Oh, Tim, if you mean homos, no need to be coy,' Mungo expostulates.

'Excuse me, sir.' A tall young man who might have been called Bradbury, in a Burberry ensemble spattered with the crumbs of a blueberry muffin, appeared at the table in an instant – well faster than he did the first time when they were looking for service, the sloth. 'That language, sir, you cannot use it.' And with that Bradbury strode away with a very determined and muscular gait.

'*Gay*, Mungo, that's the accepted term,' Tim explained crimsonly.

'*Gay*, but they never seem in the slightest bit *gay*,' Mungo began, his voice rising as this was a cause he was deeply devoted to in principle, for, despite his haute bourgeoisie background – especially that appalling private school – he celebrated diversity in all its forms (apart maybe those barbarians that liked to snip off the wee bit at the end of the willie of boy-weans[27]).

He continued, his voice rising to oratorical heights, so carried away was he with the thought of the power of his

---

[27] *Thus demonstrating how even-handed Mungo is: now he's got Jews, Muslims and some of the Bantu and Nilotic peoples after his arse. And as for FGM, not a laughing matter in any way; those are the real savages. It's happening in this country today. 'Celebrate diversity'?! Get the bastards!!!*

rhetoric, 'And why would they be *gay of spirit*, given the scandalous discrimination and abuse and ridicule to which they are subject on a daily basis?' Mungo said loudly and looked about and a ripple of applause disturbed the sultry air (it had turned sultry and it looked as if another tropical downpour would be needed to cleanse the now apposite curry from the pavement).

'Carry on, Tim, I'm fascinated with your explanation of whatever it was that brought us on to this stuff,' Mungo said generously, and nodded to the people of all ages, genders, denominations (and even a few that looked atheistic) as they drew their chairs nearer to be close to this wise sage. Then Mungo, never knowing quite when to quit, added by way of a codicil, 'Just like the way they treat the elderly, that's what it is.'

'Oh ph*que off, you old tosser you, and take your bus pass with you. We're subsidising the lot of you.' This came from an accent that sounded suspiciously like Jordanhill or Hampstead.

And, amid the scraping of chairs as the mob shrank back from the old coot, 'Free TV licenses you lot get.'

'And the winter fuel allowance.'

'Cold weather payment.'[28]

'Ph*cquing bed-blockers.' Now that was definitely Ubiquitous Chip clientele.

'Pensioners. Never had it so good, you lot!'

'Bus passes. Cannae get a seat on a bus for them.' (A plebeian note to that one).

By the time the mob had settled down – is there anything more frightening than the middle-classes and aspirant-bourgeoisie scenting blood? (Rhetorical question, by the way, just in case like) – BY THE TIME the mob had settled down, Tim had launched into a response to the business of 'projects' but not before he had muttered to Mungo *sotto voce*, 'Times like this I wish I was made like my cousins. Would have battered the melt oot o' that lot of wankers, so a wid. Now let's

---

[28] *The plonker that cried that out doesn't know her (women can be cruel as well, you know) Cold Weather Payment from her Winter Fuel Payment, thus betraying the nature of prejudice – pig-ignorance.*

83

ignore them. Projects, Mungo, that's what it was about. Places in the sun or Cornwall. Anyway, these tossers on the telly of whatever gender combination, they've got loads of money – no explanation of its source (we hope HMRC have got spooks that watch these programmes) – and they want to buy a place in the sun or Cornwall. You'd think that would be easy. But no, they want *a project*.

'Projects come in two forms: utterly uninhabitable ruins that you would not let your neighbour's rabid lurcher even piss in (keenly priced, and usually in Croatia or some other former Yugo republic war-zone of recent or future vintage).' Tim took a sip of his *Caffè latte suprème* with the lightest dusting of finely ground chocolate which had developed a skin that suggested it had been trialled as a ballistic vest for shooters in the Vietnam War. He continued:

'The second type is an impeccable villa with sea view, swimming pool, vineyard etc., and the two tossers go in with the camera crew and say: don't like the work surfaces – rip them out; don't like the footbath (we told you they are tossers) we'll put in another one. That is the nature of their *project*. Yes, let's put in a *cheeky offer*, they say spontaneously following the script (replete with phrases like: *double aspect* (two windows in a room!); *blank canvas* (white and bland throughout); *put our own stamp on it* (f*ck-up what is a perfectly good *hacienda, finca or bordello* (is the last a wine-shop in Spain or a little known gem of an Italian wine that the Sunday colour supplements remain ignorant of or keep to themselves?). ANYWAY, one of the tossers – usually the male – gets all tearful and choked with emotion.'

'Tearful and emotional? Men do that?' Mungo expostulated, and such was the accompanying susurration, he almost choked – *but not with emotion.*

'Disgusting,' Tim said patting Mungo on the back. 'Anyway, the absolutely ethical and morally unreprehensible estate agent has told the TV people that though it's priced at €2,000,000, *THE VENDORS* – you have to use that term, Mungo – will be prepared to accept an offer of around €76,000 and will throw in the Suzuki run-around (emissions compliant). Seems fair enough. The cheeky offer is accepted and the TV person – and one of them is the most beautiful creature outside of Nardini's in Largs (Jasmine: a Divine Goddess) – says to camera, 'Well, we wish (the two tossers) a happy life in their new place in the sun (or Cornwall).

Voiceover: 'Unfortunately when Gideon and Chardonnay returned to the UK the rozzers were waiting for them. See ya then for another edition of …'

Chapter 13

The Turnip Prize

Later, having satisfactorily put Tim's mind at ease regarding the facility with which Ethel got her hospital admissions thing – and incidentally having convinced Tim to try WD40 on his knee, before opting for the full *knee-ectomy* (medical term); and having exhausted their eyes on the moveable feast that streamed past in the hot sunshine – it was mid-January after all – one of them, in a moment of madness (not that type of *moment of madness* when married male politicians are caught *in flagrante* with young men in a park, or when a leader of a city cooncil is caught in a car in Linn Park in daylight and the best he can hope for career-wise is a professorship at a nearby uni); ANYWAYS, the innocent moment of madness led one of them to suggest moving on and lo…

'Shall we take in the Arts Centre and see if it gives us inspiration regarding THE PROJECT?' (which doesn't sound like either Tim or Mungo's speech patterns, but there you go…)

And so the two friends, from greatly different backgrounds, moved on having for the moment neatly procrastinated on the big question for the day.

Now, to the few of you who are not *au courant* with the world of Arts and Culture – perhaps you are from Glyndebourne or Haywards Heath and you've served your debt to society, or you remember the Tate Modern when it was a power station and was of benefit to the Commonweal – Borrfoot Arts Centre had, almost unnoticed – in fact definitely unnoticed – had become a thriving centre for new ideas. In fact, so much so that just at that very moment it housed the pre-Turner Prize Exhibition. (This outreach business with the cultural folks has become an obsession and they really need to get a grip, dig their collective heels in and say to governments: *'we're no' goin' oot tae visit the philistines; just*

86

give us the money for the Monet.' Anyway that's their business.)

Of course in the past there had been in the rival metropolis of Nullson, a long established Turnip Prize. This was the gold medal event, the Pythian Games, the Olympics of the Root Crop world – without the drugs (allegedly). And while the *bumi putra* (Malay: *sons of the soil*) of Borrfoot had long taken up the challenge to try and win the Golden Hoe, they had failed (hey-ho).

But now things had changed for the two towns were on culturally level terms: the Pre-Turner Prize Exhibition would outshine (just about) the annual Turnip Prize which with the Nullson Cattle Show, marked the end of the cultural season as they knew it; and the end of culture as everybody else knew it.

And so Tim and Mungo went inside as just at that moment there was a torrential downpour of a tropical sort, otherwise they would have given it a body-swerve. And wandering about the exhibits and wondering about the exhibits – they discovered:[29]

- a building project
- chairs with fur coats
- a table with pamphlets (so obviously representing 'myth-science of energy and consciousness research' as to be *trop outré* for our taste)
- a performance of nine songs for six voices - which we find to be too obvious and insufficiently subtle since it definitely borrows 'from conventional modes of narrative in order to create elaborate imagined forms.'

As the two neophyte art critics dried off by a radiator – having established that it was not an exhibit in contention for *The Turner* – they watched a chap and his wife wander about the place. Mungo speculated that he might be the art critic of *The Telegraph* given his noble *mien*. Tim postulated, in Holmesian

---

[29] *God's honest truth, right hand up to God an' that. (Okay, it was not held in Borrfoot, but by a certain rearranging of the alphabet it can be translated as Edinburgh. Everything else is true, including the true profession of the featured art critic.)*

tones, that this guy had been a postman, had a bad knee and was probably called Tommy.

As they observed, this chap went about and after assessing each exhibit pronounced, 'Shite.' The '*e*' at the end of the word weakened Mungo's thesis that he was from *The Telegraph*. After a bit the ex-postman's wife said for to him to moderate his language, after which on his third or fourth circuit, he pronounced each exhibit as 'Pish.' Evidently the exhibits had either grown on him or he had listened to his wife for once.

As Tim and Mungo made to leave, the art critic called to Tim, 'Knee still giving you gip, Tim?'

To which Tim replied, 'Aye, Tommy.' At which both – all four – made their excuses and left.

So. Outside, they continued their peregrinations which is where we will leave them for a bit.

Chapter 14

AT LAST MUNGO MAKES FOR the Queen Mary and Ethel (no relation)

So. Moving on, and having lost contact with Tim at B&Q where he was negotiating a special deal on 'extra water-retention' buckets, Mungo recalled to mind his quest that Idris had set him for the day. It is time that he gets to see his beloved Ethel and so, eschewing the taxi rank by the site of the projected Opera House, he, sauntered to the rank outside the site of the projected National Stadium. With his usual panache (he had again left his ash-pan behind) he asked the tattooed gal with the crew-cut to take him to the *Queen Mary*. On the journey, Mungo's attempts at engaging the cabbie in desultory conversation or even philosophical disquisition hit the buffers rudely after about two minutes into the journey when Mungo, having espied the strong jawline of the driver in the mirror said,

'I say, your name wouldn't be Betty would it?' This was greeted with a glance in the mirror, an excessively extravagant change of gear from fifth to second and a swerve, all of which contrived to throw Mungo on his face on the floor. Thinking the good lady had been taken aback by the fact that he had recognised her, he pressed home his advantage.

'Port Klang, Malaya, 'sixty-one. Just before the ethnic riots – not suggesting for one minute your good self had a role. If I remember correctly, Betty, you were chief stoker. Iron ore-carrier. Never forget a tattoo.' He ended with not a little self-congratulation.

Pin-sharp as ever, as he was being wrestled from the interior of the taxi, Mungo had the presence of mind to take down the cabby's details from the little plastic thing that irritatingly swings about. His last words to the … person … were, 'I warn you, so-called Jackson Brown, you'll be reported to the taxi czar for impersonating a man, and for downright rudeness. We all make mistakes, you know.'

Just at that a passing McGill's bus – '*Sorry not in service*' on the front – stopped and after an exchange of pleasantries in at least two languages, none of which either Mungo or Lech the driver knew, he was dropped off at the *Tail o' the Bank* in downtown Greenock right outside the *Queen Mary*, but not before he had supervised the dis-loading (Lech's term) of various white goods, in which Mungo's experience of being a National Service whitey at Klang Port, KL, stood him in good stead. Mungo had been nominally in charge of supplies but the natives did what the bersetubuh[30] they liked; this being much more efficient than anything Mungo could have devised.

To the *Queen Mary*… as luck would have it, the great Cunarder was paying some sort of courtesy call, which Greenockians – famous as far as Port Glasgow for their own brand of courtesy – reciprocated by ignoring 'That Shuge Big Boat Thing' that had appeared overnight. Mungo's steel-trap mind took in the situation in an instant – that big boat thing did not look like a hospital ship. Or at least not one in which his Ethel would be ensconced. And why was he in Greenock? How did he know he was in Greenock?[31] Elementary: it was full of old, abandoned sugar mills and derelict rope works.

As for the handsome inhabitants of that place, they went about their lawful (mostly) business, which involved going up the hill and looking with nostalgia and other forms of disease of the soul, on the derelict sugar mills that had sent out their product and had rotted the teeth of generations without fear or favour or discrimination on the basis of colour, creed, ethnicity (technically not quite the same as colour), sexual orientation, gender, ability or disability or … eh… any other term taken from The Equality Act 2010, and any other act we have missed but promise to abide by as ignorance is no excuse, m'lud.

A few semi-upright stragglers, of a radical bent, chose to ignore the old sugar mills, and instead visited the equally

---

[30] *Indonesian; like the French not having a word for entrepreneur (G.W. Bush), there is no word equivalent to 'f*ck' in Malay. Hasn't stopped them though, and why not?*

[31] *From the Gaelic 'grianaig' for 'sunny". Those of you who know the Tail o' the Bank will appreciate that the ancient Gaels were as big on irony as yon Greeks.*

depressing or culturally stimulating site of the rope works. What their thoughts were as they thought of that product – *Ropes no more*, in words that Sting, Stung or Stang might have pinned, punned or panned – we will draw a veil over, (though not a *niqab* we hasten to add – one of us has a wee fancy for the *hijab* (not to wear we even more hastily add), or even better the *shayla* – which has no connection with Australia or one of our wives. And we do not mean any disrespect[32] – honestly. In fact, we might go back and delete the previous, for no amount of Kaolin and Morphine is gonna stop the skits if that mob reads this book).

So. It was a sunny day in Greenock. Never being one to miss an opportunity – and by his timepiece (sorry pawned, and anyway Mungo has no need for conventional measures of time) it was too early to get back to Borrfoot and its hospital which is in fact Queen *Margaret* – Mungo gets *Margaret* and *Mary* mixed up (easily done) – wherein abed (and in a bed) his beloved Ethel awaits.

SO. Mungo decided that he would grasp the moment, and as he had never been in Greenock before – that he remembered (always an important caveat for Mungo) – he thought it an opportunity not to be missed, especially since it reminded him of Klang Port, with its hot sun beating down, the shimmering water, the smell of curry for breakfast (all day too).

So. Head down, Mungo pulled his faithful charcoal Crombie (original red-lining '*a touch of the dandy that reflects the wearer's personality*' £895.00. Shopper's tip: you can get a Snorkel in Peacocks or Primark (with ersatz fur trimming in the hood – no animals harmed, etc. **– THE ONE BELOW:**

---

[32] *We are with Lord Blunkett on this: Sharia is fine by us; where we differ from the 'noble lord', is, firstly we don't have a blind dug; secondly we would so much prefer Sharia to be applied in some place with lots of sand (not Saltcoats, Ardrossan or Chesil Beach (the beach, not the book), and certainly not the hallowed bunkers of Royal Troon or Birkdale. (We concede – let the women in).*

look at the price!

Faux Mongolian Fur Collar PU Jacket for £30.00! Where
are you going to beat that for style and price? Can you not
just see Mungo in that? (Crombie no more!)

Anyway, that's not our concern. So: with that Crombie draped about his thin but erect shoulders he raised the collar against the warm breeze that had blown up from the Sahara (there are some pluses with global warming, including getting rid of those neck and shoulder pains without recourse to drugs or legal highs); and the brim of his old black homburg (Christys' and Co; £125 atow) [For alternative see below: competitively priced *Black Aztec-Band Fedora*, Primark, where else? Seriously!] WE SAY, his old homburg offered protection against the glare of the midday sun (it must be later than that! He thought, searching in his waistcoat pocket where his watch should have been (Gold Full Hunter, B'ham 1906; approx. value today: £2750; sold at Cash Convertors for... a lot less).

He couldn't have cared less. Not about the sun and the scorching Sirrocco (if that's what it was and if that is how you spell it – the hot wind from the Sahara, to be clear; not the car from our great friends the Jerries, nor *the rooftop restaurant that Bangkok proudly calls its best*[33]). Nor did he care a toss for the heat and dust that reminded him of India (well a film with the lovely Julie Christie in it; without Googling we think another Merchant Ivory piece of candy floss dressed up as socio-historico comment); nor the blistering tarmac beneath his feet (encased in semi-brogue Oxfords; *Crockett and Jones of Northampton* £209 atow) that had been reserved for just such days since he was entering manhood (the spots are still there for another four or five years, son).

Hint: have a look at the next image – not wishing to be dogmatic, just saying like.

Black Aztec Band Fedora for £8.00 at Primark. This is top of the range. We think that Mungo would look spiffy in this. For eight quid? Who can dissent with that?

---

[33] *Actually see TripAdvisor where it came #96 out of 8721 restaurants in Bangkok! So. Where did it all go wrong George?*

[While probably not suitable for Mungo, we can just see Ethel on one of these. Even both? (Price on request)]

All of these thoughts and much less, sped through his steel-trap mind as he headed along the front towards, what he did not know was, the more salubrious pairt of Greenock called Gourock.

After a time, the weather changed and a solitary cloud materialised in the shape of New Zealand's South Island (*Te Waipounamu* to give it a name that celebrates diversity but not dyslexia) before it dissolved and the sun reappeared, and Mungo felt rejuvenated and tired at the same time. He paused for breath, sat on a bench, and taking offhis bunnet (yes it's his Homburg; it could so easily be that Primark *Black Aztec Band Fedora* – quality, man, sheer quality; in fact, we'll throw in two for £12.00. Who can argue with that?).

ANYWAY, Mungo wiped his brow and felt at one with the world. A moment later he felt something in his bunnet. Some scoundrel had put loose change into it as if his bunnet was a recycling bin. Before he could gather his thoughts and count the change, another splash of small copper *sans argent* (silver) hit the interior and the label.

For a brief moment he wished he had brought his moothie (mouth or mooth organ: Victory, £4.00, includes case and wee chamois (the cloth not Bambi) Lidl, where else?). He had worked on his *Red River Valley* since he had picked it up with the *multi-use ladders* that he had not been able to get out the box, and felt that a little bit of busking would recoup his – taxi fare as there was no guarantee that Lech the bus driver would be back to get him in front of the Big Boat, as promised. Though a promise by a Pole is like a... like the best kind of assurance you'll ever get this side of PPI or *Webuyanyshitedotcom*. But he didn't have his harmonica with him – in fact he hadn't seen it in four years.

So. So he sat back, bunnet in the recumbent position on his knee, and he half-closed his eyes. Suddenly! Bunnet, change and all were gone! Mungo glowered as the wee bastard kitted out in fetching Velcro on a skateboard thing wheeched and whistled away.

Ho-hum, Mungo thought with that *insouciance* he was in danger of being stereotyped with, and resumed his perambulation – what he had never earned, he had never owned, or some homily like that came to mind and was supposed to console him. But his ph*cquing Homburg was gone! Still, 'lose a bunnet keep the heid' the Bard might have said and that little epithet would go into his collection beside 'If music be the love of food… turn up the volume and scoff the lot.'– *Anonymous… Fat Bastard*

So much for Gourock being the better pairt. He went back towards Greenock (pronounced *Gren*nock, by the guid burgers of Gourock— who has not looked with wonder on Rodin's the Burgers of Calais and thought of those effete fuds that they are; the Greenockians, that is, though those of Calais run them close, by jings.)

And lo! A shimmering image approached, or seemed to, and he saw an oasis in the desert of old sugar mills and abandoned rope works: a Turf Accountant. 'Now yer talkin,' he might have said had he been brought up in the denizens (or Dennistoun for that matter): this was his lucky day. Why before he had left the house – Villa Idris – the eponymous Idris had slipped him a copy of the *Racing Post* and with a little wink, had whispered that he must not let Ethel see it when he got to the hospital. And why, had he not on Lech the driver's bus, had he not spent a greater part of that provocatively circuitous journey studying form? And had he not, isolated a nice little double across the jumps cards at Towcester and Hexham. Forsooth, enough – get the deed done – to the Starting Post!

And so it was with a spring in his heels and a wad of cotton in his leaking ear, that he entered the said Turf Accountant, Miliband Brothers.

'You're barred. Oot!' He was exclamated at by the disembodied voice behind the quadruple-glazed window.

Mungo looked to see who had followed him in. No one. He approached the defensive screen and the little fellow behind it stood on the tip toes of his elevator shoes (Otis, £47.99) to hold out what looked like a hand grenade, but was only a pepper spray with a little side-jigger of mace.

'Ah'm no' afraid to use this,' the amiable-looking fellow yelped.

Mungo began, 'I'm sorry, there seems to be some mistake. I've never set foot in this little town let alone inside this … (he was about to say 'hovel', but felt that was maybe praising it too highly and settled for 'cowp'.

UPON WHICH a debate sprung up among the clientele, the essence of which was that one client of the punting variety offered that it was he, Mungo, who had been there before and was banned for behaviour that cannot be repeated in newsprint because said scoundrel – Mungo or otherwise – looked like the type who might have relations within the legal fraternity. Then another punter (to give them a name that carries no stigma) says 'no' with all the certainty that suggested he might have been an economist: it was Mungo's identical-double but different – the other one was dressed the same; but was taller – well not taller, but appeared taller than Mungo. If they were twins, the expert in genetics and heredity (for it was he and he looked up into that same Petri dish in which he had conceived Dolly the Fuc*ing/Fuc*less/Fu*kinguseless Sheep), opined that they most certainly were not *monozygotic*. The other punters considered this for a moment, then the house divided between those who supported the conjecture, and those who favoured *dizygotic* twins.

'Torquil!' Mungo mumbled (he had dislodged that caramel from a cavity a couple of hours ago).

Chapter 15

Doppelganger on my shoulder and nae big bright moon above

'Torquil!' Mungo mumbled (he had dislodged that caramel from a cavity a couple of hours ago).

Explanation: Torquil, formerly known as Buffy, was his brother who always appeared when least expected or least wanted and who had, despite being a Major in the army, had never been convicted by any courts martial of any malfeasance (nicking regimental funds) moreover. He tended to infuriate Mungo by being perfectly pleasant and a source of munificence and bounty in the form of crates of … postal orders and cheques of uncertain provenance, some of which he had not printed himself, a few of which had even been honoured.

In Greenock the town had long been divided along these lines – *genetics and the development of the zygot* into one or two (or more) embryos. Families were divided in this ideological dispute.

In many ways this controversy is mirrored in the still to be mentioned difference between Borrdookians and Nullsonians in terms of their preferences for speech patterns – Nullsonians spoke in *iambic pentameters*, while Borrdookians favoured the *dactylic pentameter*. While this is hardly relevant to the dilemma facing Mungo who desperately need to get his line on (argot for *put* a bet on), it does illustrate how at the base of all disputes there are matters intellectual, no matter how impoverished of spirit these communities might appear to the mean-spirited outsider. So there!

ANYWAY the debate in this case was largely irrelevant as MUNGO MADE HIS EXCUSES AND LEFT, but not before drawing the attention of the patrons to a monograph he had penned: *On rainfall and inherited regression with special reference to The Tail O' the Bank – a speculative prolegomenon.*[34] which, as it turned out, united the patrons across the divide as they chased him from the premise. He was saved by the magic words of the tannoy announcer: *they're at the post at Badminton…*

ANYWAY, as his steel-trap mind foggily came to the vague conclusion that it had been Torquil that had upset the natives in this Greenockian bookies, he made his excuses and left and to his joy, in the window of the shop next door – a charity shoap – he espied his Homburg. After some negotiation he emerged with his homburg and a lovely sequinned purse in mother-of-pearl; a salt and pepper set bearing the image of Cliff Richard, and a tape of Shani Wallis playing the bleeding zither (though one of us thinks it was probably Shirley Abicair).

---

[34] *Alas the book for which the prolegomenon was to be the introductory essay, was never writ.*

Chapter 16

Later: Home is the sailor... getting closer to the hospital

So. After a busy and largely educational half day spent in Greenock, during which he had learnt precious little, Mungo wended his way back to Borrfoot. The driver had taken one look at the proffered entitlement card (bus pass by another name) and looked from the photo of Idris (the genuine entitlement card) to the visage of Mungo before him, had shooken (he's not quite mastered the native grammar) his head and issued the *billet* without obvious rancour. The Poles were great chaps for recognising a fellow alien either that or they were broadminded and well-bred enough to tactfully turn two blind eyes to a transvestite operation well-bungled.

With a bit of luck visiting time would be over should he ever make it to the hospital that was giving succour to his precious Ethel. And on that journey by bus Mungo looked out the window and reflected on how, as well as having been a learning experience it had been in some other ways too, a profitable day: he had cleared sixty-five pence at the Miliband Brothers – where strangely his doppelganger – for it is Torquil, his brother – had not (yet) been barred; he had had two good plates of soup at the Seaman's mission. The only skelf in his bum so to speak, was when he had asked the kind lady serving the soup what kind it was.

"sf*ckin'soupsoitis!' she had fluted, adding some of her sibilant saliva to the tureen in the process. Mungo had made a mental note not to bother with a third plate. And when he had taken a closer look at the good lady – he had admired and then perused her tattoo, but did not comment audibly on it, as far as he knew – he thought he had encountered the said lady in the dim and distant past, maybe even on that short taxi-ride? Nay! – Malaysia, could have been – yes! That was it! She had been a stoker on a ship that had called into Klang Port for refuelling. The ship that is, not the lady. He would maybe ask her later. But he was pretty confident. He had that kind of mind.

So anyway, another bus driver – and probably a Pole, for they are renowned for their ubiquity, cheerfulness and their delight in surviving another day, as we would too if we thought each day we were going to be invaded by Putin's hordes (only kidding Vlad) – so anyway this Polish bus driver apologised for not being able to take the bus right up to the hospital door for Mungo (he had already gone out of his way by pulling into the car park at Asda to pick up a telly (one week only: 49" flat screen LED: £499.00 atow) for the woman in the side seat with the Rottweiler that had been making admiring glances at Mungo; so Mungo thought it would be churlish to insist that *he* be driven all the way up to the hospital.

And so, at last having swapped business cards with the driver – Mungo's had actually been taken from Miliband Brothers, Turf Accountants – he began his pilgrimage up the long hill to the red-brick Victorian hospital, now a worn-down grimy grey, in-keeping with Old Town Borrfoot itself (as it was designated on the Heritage Trail plates that had once graced the pavements, walls and bunkers (Cold War era) of the town).

A motion had been passed at the Cooncil to change its name *to La Vieille Ville Borrfoot*, as it was twinned with *Rennes-sur-Pigeoncrottes*, but the meeting was inquorate because the chairperson and her deputy were passing their own motions after a particularly virulent left-over curry working-breakfast that worked remarkably quickly and left nothing left over but (left) everything else working over-well.

Anyway, Mungo laden with his *Bag for Life*, trekked all the way up to the hospital and as he passed through the gates, made a note to pen a letter to the local journal on the need for some serious weeding to be undertaken at the hospital as well as someone to fix the gate that was hanging off its hinges. The other gate was presumably being melted down in China or Nullson right at this very moment. And what about those windows?! All boarded up. Surely that cannot be conducive to patient care and welfare. Or perhaps not: Health and Safety. Stop deranged individuals – some of them patients – from jumping to their doom.

And then as he banged on the front door with its padlocks and chains and the notice warning of *Danger Unsafe Structure* etc., Mungo's steel-trap brain took all of this in, in an instant in Mungo-Time and realised: THEY HAD CLOSED THE PLACE DOWN. (And no' before time!).

He trusted it had nothing to do with the arrival of Ethel.

Chapter 17

Mungo meets Albie

So. Having realised that he had mistaken the name of the hospital that contained his wife it was with a spring in his step and yet another caramel in his mouth that Mungo set out back down the hill into the town to ascertain the precise location of the new Queen Margaret (not Mary) Hospital, for the day was proceeding, the sun was below the yardarm and Ethel would be getting rather testy in hospital with all the healthy food they would be forcing on her, not to mention the fruit-juices and lactose-based fluids with which to wash the nutritionally-balanced diet down. She would be having the heebie-jeebies, or both separately if not one at a time, by this time more than likely if he was much longer.

Mungo quickened his pace at the very thought of his lover suffering so, and looked to find a source of information. He reasoned that with all the changes in the old town, there was bound to be a Tourist Information Centre and lo! There it was. But even more lo! Next door to it was a Turf Accountant! The very place! For the clientele of such establishments usually have a close affinity with those in need of hospital care, indeed often the two categories overlap – what mathematicians, in that earthy way that endears them to us civilians, represent using set-theory as in the Venn diagram below: (which is largely self-explanatory, but for the sake of equity we will go through the motions).

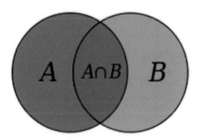

Let *A* be the set of all punters and *B* be the set of those needing hospital care; then *A∩B* is the common set (those who are punters in need of hospital care). Incidentally, this is a good illustration of the axiom that mathematics is a language that expresses the commonplace in a complex manner. So, if you were not strong in maths, no need at all to worry about it – the fault, dear reader, is not in ourselves, but lies elsewhere (Hint: it's the mathematicians to blame). Additional note: if your reading in black-and-white, *A∩B* is sort of purple.

THE POINT BEING: Mungo would be able to obtain the information he sought more efficiently from the bookies than from the Tourist Information Office (which was shut anyway, it being a public holiday).

It seemed as if it was nearly sixty years since Mungo had been inside a bookies. He had already forgotten about his morning visit to Milibands and anyway that does not count as it was in Greenock...

All his post-teenage myriad bets had been strictly laid by telephone accounts. But then on his voyage of today – which had more of the Iliad than the Odyssey about it (it would end in tears) – to the chthonic (not the Taiwanese metal band – the so-called 'Black Sabbath of Asia') environs of Greenock that very bless'd morn, he had rediscovered his fondness for the camaraderie of the lost souls, the sweat of the punters, the roar of the tannoy, the smell of the toilet on fire. Then, he remembered that bless'd morn, seemed like it had been decades before, Mungo had had little chance to study, to embrace the atmosphere as he was turfed out tout-de-suite due to the (apparent) misdemeanours of his brother, Torquil. But now he was drawn in and this looked the type of place that would welcome even the normal.[35]

He entered and inhaled and it was as if the horses themselves had been stabled therein overnight. Then he saw that it was an Alsatian (canine variety) of indeterminate gender that had left a little reminder behind. The sooner that new Korean chippie gets a licence, the sooner the streets will be clean, he mused.

Mungo doffed his bunnet and smiled at the man sitting high up behind his security grille. The bookie, one Albie Freeman gave Mungo a stingy-looking nod and turned to his lovely companion. But before we tell you about the lovely companion, (OK, she's called Raylene, but that's enough for now), we'll dwell a moment on the emotions that boiled-up in Mungo as he looked around: it was his yoof all over again.

If indeed, as his faulty memory told him it had been sixty years since last he entered such a place – and let's face it, he may have been suffering from 'self-inflicted-memory-loss' (a term he had penned in an authoritative article for Wikipedia and which now was part of the currency of the gibberish spoken by psychologists and BBC experts on gardening, cookery and antiques – often the same person: a beanpole clothes horse of indeterminate gender), anyway it seemed as if it was sixty years since…

It seemed nothing had changed in the interim apart from the punters now being (allowed) encouraged – nay compelled to *linger*. In Mungo's illicit, underage sojourns into unlicensed betting shops (pre-1961 – usually up a close or, he remembered the deliberately unwelcoming premises that discouraged punters lingering/remaining longer than it took to punt). This 'shop' - what little he could see of it through the thick fug of cigarette and suspiciously sweeter substance smoke - was less than Spartan, albeit surprisingly spacious and then there was … *the smoke*!

Cigarette smoke! Even one old chap sitting at the centre table puffing on a *pipe*! Could it be that by some peculiarity of Scot's Law, this little enclave was immune from the predations

---

[35] *Gaussian definition, for those of a sensitive disposition.*

of the Smoking, Health and Social Care (Scotland) Act 2005? Mungo's steel-trap brain recalled – as he lit up a small cigar – that there were a number of exceptions to the ban in public places: if he recalled his Wikipedia properly, this included prisons, care homes and police interview rooms. He 'scoped' the clientele and it seemed clear to him that they would all be equally at home in at least two out of three of those listed. He sighed luxuriously, 'Home at last,' and with that, his troubles were banished again from that wee space in his brain that held annoying things.

Mungo smiled at the man sitting high up behind his security grille. The bookie, one Albie Freeman, grunted winsomely in return, and turned to his lovely companion. But before we tell you about the lovely companion (okay, she's still called Raylene, but that's still enough for now), we'll concentrate on Albie.

Albie Freeman was born *Andrew Albert Christian Edwards*. And all was well for Andy Edwards when he inherited his Turf Accountancy profession. Even when betting was licensed (made legal) in 1961, he sort of thrived. Then one day 'a voice cried out to him, like a thunderclap from above', which turned out it was. The woman upstairs called down for him to make less noise or she would send her daughter down to straighten him out, which she duly did. And when his eyes alighted on the princess that was Rachel 'Dixie' Freeman, his fate was sealed as were certain changes to his name(s).

For starters, Dixie was of the Hebraic persuasion (we're not sure if it's okay to use the term 'Jewess' so we have circumlocuted a little), so during the negotiations over the marriage, the 'Christian' fell by the wayside promptly without so much as a Publican crossing the road to render first aid. Secondly, as Andrew Albert, had long been an admirer of the accountancy skills of the great Myer Lansky ('the Mob's Accountant') – the character of Hyman Roth (a less-than nuanced performance by Lee 'The Method' Strasberg, (6/10) in *The Godfather Part II*) was based on Lansky – Andrew Albert grabbed this opportunity to move towards the Hebraic end of the religious spectrum and decided Albert – better yet, 'Albie' – was more consonant with the self-image he was rapidly forming. From there it was but a short step to embracing the whole *flaky borekas* when he married Dixie: thus he became Albie Freeman, Turf Accountant.

Along the way there were a few hiccups, like when it was pointed out to him by Dixie's uncle, a Rabbi, that observing the Sabbath (*Shabbat*) would mean closing the shop on a Friday evening *through to, and including all day Saturday*! That was a problem as Saturday was his best day. When after a few months of marriage this was again pointed out to him with emphasis that as a fully confirmed member of the Hebrew faith, he should observe Shabbat, Albie rent his gown and pulled his hair and cried out, אלוהים, אלוהים, אני חוטא, which is self-explanatory, and he carried on raking it in on Shabbat, (but felt guilty, even remorseful, by the way). As to the old circumcision, he felt it was not too big a drawback to pass over that one.

When Dixie eventually left him for a real accountant, punters and his friend would say, 'But Albie, you're not really a Jew, your middle name was Christian, you're probably in line to the Head of the C of E, so why don't you forget this whole Hebrew business and stop suffering with your conscience?' And he would reply, 'You don't just abandon six thousand[36] years of history lightly.'

Six thousand years or six years, since Dixie departed Albie's returns were shrinking by the day. And where was he? Stuck here. The smallest small-time bookie as far as his glass eye could cry over. So small and decrepit was his operation in fact that even Benny Queen, the Sweeper-Up of one-man bookies, would not buy Albie out. Benny had laughed in Albie's face when Albie had offered to sell his business to him. 'I might not have much taste Albert, you need only consider my portfolio to know that – twenty-seven shops deliberately sited in all in the worst areas of the West: Borrfoot, Paisley, Clydebank and Glasgow, even as far north as Bishopbriggs

---

[36] *We think the figure of six-thousand years is Albie's rounding-down of Bishop Ussher's (1581-1656) dating of The World to 4004 BC. Seems close-enough. Further note: aye wi' the three 's's in the good Bishop's moniker.*

but I draw the line at a shop in The Park. F*ck's safe, Albie, you think because I'm ten years older than you, I'm going senile, old son?!'

Albie could just remember (he was sixty-three now and looked much older) when his dad's shop had some, if not cachet or prestige, at least decent takings. And decent customers. Then they knocked down the Victorian dwellings relocated the Victorian dwellers to build The Park. High Rise would have been an improvement, but by that decade even High Rise flats were passé if not actually commencing the slow, painful process of inexorably falling to bits and ending in blissful demolition if enough bits had not self-destructed.

And now his 'clientele' – no, his punters, had shrunk to meagre rations. He had looked about his shop just after Mungo had first entered and thought: Is this it? It would not take much for him to throw in the towel.

Next minute, as if to kick a man when he's down, that old stranger in the old Homburg and shiny Crombie and that worn, frayed shirt-collar (looks as if his mother turned the collar for him fifty years ago,) he's collecting his winnings. And he's just in, and he'll probably disappear never to appear again. Or if he does, it'll be to relieve his bladder (Albie does not know about Mungo's pelvic-floor exercises).

At that moment Albie wished he had gone to those Yiddish night-classes Dixie had tried to force on him. Then he would be able to come out with some stereotypical mouthings of desperation or of calling down the curses of *Yahweh* on his own head and on the heads of his enemies. (You know the sort of really annoying thing that a character supposedly of the Hebraic persuasion says on TV: *A falsheh matba'ieh farliert men nit*; *A klog tsu meineh sonim. Geh in der klozet).*

Funnily enough, re that last saying, Mungo collected his thirty-two pounds shyly and asked to use the toilet, which on viewing he suddenly felt that his needs were no more (for which there is another Yiddish phrase), and instead did his pelvic-floor exercises (which need not be done on the floor, and one of us can testify, actually work!).

The bookie mumbled out of the side of his mouth – an aside to a youngish female sitting on high next to him (yes it's still

Raylene – she's a cracker). She looked as if she might turn a pretty ankle, Mungo thought – though in an unpolished way, the very best of ways as far as Mungo was concerned. The security grille she sat behind added to her elusive, somehow illicit allure. He watched her through hooded eyes as the bookie continued grumbling.

'See this betting business, CChhrraylene, it's goin' cchhrright tae the dugs, ah'm tellin ye. For twa pins or cchhrreeree bob I wid ...jack it in the mocchhrrra ...' then he breathed a sigh of relief: the old boy in the homburg had returned toute de suite from the toilet and was lingering, scanning the runners and riders again. Great (or *oy vey* or something apposite) Albie said to himself – I'll get that thirty-two quid back and more before the sun sets on the malahwach-bakers of Yemen.' (We made the last bit up; but he did say that about getting the thirty-two quid back from Mungo.)

Mungo's sharp ears missed nothing of this despite the extreme throat-clearing 'cchrr' and rolling Rs – on second thoughts, that might fit in to odd vocalisations. (We'll write this one up as a discussion paper on conversion or even *conversation* disorders and have Mungo send it off to his publishers.)

Meantime, Mungo's gimlet eyes missed nothing of Raylene who was ignoring the bookie, busying herself with checking betting slips as her boss grumbled on:

'You'rre smarrterr than me, hen. Always werre. Getting' oot in time. Oh you'll be aw rright overr at Hillbrrokes, Ms Rraylene McMasterr... wi yerr pension scheme, company sharres and whitno'. Oh an please dinne you worrrry aboot me stuck here wi' ma Sweet FA...an' don't botherr yerr err*e sending me owerr food parrcels or anything cos ah'll be in the canal. Deid. Drroont. Corronerr's Verrdict? Pissed as a newt but no' as guid a swimmerr...' The bookie dry spat, probably due to the condensed overload of Rs, (RRs) Mungo guessed. (Mungo wondered later whether there was a perverse attention-drawing Freudian or Jungian trope in operation here. That is, sufferers such as the bookie seemed to unconsciously *choose to use* words containing the letter R. Mungo had a younger musician relation who suffered similarly and insisted the 'genrre the grroup' he was in was 'RRorry Gallachrr Trribute Trrio'. As for lispers and aspirants and choosing 'S' words, Mungo did not want to think of that ever again as it conjured up memories of a dead police constable. (See near the end of our first novel *Skelp the Aged*. Well worth a read and a bargain still at £8.99 atow... ANYWAY, Mungo's antennae were now in full receive mode. He stood just close enough and long enough to hear as much as he needed before giving exactly half his winnings back to the bookie by leaving a £15.00, Lucky 15' (15 lines at £1.00 per line *—see also glossary for full instructions/details*) across the late afternoon cards at Wincanton, Kempton and Punchestown, hoping that the form he had kept aware of, and up with, all his adult life and during the all too short months in the Algarve would stand him in as good stead as the earlier certain knowledge that that canny North of England racehorse trainer did not send one lone member of his tiny but select stable all the way south to Kempton Park for a day out or for a change to Southern air that the odds of 14/1 Mungo got might have previously suggested.

And with that, Mungo left with a cheery wave to his new friend, Albie the bookie and his lovely assistant, Raylene.

To the hospital at last.

Chapter 18

The hospital at last – reflections in glass double doors

The hospital's glass double doors sighed open and sucked Mungo in to the generously proportioned reception area that was redolent of a five-star hotel, the air fresh and subtly scented, the floor polished and yet soft beneath his feet. For a moment Mungo thought he had been transported back to KL and he was no longer barred from the Pan Pacific. He looked around him as the bright receptionist – Venezia, according to her name badge – punched his name into a computer then handed him a slip of paper with instructions how to find his Ethel. Maybe Tim was right – maybe this was a private hospital. Sunny Portugal though just less than a week hence now seemed a lifetime away, a lifetime as long as Mungo's. He took the slip of paper and the smile from Venezia and mulled what all of this meant: it came down to one thing: modern visiting hours are insufficiently restrictive of the visitor.

As he moved toward the bank of lifts he mentally penned a paper in which he would argue that unrestricted access was harmful to patient and visitor alike (and to staff – but they would feature in another paper). The visitor had no excuse for not visiting at some point in the day; moreover, it made it difficult to just get up and leave the patient – no bell ringing to call a halt to the penance; no sour-faced matron telling one to bugger off (no sour-faced matrons at all now). And from the patients point of view it was simple: they had to pretend interest and appreciation of the effort made to come and sit with them. In the conclusion to his paper, Mungo would call for strict limiting of visiting hours, not just for the psychological damage inflicted on patient and visitor alike – and here was the clincher – but also if for no other reason than to say that all the problems with germs in wards comes from the visitor. Yes, this paper would do for hospitals what his paper demanding equal treatment between alcoholics and heroin addicts had done for the treatment of those with addictions. (Simple: alkies to get a wee shot of *goldie* in the morning[37] in the same way that junkies (excuse the language) get a little *greenie* of methadone.)

Mungo's view of hospitals was a very simple one. He did not like them one bit. He viewed them as a category of modern institutions like prisons and Royal Caribbean cruises to the Western Mediterranean (*Western Med* in the language of the street): in each of these institutions you find yourself in company that you would not normally choose to be in. But hospitals were even more *anathemic* to Mungo because they were dangerous places: they were full of people who were sick and injured and in other ways disadvantaged. Then there were the patients.

Hospitals were, like prisons and some cruise liners, very dangerous places. There was a very good chance that you might go in (go aboard) perfectly healthy (limbs, psyche, organs and bowels all intact) but you would probably come out (disembark) with something egregious. It seems obvious at one level – you visit someone in the infectious diseases ward (very brave), you catch something. That was all in the risk sheet given to you. So far so straightforward. Now here is the sophisticated part of his thesis: you visit someone on the fractures ward, you come out with something broken – if you're very lucky it'll be that tiny wee bone at the base of your hand, on the wrist sort-of, just below where the thumb joins the rest [this could probably be best described by a Venn diagram but we'll soldier on] – it just came to us: could be the *scaphoid* – you'll know it, for who among us has not fallen over on a Christmas night-out, out with the workmates – celebrating Santa's birthday; who among us has not got lodged in a too low hawthorn bush and contemplated the stars and wondered: which one is the Star of Bethlehem? Only to find that having been extricated by a passing publican that a couple of days later, you have this little pain where it was described above in

---

[37] *At least one enlightened treatment centre for alcoholics (sorry, it's in Canada) has adopted Mungo's suggestion – although they hand out wine at hourly intervals and not wee goldies. http://www.bbc.co.uk/news/magazine-36717557*

lay terms. If you're over forty, that pain is with you for the rest of your natural even if you do not go out on another Christmas work's night. Ever.

ANYWAY: Mungo's conjecture is that there is a good chance you'll fall over in the fracture's ward because of the crutches and other things for helping the fractured hobble about. Even if you're visiting a patient with a broken arm, he/she might *stookie* you by accident when illustrating a point. [*stookie* being the technical term for being damaged – intentionally or unintentionally – by someone else's 'plaster cast'. Note: as well as being a transitive verb, *stookie* can double as a noun viz: the plaster cast *per se*.]

Saddest of all cases is that of the psychiatric ward. To see a loved one losing touch with reality would make anyone chronically depressed as would reading about it, so we will pass on, for Mungo has been sucked in by the sighing, glass double doors and it is time to follow him.

He passed through myriad corridors, a virtual labyrinth, half expecting a charging Minotaur round every corner, only having to double, now treble, back and peer at the Giant Noticeboard in Reception all of three times having forgotten his glasses then forgetting what he thought he had discerned by way of directions to the ward containing his sick wife. (That piece of paper handed to him by Venezia, had been tossed into a chrome waste bin, as Mungo had memorised the directions. Now if he could just remember which bin…

By the time he reached Ethel's ward he was knackered and certain he was completely contaminated and would spend the rest of his life plagued by MRSA, or e-coli, or salmonella or athlete's foot, front *and* back or whatever the latest Super Bug that reportedly lurked all over hospital nooks, crannies and corridors these days. (*Sunday Mail, Mail on Sunday, Sunday Post* … take your pick of these authoritative sources on medical matters).

Just outside the swing doors of Ward Ethel he greedily dosed his hands, wrists, face, neck and semi-exposed ankles with the walled dispensable goo that claimed to kill *most household* but apparently not nearly all hospital germs.[38] He thought about cleaning his shoes then thought better of it as the goo had run out.

Ethel looked better now, Mungo felt. Then he realised: that's not Ethel! Wrong ward! Still she was very pleasant to him and would not let go of his hand until he had plumped up her pillows and planted a gentle peck on her rather peachy complexion and had promised to visit her again. As he reached the door a ph*cquing great hair brush caught him on the napper. He turned as his new friend waved and called to him,

'You'll no forget noo.' Of such little things are memories made. Or not.

At last he found the little room that contained Ethel and who accounted for seven-eighths of the visible space, like some great inverted iceberg. It even had an *en-suite*, with a footbath – quite tasteful too. Wouldn't mind a few nights in here meself, thought Mungo as he set out his myriad goodies on the tiny cabinet by the bed. We would like to say that Ethel interrogated Mungo as to whether Idris was looking after him, was feeding him all right, how many of the dugs had bitten him, had 'that Tim' made him go up into the loft to change the buckets, was he sleeping all right, did he have enough pocket money, etc., displaying her infinite capacity for *solicitousness*. But her first words were:

'Mungo, did you bring some?!' Ethel tugged the cover up about her generous bosom, in an unnecessary display of modesty. Her lips closed tightly on the last syllable. She waited.

Mungo thought to himself, 'Why does she not ask how my day has been?' He sighed and sat down.

'Okay, Mungo, how has your day been, dear?'

'Uneventful, dear, humdrum.'

'Okay, Mungo, did you bring some?!'

Mungo looked about but not one of the staff in the corridors was paying a blind bit of attention – they had judiciously assessed Ethel and were confident she was much better off in

---

[38] *Dettol Surface Cleanser is claimed (by Mrs Dettol) to kill '99.9% of bacteria and viruses' and 'Proven to kill cold and flu viruses'. So where is the problem?! Why bother with the winter 'flu jag'?*

her own company – and so he brought out the hot-water bottle and gave it to his wife. Ethel examined the wobbly object on her lap, making no comment. Not wholly unattractive, the water bottle was a delicate pink-and-white pattern that reminded both Mungo and Ethel of the scrotum of a Golden Retriever (Laddie) they had once owned. For some reason known only to ~~those scoundrels the~~ vets, Laddie was incessantly licking his ~~balls~~ testicles, especially in company. Once, when Mungo's brother Torquil on first seeing this display remarked that he wished he could do that, Mungo said, 'I'm sure he'd let you, gentle sod that he is.'

Ethel restrained the tear that threatened to spill from her good eye and, ignoring the tug at her heart strings (twang!) said with just a hint of edge in her tone,

'Mungo, if this is your idea of a joke then I consider that we have no future together.'

Mungo put his hands to his lips, retrieved the object and unscrewed the cork, which, like the grandest sommelier, he waved under her great nostrils. A gentle expression came over Ethel's fizzug as the restorative fumes gently caressed her being and with not a few finding their way past her imperious philtrum where they briefly separated as they entered each great nostril, channelled up along the nasal septum. From where they activated the elbows of those little neurons and sent a happy message to the part of the brain that deals with happy messages. Such a man she had in Mungo; twice blessed she was – Mungo and Buckie!

[See appendices containing medical notes on cocaine and Buckfast.]

Chapter 19

Reveille for the reviled

Zzzzz… When he awoke Mungo found to his delight that once again the music that bound their soul had caused him to tumble into bed with his beloved and that they over the piece – or *pax nobiscum* he might have said had he not been excluded from Latin, as we have previously remarked – WE SAY that they had killed half a bottle of the 'tonic-wine' presented sympathetically as it was in a pink-and-white rubber hot water bottle whose exterior filled them with nostalgia and whose interior contents filled them with a nice blend of euphoria and somnolence. And all of this despite or because of the coast being clear of state nurses, registered nurses, state registered nurses, trainee nurses, sisters, matrons, green ladies, cleaners and the rest of the plangent sorority of carers excluding the Dagenham Girl Pipers or Ivy Benson's All Gal Band. (Somewhere in the hospital at that moment there was an Elvis impersonator. Probably in A&E).

Despite the cynicism that perhaps colours the preceding, there was some evidence, unbeknownst to Mungo at the time, that there were somewhere on the hospital premises some Consultant Professors of Unspellable Specialities (not all of which were invented or *soi disant*) on the grounds that in the car park and environs there were to wit: three Porsches, two 7 Series 'Beemers' and a very limited edition (one of one) Ferrari coupe crashed into a pair of trees. But at that time Mungo could not have known this, though later on the way out of the main gates he was splashed from head-to-foot by a Lamborghini – that would be Mr Sartram the abdomenoplastician since he and his wife also ran care homes for pin money. Mungo took this with sangfroid (a change from insouciance), reasoning that if he had to be splashed by any man-made object, then a muddied imprint from a top-of-the-range Italian job could pass muster as some sort of cachet, if not impermanent imprimatur.

But that was for later when he was exiting. MEANWHILE, having supped of the juice of the Buckie with his mistress, his revivification was completed by the fact that he could not move because Ethel had hefted one of her legs – the one with the nicer ankle – over his right buttock – the less arthritic one. It was like old times. He thought that if the day ever came when he had to have a leg amputated – a *legoctomy* in medical speak

[SEE APPENDICES FOR MEDICAL NOTES and how to sound convincing at dinner parties or on buses to Largs with ~~old age pensioners~~ ~~silver surfers~~ eh… venerated people of age with ~~bus passes~~ Entitlement Cards]

WE SAY, that in the question of which leg to have amputated, then Mungo would choose Ethel's other leg to entertain the knife. But that was all speculation at this point and there was no medical evidence that suggested she need to have one off. Yet.

Anyway, Mungo had now re-joined the living and Ethel was snoring gently; on which subject Mungo had penned some years before a contribution to a *Festschrift* celebrating the life and death of yet another salesman in quack remedies in which the difference between *stentorian* and *stertorian* had been explicated (*explained* for those who did not take sociology or are just plain speakers) in a manner that had confounded the readers of the *Anglian Times* – he had actually sent it off to the *Angling Times*, but the recent practice of the Royal Mail to outsource … well you've all experienced it. Anyways, Mungo found that there was a real debate going between the more intelligent inhabitants of Norwich and Ipswich. This led to riots – Ipswich winning hands down because not only were they more *au courant* with the philosophical debates of the times, (the egregious influence, no doubt of the legacy of Terry Butcher) but because they had more scaffolders than Norwich. This might seem an obscure, even arcane point, but anyone who has had to fight a scaffie, knows what one of us means.

We rest our case on the preceding point and search for the central point.

AND AS ETHEL CONTINUED TO SLUMBER Mungo's mind with that facility for which he was noted, free-roamed for a moment during which as he settled once more into the rather plush bedside chair, thought: where the blazes is the NHS getting the money for these? But then it left its frail eggshell of a skull and soared out of the window and above the town below (narrowly missing being knocked down by a flock of marauding gulls on the way back from Borrfoot Harbour, where they had stuffed themselves with the previous night's discarded burgers, pies, chips, cardboard and polystyrene.)

And so his mind drifted over the town and to thoughts of what he would do if his nags came in with that delightful bookie fellow Albie, who seemed to have warmed to him at once, even though he, Mungo, had socked him for thirty-two pounds. But then, one of Ethel's legs jumped – proof if ever it was needed, that she had indeed 'jumpy legs syndrome'[39] (which sounds better than Willis-Ekbom disease!) **WE SAY, one of Ethel's legs jumped and disturbed Mungo's train of thought, which we will try and piece together in the next chapter.**

---

[39] *While statistically women are more likely to moan about this condition than men, it is men who suffer most from it as they cannot get a decent night's sleep for their wife's (traditional language) jumpy legs. We realise that by using the term 'their wife's' we are being less than inclusive. Sorry.*

Chapter 20

Carnival relations

So. Having been disturbed by an exhibition that Ethel had Willis-Ekbom disease, Mungo gathered his thoughts and put together a 'narrative' which consisted of a recitation of the fact that after a day of peregrinations about Borrfoot and its environs, he had visited Ethel, had shared thoughts of Laddie and a rubber bottle (pink-and-white) of Buckie with her, had climbed into bed with her and had fallen asleep with her. That's what married people do, though not always in hospital. But if you think about it, if blasted felons can get their end away at taxpayers' expense – human rights, M'lud – then why not just draw the curtains around the bed?

Mungo was in contemplative mood as he sorted out in his mind where he was, and where his mind might be, what he was doing there and who was that big lump of a woman in that strange bed. (Note that, if he happened to be euphoric at that moment as well, he would have been displaying some of the symptoms of a coke-head. But we know he had been having a wee harmless Buckie. Things are not always as simple as they first appear. Note also that the condition, come appellation, *Buckie-Head* is not to be confused with the north-east of Scotland's south-west headland of the fishing village of Buckie.)

But anyway the important point is that this brings us back to the Condition of Ethel. Now read on:

If ever a positive case could be made for tonic wines made by priests – or at least licensed out by priests to some contractor, and choosing a name at random, say called Buckfast (or Buckie in the vernacular), then had there been a time-lapse camera fixed on Ethel's fizzug (alt. phizzug) then this was QED to the nth degree – Murray Walker might have said not only was it perfect, it was *pluperfect*. (A guide to Latin grammar is available on the MungoApp).

Ethel had looked hellish twenty minutes before when Mungo had entered her room. So bad did she look that he even considered returning to the violent-patients' ward to be with the lovely lady that had sconned (*thumped* but not *skelped*) him with a hairbrush – he was actually impressed with the accuracy of the throw given that she appeared to be under some sort of restraint apparatus *and* medication.

But then love took over. And as he stood over the snoring form before him, a tear came to his eye. This was a delayed reaction to the hairbrush incident, following on from the iris-tie incident – but he manfully put all of that behind him and looking down on the great visage of his beloved, he thought he might get away with having a quick slug of the good stuff before she awoke from her slumber. But she was still an awful, lambent white, congruous presence, virtually camouflaged in the décor of the small room; totally vulnerable with a not wholly attractive plastic tube inserted in the back of her right hand for some ingress or egress of fluids, extraction or injection of blood or for other purposes Mungo did not care to think of.

With a great effort of will, Mungo restored himself to the chair by Ethel's bed having raised her upper torso using the very complex array of buttons on the side of the bed; at one point both her legs, had almost touched the ceiling – no mean feat (and feet, and we mean feet) for a non-industrial crane. WE SAY he at last mastered the machinery and she was in what could be termed a conventional position for a hospital bed – that slope of the torso and the awkward angle of the head where the chin is pressing down on the *manubrium* of the *sternum* which is just the moment they bring your soup – *sans* straw of course.

[Parenthetically, unbeknownst to Mungo, each room (*ward* in the vernacular; *treatment space* in the techno-babble beloved of university deans and other *flâneurs*) was hooked to CCTV – *for security reasons* and not for voyeuristic purposes. And even as Mungo settled down the little film-clip of him making an arse of raising Ethel had soared (like her two legs, and feet) to number one on the alternative internet, having been excluded from YouTube on grounds of national security. No matter.]

It was now time for husband and wife to have a little natter as Ethel appeared to have resurfaced and below is a pretty faithful rendition of what was said – this was also taped for security reasons but failed to make the charts.

'At least you were fortunate to gain a private room, dearest,' Mungo tried. (Mungo at this point did not realise that all new hospitals in the 'Northern Powerhouse', as we and he must learn to call our country, have single occupancy.[40] Northern Powerhouse does not have quite the ring to it as Scotland (try singing *Northern Powerhouse the Brave* or *O Flower of Northern Powerhouse, When will we see your...* at this point, we cut away as to go further would incur royalties).) Yes, all new hospitals now have individual rooms! If you're a tax payer, the cost is likely to make you sick; but think what a pleasure it'll be when your sickicity gets you one of those little rooms.

Well dash it, we say: if prisoners can get housed on their ownio at +£40k per annum... we rest our case. (And don't forget those felonious bastards are getting their end away as well, as was proved a few paragraphs above - *proved* in the sense of having been 'asserted without an iota of evidence'; but that's journalism for you where they cannot use the word 'refute' and its variants, in the proper sense (we assert without a shred of a *soupçon* of an iota of a scintilla of a Higgs-Boson of evidence).)

'Private room?! *Private*. Mungo, it's like Sauchiehall street in the... in the days there was one. Can't get five minutes to myself. Blood, urine, bowel movements, you name it they want it. Food? All that dietician stuff – nutritional junk. Now never mind that. To important matters. The Project? Idris would have passed on my message? You can tell me later. And have you checked up with Mourinho on the house business? And what about that piece of nonsense with those financial friends of yours? Can we see the trees yet, Mungo, let alone the wood?'

---

[40] *Actually Mungo had not fully read the government paper: The Northern Powerhouse. One Agenda, One Economy, One North. It applies to the North of England. But still, it's the thought that counts. And it is a great read, despite the questionable capitals after the commas. https://www.gov.uk/government/*

How the hell did Ethel know about Mourinho's suspected perfidy? Prescience? Omniscience. Witchcraft? Mungo wondered. And as for the exploratory meeting with Meg for a loan… Had he been thinking aloud again…? You betcha!

THIS WAS A MOMENT OF GREAT STRESS FOR MUNGO AS ETHEL INTERROGATED HIM. TIME FOR AN APPROPRIATE RESPONSE FROM HIS PORTFOLIO OF RESPONSE MECHANISMS:

At times of great stress Mungo developed three response mechanisms and in any given situation it was simply a question of calling on the one most appropriate to the situation.

1. Assume most empathetic smile: this he did on this occasion, but quickly dumped it as he felt it was nowhere near sympathetic and probably simply pathetic.

2. The second response that he considered evoking (and in this we admit it does him no credit in terms of originality of concept) *a fainting fit* (*syncope* in the jargon[41]). Since he was in a place that (in theory at least, if not in principle) was replete with folks who knew a little about *syncope*, he considered it only briefly before discarding the idea, of going for the full-on *vasovagal syncope* (which is a better class of 'faint') and though harmless (unless you crack your napper – cranium – on the way down) sounds much better, more convincing. Mungo reasoned it wise not to adopt that strategy in the face of Ethel's interest in matters that he knew were reaching crisis point and for which he had as yet not a scooby as to how to solve, and he felt it might be best not to mention his assignation with Meg earlier that day.

3. And so he called upon the strategy that had served him so well in precarious situations throughout the world – most of which were in pubs, or social gatherings of a different type such as dinner parties.

---

[41] *According to Wikipedia – and who are we to argue with them? – one-third of medical students describe at least one such 'event' at some point in their life (presumably their life up to that point). Encouraging, what?*

And that was of course to stand on one leg. Now there is controversy in the precise ethnography of this posture. In Mungo's researches into *the arcana*, he had come to the conclusion that while among academics and others who should really know better, standing for more than fifteen seconds on one leg was associated with the Zoroastrian *one-legged dance of Yü*. Furthermore, Mungo had refuted (in the sense that journalists with the BBC use the word) any association of it with the belief – probably held by many of you – that it traces out the stars of the Big Dipper – although Mungo sometimes confused this with the Big Bopper (RIP).

As most of you who are of the Zoroastrian persuasion will know from practical experience, the so-called *one-legged dance of Yü*, quickly becomes a limping dance. And indeed it has been rumoured that there was once a tribe in the Amazon rain forest – or somewhere else quite wet, though not so much under anthropomorphic threat – that went into battle doing the *one-legged dance of Yü*. Should we be surprised that they no longer exist?

Anyway, during all of this rumination on how to answer Ethel's rather to-the-point questions affecting their financial well-being, Mungo had unwittingly assumed the one-legged position as a precursor to engaging in the full dance of *Yü* when Ethel said waspishly,

'And you can cut out that dance of *Yü,* crap Mungo, it simply won't cut the mustard with me… and it certainly butters no parsnips!'

At which juncture Mungo limped away (his standing leg was in a cramp) and in that posture, just as he was trying to lower his *Yüvian* limb (always the non-standing one), a young doctor arrived at the bedside and before dealing with Ethel – at least we trust he was a *real* doctor and not one of those PhD johnnies – he turned to Mungo and said:

آیا شما ردیابی دب اکبر؟

Which, because the question mark was at the front end and backward and since, like Latin, Mungo had never studied Persian in depth, he turned away from Doctor Ahura Mazda (according to his badge) and looked into the middle-to-far-distance through the window.

As Dr Mazda fussed with Ethel while she simpered winsomely (how quickly some women can turn it on and off!), Mungo's mind had in a nano second or even a lot quicker, had seen the badge and he recalled that *circa* (Latin) 1964 he had bet on a horse called *Ahura Mazda*! One shilling each way at 14 – 1. It lost as well. What were *The Fates* trying to tell him? While he considered this, the real Ahura Mazda (MBChB etc.) checked-out Ethel and said she was fine, but if she wanted to bed-block like the rest of her generation for another week or so, then she would not get any arguments out of him. And with that the young doctor limped away on his one good, God-given leg.[42]

Mungo was confused – he would need to face Ethel and so he pirouetted on the leg that was in touch with the floor and found Ethel shaking her empty NHS tumbler meaningfully in his direction. Such was his state of mind that he took the few remaining coins from his pocket and with an *insouciance* that would not have been out of place with some old French well-past-it singer, he tossed them into the cup and swept out of the ward ('recovering space' in the jargon) on two whole legs.

---

[42] *Medical note: it has been shown irrefutably (BBC use of term) that a good indicator of the likelihood of a person over the age of fifty suffering a stroke (cerebrovascular accident in medicalese (CVA)– now is it not easier to say 'stroke'?), is the ability to stand on one leg for more than fifteen seconds without falling into the fire. www.prevention.com/health/health-concerns/quick-brain-health-test-stroke-risk. The good old one-legged dance of Yü comes up trumps again!*

Chapter 21

Another chapter in the same recovery space

Mungo was beginning to become concerned as to his state of mental well-being. He was starting to raise questions that he would never have raised before. After much reflection and self-analysis (he had bought a book called *Psychoanalysis for Complete Dunderheids* or something like that), he was convinced that these insidious qualms, these new uncertainties whereof before only certainties ruled his intellect, all of these were no more and no less than the egregious[43] influence of all of those government-sponsored ads exhorting us to eat this, avoid that, do this, don't do that. And to what purpose – *cui bona*? (More Latin, sorry, it asks *Who benefits?* we seem to remember, Lower Latin was a long time ago... as you may discern from the adjective): the bleeding advertising industry and the TV companies that's who benefits.

Meantime these deeper philosophical matters that Mungo tended to wrangle with on a daily basis, were not occupying the frontal lobe of Ethel's brain – or any other lobe for that matter. And even though there was much evidence of *endorphin limitation* (she was a wee bit crabbit), there was absolutely no risk of schizophrenia in Ethel's case: one of her was enough even for herself. And so with an acuity of thought she cut away the central plank of Mungo's thesis on wisdom and its variants, poured the contents of her cup into her purse

---

[43] *Second time using this word – got it from The Practice: a series about a Boston law firm. Worth a look; even if its just for Kelli Williams as Lindsay Dole; and Jessica Capshaw as Jamie (honestly) – although some might prefer Dylan whatsisname, the guy. But here is a really spooky coincidence: the best actress (archaic usage permitted) is Camryn Manheim as Ellenor Frutt (honestly) – and who does she look like from the neck down? Yep: Ethel! Spooky or whit?*

and reaching behind her wee bedside cupboard, extricated the hot-water bottle with the Buckie, momentarily an image of Laddie's balls flashed through her head, but then sweeping nostalgia to one side, and just as she was about to pour herself a good jigger's worth a voice inside her head said,

'Ethel, do you think that wise?'

To which another voice inside her head said, 'Wise? Wise?! Who said anything about wise – does it say it on the label? No! It's prescribed. Just what the doctor didn't order!' And with that she tilted her fine wrist deftly and did the needful. (We withdraw earlier comment about Ethel being a schizophrenia-free zone).

Meantime, Mungo had recovered his composure and had returned to the recovery space ('ward'), where at Ethel's invitation he took the water bottle and tried not to think about Laddies' ball-licking, and having ascertained that it still had some liquidity by sloshing it about, he examined the label where he was pleased to see that it carried no warning against over-use or abuse of the contents or twenty-three pages of appendices of possible side effects. It did not even mention allergies or containing nuts, or dairy produce or things with E-numbers, not even 'best by' dates. It said nothing about *if using this hot water bottle do not drive heavy machinery*. So, taking the absence of evidence as evidence of absence, he quaffed his share straight from the hot waterbottle. (Poundland, £3.99 *atow*).

Which of course led to more evidence of the aforementioned endorphin limitation in Ethel's nut and if she could have got out of her bed she would have given a good account of herself in close-quarter grappling. In her youth Ethel had been a great fan of the avuncular Mick McManus, (*The Dulwich Destroyer*) and she would have bet on herself to tear apart the detested Jackie Pallo just for wearing those striped three-quarter length breeks. And as for Shirley Crabtree? *Ph*cque her*, Ethel might have said. She did have a soft spot for Masambula, it should be recorded, if only to prove that she did not have a tiny prejudiced bone in her substantial body.

But she did not leap out of the bed and attack Mungo, for she knew when she was at a disadvantage and so their cosy little chat continued to roam over the world's affairs, and, whether or not it was the influence of the tonic-wine, or Mungo's company, or the fact that this was the first time she had tasted Buckie from a rubber container, they both felt considerably cheerier and a warm glow suffused their complexions and it is possible that the Buckie reduced the influence of that little critter in Ethel's frontal lobe that insisted in limiting the amount of endorphins that got through to the parts that counted. They got merry as folk married for many years, should do from time-to-time. Even in each other's company, from time-to-time.

With a little bit of luck, Mungo reasoned, the good tonic wine would eradicate any vestige of unpleasantness that had earlier been touched upon regarding Mourinho and the state of their domestic finances. Surprisingly, that effect has never been listed in the marketing material for their elixir of choice. You will recall, (unless you've been on the stuff yourselves), that among the benefits offered by daily consumption are those pithily expressed in that masterpiece of marketing literature: *Three small glasses a day, for good health and lively blood*,[44] to which one of us can only add: slàinte.

[As an aside and related to the previous point, it should be observed that one of the key influences in the formation of Mungo's character in the … formative decade – about which there is a certain mist – was the memory of sitting in the barber's chair and seeing in the mirror a cigarette poster that read: Craven 'A' good for your throat. Actually it read backwards, but Mungo had a condition little understood at the time – probably caused by 'privileged access to mirrored graphemes', Neuropsychologia, 2003; 41(1):96-107, Gottfried, Sancar and Chatterjee (No kidding) that gave him a preference for reading things that were in mirrors. If anyone is interested in following this up, then we refer you to DSM-5; what's our point caller? That we are all at the mercy of the merchants of dreams – so much for freewill!]

---

[44] *http://www.buckfast.org.uk/tonic-wine_105.html*

ANYWAY, Mungo and Ethel felt much better after ~~Laddie's testicles were~~ the waterbottle was relieved of its contents and they nodded off again – saving the NHS the cost of another meal incidentally, for the canteen person saw that they were in a state of bliss or something and he took it back, not wanting to disturb the old dears. Mungo woke first and seeing Ethel was at peace – no not dead, we hasten to clarify – he decided it was time to take his leave. But first he thought he would improve her condition by amending the charts and things that should have been at the bottom of the bed. But drat – this was the newest hospital in the known world and instead of clipboards and charts there were complicated computer thingies on a trolley at the end of the bed.

We say *complicated*, but that is a relative term – and after pressing a few keys and things, Mungo thought he had the hang of it; he wondered if it had *Wi-Fi* - a concept he had recently been introduced to by Tim, who had learned it from Idris. After trying to get BetFair or even Packie Power on-line, to have a look at the latest results and next day's cards, the room was suddenly swamped with people in medical sort of gear who pushed him aside and worked frantically on Ethel. But since she continued to snore like … is it *Stertorous* or the other one – pub quiz question? Mungo did not bother to make his excuses and left.

Chapter 22

A forgotten project, *pro tem*

Mungo did not make his excuses and left. As he left among the unnecessary (in his opinion) hubbub, he thought about calling out that if he was needed he would be at his club. But on reflection and on balance, he thought that might be viewed as being somewhat insensitive, and perhaps would have a ring of the *poseur*. Anyway his membership had been suspended due to a misunderstanding regarding fees. Mungo had quite reasonably assumed that in decamping to the Algarve, HM Government would have included that in the package with the Cold Weather Payment, pension and free healthcare and Child Tax Credit paid to a numbered account in Ibiza or Iberia or somewhere starting with an 'I' (but not Islay). It was not to be.

Anyway, in the present, as he gazed for the last time on his beloved (that day! Ethel is not going to snuff it just yet, so rest easy on that score) through the little window of the little room, he reflected on two other matters of import that in their own way were symptomatic with what was going wrong with society. Firstly, had there been the wee clipboard and charts at the bottom of Ethel's bed as in the good old days, he would have amended some of the entries to present a better picture of his wife's condition. This would not have been artifice alone – because Mungo was a disciple – nay, a *proselytiser* – of the belief that the psychology of the mind is reversible.

This can be presented better by this example: if a person smiles when they are not in the mood for smiling, and if they do it consistently in the face of pain, then eventually the pain will ease. Why? Simple: it is the reverse psychology of the musculature of the face and the neural connections (cells with wee elbows) to what neuroscientists call 'the happy bit of the brain'. The action of the facial muscles sort of fools the brain into releasing those wee endorphins (or *endorphites,* as

Mungo had named them in a paper[45] offered to the British Society for the Advancement of Science and Obscurantism, the release of which makes the person happier and reduces the pain.

Where were we? Yes, *no more charts*. On a related issue, if there had been clipboards and charts instead of that complicated computer thing at the bottom of the bed Mungo would not have tried to open an on-line account with Packie Power, and presumably that 'browser' (technical term Mungo was learning to throw into conversations), would not have cut off the liquids or drugs to Ethel and those medics could still be sitting in rooms chatting each other up.

Which brings us to Mungo's second reflection as he gazed in the window: why no electric paddles where you stick them on the person and shout, 'Clear!' And restore them to life – dragging them back in some cases it would seem (according to sworn accounts in *The Sunday Post*) from Paradise and the Great Receptionist – or even from a nightmare about Royal Caribbean cruises. Oh well, *you can't always get what you want in life*, thought Mungo, even though he had not heard of the Rolling Stones, and off he toddled down the corridor remembering to duck his head as he passed his fiancée with the hairbrush-throwing arm, in the Violent Patients Ward. He did consider chucking the brush back at her, but thought that a cowardly way of breaking their engagement. Ho-Hum.

And so for the moment Mungo took his leave from the Queen Margaret (not the big boat) without once throwing a fridge or sink[46] from the window, and his spirit soared and raced away above the mere mortals that lay below him.

---

[45] *There will be more here on this paper and the debate that sprung up in café society. Those who are interested might have a gander (Google it) at Project Violet - The Metropolitan Police Service (MPS) response to abuse related to faith and belief. Honestly.*

[46] *This would seem to be a very obscure and misplaced allusion to a novel titled, One Flew Over the Cuckoo's Nest, by Ken Kesey, (Viking, 1962.) set in an insane asylum. Neither Mungo or Ethel would*

Chapter 23

Good news: Bad news: Worse news?

Mungo started to shake. He also was feeling dizzy. He sat down on the nearest purple cushioned stool to try to compose himself. For a brief moment – a few nano seconds – he thought it was he who had died and not Ethel (he's wrong syntactically here: Ethel is, still, repeat, still alive), and that he, Mungo, had gone to Heaven. But then his steel-trap mind grasped what had happened and where he was. And with just a little bit of self-pride at his powers of reasoning – he was alive – he rose from the little two-seater table he had found himself at when he came out of the dwam[47] that had obliterated all memory of how he got from the hospital to this … this pleasure-palace to rival Xanadu.

WE SAY, he rose, scrabbled for his glasses and approached the bank of monitor screens high up on one wall.

He was inside a Hillbrokes betting shop – the Top-tottie bookies. Recognising the remarkable makeover that had transformed Borrfoot since Mungo had left for Iberia, Hillbrokes had staked its claim to the spare cash of the new middle-classes who were flocking to get houses in what had been not so long ago even cheaper than Paisley (or Edinburgh for that matter). What with the Waitrose (Lidl's better value,

---

have qualified for admission. And by the way, if not incidentally, this is the second time we have mentioned a film that was as good as the book – a rarity indeed. Hollywood, are you listening? We are waiting… for your screen version of this book… cos it will save US coming up with something completely different to complete our three-part trilogy.

[47] *Dwam – reverie, dream-like state; drunken stupor (not in this case). According to Collins Dictionary (http://www.collinsdictionary.com/dictionary/english/dwam) this word reached a peak in its usage over the last ten years between 2004 and 2006.*

honestly) reflecting the gentrification[48] of this new metropolis (with its associated dark side: Museums, art-outreach programmes, Channel 4 News Presenters moving in, etc.), it now had the final stamp of success: decent bookies.

Mungo thought he had died and entered heaven for at that very moment a very attractive young woman in a uniform that reminded him of the good old days when he would volunteer to go down to Imrie's to buy the fruit – he had long been of the view that those ladies, young and less so, wore very little under those green tunics; it was a sad moment for society when Imrie's folded – approached him and asked would he like tea or coffee? (She almost spoiled it by mentioning water, but so charming was she that he let it pass.)

Flustered, he gave some sort of response and she went away to fetch whatever it was he had said, during which time he scrabbled in his pockets for change to pay for whatever-the-devil he had ordered. But when she returned with whatever-the-devil, it was in a real cup on a saucer and a biscuit on a side plate. She waved away his money with a charming smile. What is going on? Has the world gone mad? They, bookies, turf accountants are in the business of *taking* our money.

All of these thoughts and less flashed through his steel-trap mind in less time than it took the elderly lady at the next table to pour her tea into her saucer, drink it, eat her and his biscuit – she had long arms. A word with the management was called for, he thought, then remembered to check his results.

Mungo finally began to concentrate on matters at hand. The 'Investment Space' ('bookie's shoap' in the patois of the bulk of the clientele at this time of the day) was nearly empty as apparently there was little interest in the last live and 'proper' horse race of the day, the 5.15 from Punchestown.

---

[48] *Artisan cafés and luxury flats: How bad can gentrification really be? (June,2, 2016) http://www.independent.co.uk/life-style/ Do not read this if you are easily scared or an architect has moved in next door to you. It's the surest sign your days are numbered in that scheme (housing estate).*

Going good-to-soft, we're guessing given its geographical position – not that we would ever say anything against the Irish (or M*slims, for that matter). But Mungo was interested, avidly so, especially in the horse numbered five named *Archer's Folly*. Mungo checked the clock in the centre of the bank of screens that shone out odds for seemingly every forthcoming sport known to man or king.

He returned to his stool after rechecking for the third time the earlier results on the screens on the opposite wall. He definitely had three winners on the line of fifteen permutations[49] that he had left at the dilapidated bookies (Albie's) on the edge of The Park: seven winning lines so far, with yet another eight lines dependent on the winning of *Archer's Folly*. Potentially exponentially greater returns. Interesting, Mr Bond, very interesting.

Having left Ethel aglow in her private cubicle, Mungo took the scenic route back up to Villa Idris, when he encountered this Hillbrokes betting shop, new to him here on the right side of the Borrfoot tracks. And to give you some idea of the importance of that old cliché: *location, location, location*, it was flanked on one side by a large self-service (and many did) Lloyds Pharmacy for all your chemical-dependency needs. Now if Lloyds ever, ever gets a license to sell alcohol – well we know it has, but the other kind – then Shangri-La is here on earth. (An earthier, lustier sort than he, might have mused that all it needs is a brothel upstairs, Mungo did not dare think; he still wasn't sure if that little problem with his innermost thoughts being converted into sound waves was still on the go.)

So. He sipped at his skinny latte with the whisper of cinnamon and dusting of chocolate on top – revolting stuff, but free – and checked the results.

---

[49] *Mungo is using the term in a loose sense – he really means combinations. You will all recall from your maths class that a permutation is an ordered combination. To illustrate this …. Naw, the thing is, who gives a toss as long as the gee-gees win (or are placed if taken 'each way'). For those who do wish to pursue this matter we can recommend the Electronic Journal of Combinatorics. And good luck to you with your line.*

Three winners out of three at Kempton and Wincanton (damned fine odds too). Last one still to run at Punchestown. Interesting, he thought, and stroked where his moustache might have been. He would do a quick calculation of what was going on that last nag. And so he applied his steel-trap mind and with a will that would have been envied by someone with a really strong will, he shut-out all extraneous diversions and… bugger!

The chirp and clatter from the fruit machines and the drone of the commentary on the incessantly 'televised' 'Virtual Racing' did nothing to assist Mungo's fourth try at calculation of his current winnings. His hands shook, the bookie's pen he was holding was a waggling worm; his (steel-trap) brain turned to jelly and he struggled with his dim remembrance of primary school and his 6, 7, and 100/8 times tables.

Four minutes later he treble guessed he had already won nearly one thousand pounds. But the gambler's superstition against pre-counting (chickens-hatch-counting-before: re-arrange to cliché, but do not pass Go), his nerves and recalcitrant brain cells[50] refused to allow him the luxury of assessing precisely what an *Archer's Folly* win would yield him. 'Thousands' was as close as he got at the starting price of 15/2 just…

VOICEOVER: 'And they're off at Punchestown!'

It was the longest two-mile chase Mungo had ever experienced. *Archer's Folly* had taken a big lead at the first fence and maintained it through the next six; now the pack was closing rapidly led by the odds-on favourite *Labour of Love.*

---

[50] *One problem with humans like Mungo is that they have too many brain cells. It has been demonstrated (irrefutably) that a snail uses two brain cells: one to tell it it's hungry; the other to tell it where the nosh is. (According to Prof George Kemenes of Sussex Uni, which being near Brighton, gives it some authority in the field of snailology, though it is not clear if it is a particular snail or the set of snails). Now if snails (and humans) had a third brain cell for calculating winnings on the horses… then all their basic needs would be catered for. On reflection, maybe one more cell wouldn't go wrong for getting a mate.*

Mungo turned from the screen and removed his glasses to sit on the furthest stool from the screen showing Punchestown. With steely resolve he controlled his pulse and the twitch on his face then when the effort became too much for him – he had fallen off the stool twice at the fifth and eighth fences - he let his heart and all those other things take over and for a moment in that room it sounded like … his heart would not hold out as he felt it thump and loudly complain.

He could not watch but he could not fail to hear the commentary. He had seen enough to know that by this stage in the race his horse was extremely tired, the word 'knackered' came to his mind, as the grey had given its all in leading from the front. It would surely fall at the last fence.

VOICEOVER:

…………………….….. and Archer's Folly makes a mess of the last, but… oh brilliant riding by Ruby Walsh, he's kept it on his feet, but here comes Labour of Love, it's a short run-in here at P… but ooh look at that… oh, now that is unfortunate… and they go past together. Photo finish…I don't know about you Sean but if the favourite doesn't get the verdict… you think that was interference with Walsh's 'wobbly' there at all, at all…'

'Well Eamonn, sure you know trainer McSeugh will object for the least wee bump on his animals and that was…'

Mungo had had enough of the Irish. But not of the Scotch. He sipped a neat twelve-year-old *Glengoyne* in the lounge bar of *The Wallace* (they did not serve Buckie and hinted that they did not welcome Buckiephiles, but relented when he ordered the wee goldie). He looked in the mirror of the gantry and reflected and reflected on his winnings, consoling himself and trying not to count 'what might have been' (the curse of the loser). Within fifty pounds or so of four figures (aka *a grand* aka *one thousand*) was as close as he managed.[51] His biggest win ever in sixty gambling years. He refused to contemplate far less calculate exactly 'what might have been'. *Archer's Folly* had indeed been, by a short head 'first past the post', a winner, but the favourite had objected for 'interference' and the 'official result' was that *Labour of Love* was given the verdict,

---

[51] *Download free MungoApp at www.MungoLaird.com*

the race and Mungo's 'thousands'. Ah well – *que sera, sera*, he mumbled to himself and the vision that was Doris Day swam before him, and gave him some consolation (this is a *meme*[52] from his youth before he had taken an interest in sussies and not even Mungo could envisage Doris in suspenders – *Calamity*).

He had lived and gambled long enough not to do it: never dwell on *what ifs* in gambling nor in life. *Deal with it. Get on with it*...or as that credo often failed him *Something will turn up*. No, well, eh, but ...he was ... in fact he wasn't ... that type of chap was he, he asked himself rhetorically (not easy: try it). His cheery, sprightly exit suddenly slowed as he checked his pockets to assess what was left of his money. Enough for a taxi. To The Park. And his winnings.

This proved extremely difficult.

The taxi rank's first two drivers either laughed or told Mungo he 'was having a laugh' and the third simply grunted for Mungo to 'Gettaef*ck'. The next wanted as much as an undiscounted return fare to Faro but eventually a skinny little runt of a driver agreed, provided that is, Mungo stumped up the amount right now! The driver looked at what Mungo had on him – the money we mean – sighed and said, 'Get in ya... silver surfer you' or something a little stronger than that, proving that many cabbies have hearts of gold (and silver).

Somewhat relieved if uncomfortable in the back of the badly sprung banger of a private cab, Mungo watched Borrfoot suburbia segue downmarket as it headed very roughly and rapidly downhill to the outer edge of The Park – which strictly speaking is no longer part of Borrfoot proper as it had been zoned-out by a neat bit of jerry-mandering (not gerrymandering - it wiz a cooncillor originally frae Dresden wot did it) in the planning department – among other things, this effectively meant that old schools that were not meeting 'performance targets' were let go, as were dilapidated housing

---

[52] *While we don't really know what this term means, we feel that any sociological document such as this one will prove to be, would be incomplete without us demonstrating that we have heard of the word.*

schemes. But this is not the time for Mungo to develop a social conscience!

He grasped the betting slip tighter then slackened his grip afraid of erasing its lucrative evidence. He was glad he was not walking. Walking out of The Park with nearly one thousand pounds. Impossible.

'Would you wait, please?' he asked the cabbie, a perfectly pleasant fellow who it turned out did not know Betty the Stoker, but asked Mungo if he had her telephone number.

'Wait here? Yer f*ckin' jokin', auld yin. I'm offski!' That last phrase should not be taken as a subtle hint that he was one of Putin's plants, nor a ubiquitous Pole.

The taxi screeched away, leaving Mungo facing a grille securely in its place in front of Albie's that was definitely closed.

Chapter 24

Some days in the life of a turf accountant

Albie Freeman was feeling anything but. 'Free' and a 'man' were two of the last things he currently felt this late morning as he waited for his fate in the shape of Mungo Laird, the lucky old g*y (not *gay*, not *guy*, okay it's g̲o̲y̲) who had got up his Yankee Plus4 or Very Lucky Fifteen (again see glossary for detailed, arcane and pretty damn close to unfathomable betting parlance unless you are addicted – as one of us is, M'lud.). At bloody good odds too. And he didn't even use the lavvy.

For his heart's sake – three stents, a quadruple bypass and two veins from his leg – almost like a straight Yankee bet if you said it quickly enough – he was glad it wasn't a lady. If there was something Albie hated more than a winner it was a lady-winner. What did they know about horses? What did they know about odds? OK, knowing about odds and horses only confirms you're going to be a loser; but at least you know why you're losing. Women punters, like women civilians were irrational – this was a well-established fact; just read all of the studies by Psychologists and Logicians. Better still: just ask a man. For a start they, fillies, tended not to gamble – they were what psychologists and other people with fancy degrees and financial advisers who can read and plagiarise, call 'risk averse'. That's why they like to marry in the first place. It's why they only have a 'wee flutter' on the National. Or the Derby. Or the Gold Cup. Or... etc.

You can do all your studies all the way back to *Foinavon* (the useless bastard, should have been shot and turned to glue on the way to the start), and you'll see that women have had their wee flutter and have raked it all in. Just as well we have male punters – or in the parlance of the turf 'the mugs' to balance the books... and so on in similar vein (not the one in his heart) Albie ranted on internally. (Had he rrrranted to Raylene she would have told him to 'shut it'.)

As he reflected on these weighty matters and gave rein to thoughts that had been swirling about his brain in a chaotic fashion for four decades and more, and as they became more articulate, Albie thought he might just have found an alternative to stultifying retirement working his allotment.[53] (Glasgow City tel. **Email:** land@glasgow.gov.uk **Phone:** 0141 287 2000 **Fax:** 0141 287 3519... but be prepared to wait up to twelve years...and that's just for an answer to your phone call.)

Anyway, as Albie began to develop his thesis – *thesis*: the very word cheered him up, almost; he liked the idea of hearing the words ring out: Arise *Doctor* Albert Freeman, PhD-and-Bar. And just when those chime things and wavy lines they use in movies to tell you it's all a dream (and your wasting your time), the telephone rang by his elbow and he awoke to see before him his Nemesis in a pea-jacket (courtesy of charity shop in Greenock, we think; *Hello sailor*) he recalled the words that should have been chiselled on George Best's headstone: *Where did it all go wrong?*

But these wind chimes things started up again and the shape before him wriggled and Albie, thought, 'F*ck it, this'll be my last memory' and he lay back in his chair and watched the movie. Inevitably the movie playing in his mind was a bit of a horror that starred his former wife, Dixie.

Dixie hadn't gone far with the real accountant (it turned-out he had not taken Part Two of his ACCA exams – and although that would have got him a job with a uni that does not bother to check out CVs, it was not good enough for the Dixie chick, and quite rightly, she dumped him). Now she was virtually Albie's neighbour, the owner of the hairdresser salon only two units along the terrace, almost through the wall, secure in the now lucrative business that he had bought and signed over to her as one of her many 'negotiated' (i.e. blackmailed) 'post- nuptials'.

---

[53] *The UN designated 2015 The International Year of the Soils (no kidding); Mungo should have been invited to submit a paper on this.*

Every day he came in to work her very-going concern slapped him in the face as hard as Dixie did that time she caught him with his hand in the till prior to being foiled in the act of taking that new pert and perky blonde assistant cashier (not Raylene!) out to put that same hand somewhere nicer, cosier and considerably more rewarding. Dixie promptly divorced Albie and took him for a lot more than he could afford at the time, including his wedding gift to her – a collector's item, a vintage American Buick limo. Enormous, complete with the Confederate flag stamped large on the even larger metal badge mounted on the much larger still front grille and bumper (or *fender* as the by now pseudo-Americanised Dixie called it).

It wasn't as if Albie was skint. He was just scunnered: completely tired of and totally fed up with his lot. And it wasn't as if this old guy's win would dent Albie's bank balance – he's 'talking' about Mungo's line. Albie had laid off the £15 permutations bet smart-ish. His nose told him to do so – that and the size of the stranger guy's bet, the potential loss to Albie and the instinct of a good bookie anticipating a lucky punter being 'on a roll' after the guy's earlier each-way single had come in at 14/1.

In fact, Albie had made a 'decent' (HUGE) profit on Mungo's four selections by laying them off at Hillbrokes; then, on a hunch that went against the first law of being a bookie: *do not act on hunches* - duplicated the old fella's bet on his own account with Benny Queen. Albie had nearly enough now. Enough to Bogart off into the sunset. If only he could sell the business now. He'd tried in the past without success – Benny Queen has laughed in his face and hadn't bothered to give even one reason why not: because Albie himself knew all the reasons why no one would take it off his hands.

And yet, here he was really still scunnered with his lot despite this recent little win. It made him more desperate to get out. But not that desperate that he would pass up a chance to save himself from having to part with the winnings for which the unlucky old g*y would soon surely be arriving and hoping to lug away with him.

Albie's bookie's was over the piece run at a wee loss despite or perhaps because of the lack of capital investment.

Installing the latest TV monitors and minimum regulatory whatnots was a financial quantum leap too far for Albie. But the annual backhander to the Council licensing mob (department) of graspers (planners) and playing when needed The Park Special Needs Card to the whole Council allowed Albie to run his shop as an anachronism, totally congruous with 1950 betting shops with bare boards, rough brick walls, cracked and leaking ceiling, one ancient communal wooden table complete with the eclectically acquired dilapidated stools.

It was also probably the only bookies in the land that still operated a 'wire service' that was *'Radio Only'*. And above all was the non 'non-smoking ban' that attracted Albie's regulars more desperate for nicotine, while parked on their lazy arses (and not having to smoke standing, basking, sorry, chittering outside in a Scottish summer) than they were for punting the horses. And they often brought their mates with similar physical and mental dependencies so that they could socialise happily in the fug. Praise the Lord for fags, sloth and gambling, Albie always said, in his more charitable commentaries on his customers.

Albie had liked it all that way. He was in control of his austere facility. No TV 'virtual racing' every five or six minutes – impossible to lay off - no 'crack cocaine of gamblers' fruit machines – Albie had some philanthropy, well pride, in him that did the fruit machine addicts a favour. No stupid Sports Betting on so-called sports like golf, snooker, darts or anything else that Albie knew nothing about and refused to learn.

Nothing but proper horse-racing and fixed-odds football bets would Albie take. He hated greyhounds with a vengeance that owed itself entirely to the one night that as a cocky, callow bookie he had taken his business, most of his savings (daddy's over-generous pocket money), in the brand new Bookies Satchel with *A. Freidburger* stamped proudly large to 'the dugs' at Shawfield. Cleaned out, tail between legs, paws in the air, soft underbelly totally exposed, he had abandoned his father's reserved pitch and slunk away out of the floodlit night before the second last race and remained a laughing stock for some time. Dixie never really forgave him: they were engaged and the wedding had to be put back despite his old man partially bailing him out.

But now Albie had had enough of the business, The Park, and most of all having to pass fu*king Dixie and her fu*king salon every day and live with the sickening aroma of past its sell-by date ammonia or whatever the bloody hell it was that permeated even the fug in his bookies' shop until the chip-fryer directly through the wall was fired up enough by late morning to stink out equally Albie and Dixie's respective turf accounting and tonsorial emporia.

In the background to the foregoing those wind chimes began to start up again but in reverse and Albie knew that he better finish-off for he was returning to reality and as he came out his dwam he was smiling for …

… Yes, he had enough now salted away to retire.

'F*ck!' Albie expostulated as he came back to earth – actually he had fallen off his chair onto his arse and there before him was this old guy who, if things went Albie's way would …

Chapter 25

Joint enterprise (see Supreme Court's recent ruling on this: Feb, 2016; what a farce, M'lud).

'So you'll come then, Tim? Agreed?' Mungo said, hardly believing his ears. Was Tim totally mad? Did he have no sense of judgement, Mungo wondered? Had he not heard of his, Mungo's, record of disaster in the fields of enterprise? Had no one told Tim of the brewer's fiasco – about Laird's lager? And at the end of this litany carried within the interior of his brain somewhere, Tim said:

'To take them in order: aye, I'm probably mad; Idris has always said I'm too trusting; aye I've heard of your catalogue of Donnybrooks. And first time I tasted Laird's lager I knew – this is a bummer. Of course I've heard about all that. But you're bound to get something right someday. Law of large numbers or something. Averages.'

'Hell's teeth!' Mungo said to himself. 'Don't tell me I've been thinking out loud again. Must get this seen to. Thank heavens it didn't kick in when Idris was buttering the toast.'

'Aye, the toast-buttering. Made me see Idris in a new light. Thanks for that one. Can hardly wait for the morning,' Tim said dreamily.

'Right!' Mungo said firmly. 'From now on no more thinking. All speaking alfresco from now on. Tim did I say what I just said?' Tim confirmed that Mungo was *en plein air*, though of course he did not use that phrase, preferring *à l'extérieur* to convey the sense.

'That's me away then. Again!' Idris fluted shrilly from the hall (or 'lobby' as her pere called it the one and only time he visited – the hill and the steps having well-knackered his knees).

Tim and Mungo looked at each other and waited until the door had snicked closed.

'Wonder what she meant by that?' Tim said, not for one moment realising he had evoked the memory of Talleyrand on hearing of the death of the Turkish Ambassador (or if you prefer: Metternich on hearing of the death of Talleyrand; or Metternich's barber on hearing of the death of Metternich... ENOUGH!)

To which Mungo said, having during this time glanced at the racing pages of the Sun, 'First race Doncaster. Quarter-to-one.'

Tim looked in the mirror above the old mantelpiece in the scullery and reflected, 'Mungo, if only ye'd gone tae a Benny shoap.'

'A Ben E shoap?' Mungo said slipping easily into the vernacular but still not having a scooby as to what Tim alluded.

'You would huv hud all four gee-gees up. Thoosans it wid huv been. Ben E... Benny Queen pays out on *baith* official whatdeyemacallit and first past the thingumme. A bonanza you would have had, Mungo. A. Bow.Nan.Zah.'

'Pays out on official result and first past the post? And he's still in business. What is his real business? Money laundering? Drugs?'

'Hus tae. Tae get his punters tae stay, an any new wans through the door, tae, tae, *compete* with the Nationals like Hillbrokes an' that and their free tea and biscuits and clean toilets an' everythin'. Benny's shoaps are aw boggin', every filthy wan a downright liberty, a disgrace. Mind you, nowhere near as bad as whit ah remember o' Albie's cowp in The Park.'

'Albie?' Mungo's normally steel-trap mind was having an off day.

'Albie something or ither. A wee bookie. Used to be a street bookie. Then when the law changed he went legit – or sort of. Still, he must do all right. Has a big hoose in one of those rich places – you know, full o' drug dealers and accountants. In fact, I think Albie lives roon the hill from here.'

Mungo tried very hard to take all this in as Tim eventually looked up again.

'Never mind Mungo lad, nine hundred and fifty-oad nicker is better than... than nine-hundred and forty-nine.' Then after a moment's pause – or dramatic hiatus – Tim wondered to himself, 'Wonder if Albie will pay the auld yin oot?'

'What!!' Mungo spluttered and almost had a cerebrovascular accident. 'You think he won't pay out? But…'

Right at that moment, had he only known it, Tim had encountered a genuine candidate for an entry in DSM-5 (and maybe DSM-6 and counting towards double figures); for it was the first evidence that Mungo's condition of unknowingly articulating en plein air, his innermost thoughts, had been passed on to Tim. We can speculate how this infection occurred – we can aver it was not occasioned mouth-to-mouth so to speak, as both of them were unreconstructed males of the old school who were revolted by the modern tendency for the new touchy-feely between consenting adults. So we'll blame it on the toast, for it is possible that during their discourse at the old kitchen table (ReUseit, £15 or zł 88 atow), one or the other grabbed a bite from the other's toast. In which case the evidence points to Mungo, for over the years he had to resort to such stratagems when dining with Ethel, for if he turned away for a moment she was into his breakfast/brunch/lunch/afternoon tea/dinner and supper.[54]

But to matters serious: Tim had caused Mungo concern by the very question as to whether the bookie would pay out. Tim had raised that concern (within himself, he had thought, not wishing to cause his dear friend any anxiety), because it was rumoured among his, Tim's, brothers, cousins etc., that Albie was getting deeper into debt since his Dixie had departed. Not only that, as we should have mentioned earlier when Mungo first espied what turned out to be Albie's Bookmakers Emporium, there was a large (homemade by the looks of it) sign with the legend: *For Sale: Inquiries Within – Time waster's welcome.* And indeed, as we further failed to mention, before entering, Mungo puzzled over that apostrophe for quite some

---

[54] *Social Comment: This is not such an unusual practice among couples who have been married for forty-nine years; as to whether the same behaviour will be practiced among those in civil partnerships, we will just have to wait another forty years or so. One for the social anthropologists of the future.*

time, and made a note to raise it within. Which he duly forgot once within.

ANYWAY, Tim has raised the prospect that there might be some doubt as to whether Mungo would be paid. Mungo in turn became hysterical – well *hysterical* is a relative term, and Mungo did not even have an iota of the hysteria stuff in him – he might be termed totally womb-free. What Mungo said was:

'Oh no. Just my luck.' Which is as near an expression of hysteria as Mungo is ever likely to produce. You don't see it in the line of dialogue, but there is an implicit 'ho-hum' there.

Detecting that the old boy was distraught now that he had thoughtlessly sown doubt in his mind, Tim made to repair the damage by suggesting how they – Team Mungo – might go about securing his legitimate winnings from the cruel and ruthless Albie.

After he had explained his scheme to Mungo, Mungo expressed some reservations, 'If we need to do that to get my dosh, perhaps it's best we just leave it as a lesson learned. Now, about these buckets. I've got a idea for a conveyor belt that …

'Mungo, never mind the buckets – there might be a dry spell on the way up from the Azores any month noo… that money is yours. You worked hard for it … well you know what I mean. Think of it being like that time Ethel shot the cop.'

'Well he was not actually a cop at the time. He was doing his part-time work as…'

'As a thug and enforcer for gangsters.'

'That's a bit extreme, Tim. He was pursuing the legitimate goals of his second employer who happened to be a loan shark of a legitimate type who employed less than legitimate means. He was licensed by the Financial Services Authority after all.'

'He had you tied up and was about to smash your toes aff.'

'There is that consideration, I suppose.'

'Well, Mungo, let's try this out. Trust me.'

CHAPTER 26

Emissions complaint – not compliant

A mile or so away from The Park, travelling quickly, Mungo sat next to a subdued Tim. The driver was burly, early thirties, tattooed and ear-ringed, wearing a fetching string vest that showed her toned pectoral muscles to advantage. But it was the scars that reminded Mungo of that self-same woman at the Seaman's mission in Greenock who had added an extra bite to the soup with more than a soupçon of sputum, and who, Mungo was convinced, had been the stoker from the iron ore ship (boat) at Klang Port.

As these old happy memories flooded back, he fell into a comfortable dwam, and nearly fell out the car as it took a bend and the door flew open. They don't make VW like they used to (cough, cough); still it had passed its emissions' test so what's a loose door in the grand scheme of things when Angela M assures the world that her favourite GmbH (jerry for limited company) is looking after their green credentials? (wir feiern Vielfalt, Wir werfen keine Steine zuerst.)

Tim's Uncle Richard did not give a shoite (he had spent a stag night in Dublin), for the door though he was very green (*very* Irish) in his credentials, so he shook his big, solid, shaved head and turned a little to address Mungo, enough for the long scar that ran from his right ear to his upper lip to grab Mungo's attention.

Anyway, as Mungo recovered with the aid of his bacterial mouthwash, he tapped the driver on the shoulder and said,

'I say, ever been into Klang for servicing, dear?' He turned to Tim, explaining, 'Big Betty the Stoker. After all these years too.'

The emissions-compliant car (VW) pulled up outside the Bookie's. It's very presence, it seemed to those who know about these things, helped clean the air even though the engine was left running in case there was a need for a quick getaway – and because the battery was rubbish (though no fault of the Jerries, we hasten to add). There was no one in sight. The pub was still derelict, the hairdresser's was closed on Tuesday as this was and the chippie did not open for another half-hour. The important thing was that Albie's turf accountancy was open and the security grille had been removed (it had been nicked some time past).

The four men (including Mungo and Betty the Stoker) observed the building and Betty drummed his tattooed fingers on the steering wheel as 'love' and 'mammy' blurred in syncopation of a tune that sounded to Mungo suspiciously like the theme from The Archers (which from memory, Mungo thought, had been Betty's stage act at the Coliseum Café, despite Betty's denial that he was she).

Tim's Uncle Richard gave a sigh and stuffed the sledgehammer back under the front passenger seat.

'C'mon then, Mungo.' Tim nudged Mungo.

The three of them waited on the sunlit pavement as Mungo slowly exited and straightened up with difficulty from the depths of the extremely low, low-emissions VW.

Mungo had given considerable thought to the situation and the agreed plan during the very low-emissions car journey and now said,

'I've given considerable thought to the situation and the agreed plan during the very low-emissions car journey, and what say that we give the chap – the putative damned rogue – one chance to do the right thing. You, Richard and Betty... and you dear Tim, you wait outside and if things do not go as I hope for, you will have your day. I'll call for "back up", as I believe they term it, if required, as it were...'

Mungo was just more than a little uneasy. What had begun as an innocent remark to Tim, a moot and rhetoricalesque question almost, had now become like a scenario for one of those movie things by that fellow Tarantula (Reservoir Dugs not Spiderman) though of course Mungo didn't know that fellow's name or the movie called Reservoir Dogs. But if he had been writing a screenplay, Mungo would have called it Reservoir Dogs and would have assumed the pen name ... Mr Thick...or Mr Dwam...

And the thing is, it was all because he had hit the mini jackpot with one of those once-in-a-lifetime bets, a fairly 'long shot' that should not come off once even in Mungo's very long lifetime. And now he was here to collect and … oh he suddenly wished that Ethel was here; she could do the job of Betty and Richard and the sledgehammer. *Sledgehammer*! he expostulated – to himself of course – where did the sledgehammer come from and why? Maybe there was an innocent explanation. Of course that's it: Tim's relations looked the road-crew type of chaps: tough but honest; hearts of gold under that granite-like, grit-spattered carapace. Indeed, if one ignored the scars, the missing little bits that gave them character – the top of one ear in the case of Betty; the bottom of another ear in the case of Uncle Richard; the missing finger tips, the glass eye and the stainless steel teeth, why they could have been the authors themselves or even civilians – unemployed civilians of course.

And at these thoughts, Mungo felt not the slightest bit better, for, even though there might be a reasonable and innocent reason for them being here now – but perhaps they were dropping Mungo off on the way to dig-up the road at some crucial interchange that would snarl-up the traffic for a putative fourteen weeks and they would erect a sign with a telephone helpline that if you dialled it would take you through to some yurt in Mongolia where a recorded message would say that 'your phone call is important to us' (annoying baistarts) while background music – probably some rapper (we celebrate diversity but draw the line at rap) …

'Suit yersel'.' Uncle Richard lisped attractively and Mungo felt vindicated.

Just then there was a milk-curdling, yoghurt-producing howl that Mungo now knew definitely came from the boot of the very emissions complying VW.

'Fuc*ing Montgomerie! Christ ah furgoat aw aboot him!' Betty made very slowly towards the boot.

'How long's he been in there ya wee stumer?' Richard asked.

'Since last night.'

'Whit?!' Tim exclaimed.

'Serendipity boys. Serenfu*kin'dipity. If Sir Mungo here calls for us in there,' Richard indicated the bookies shop with a nod from the scarred side of his head, (i.e. the side Mungo could unfortunately see) 'we can tie Montgomerie tae the motor tae keep the thieving Parkie's hauns aff. Then we can *aw* have a meaningful discourse with Albie.' (Richard had taken to using that language since during one of his rehabilitation-to-society-seminars (no, he was not the seminarist), he had been introduced to the ideas of Foucault – and had taken to them like a zealot (no ethnic slur intended), for had your man Foucault not demonstrated convincingly (to recidivists and sociologists and Glasgow City Labour Party (membership of all three groups frequently interchangeable) that *the criminals were never to blame*. Seems fair enough, when you think about it, but this is not the place to think about it for Mungo was about to go in and try and persuade the notorious bookie Albie the ... Monster... to pay out his winnings.

The boot flew up and out jumped the blackest, biggest, hairiest, snarlingest Alsatian (or German Shepherd to be pedantically Cruftian) dog Mungo never hoped to see again. It made straight for Betty, its pink lips curled back, yellow fangs bared but Tim grabbed it round the neck wrestled it sideways and held it in what he hoped Monty would regard as a friendly cuddle, all the while cooing softly in its big, floppy, black and golden lug.

It seemed to work. Mungo now watched Monty run his monstrous pink tongue all over Tim's face as both he and the dog stood up. The dog, its paws now on Tim's shoulders, was so big it had to lower its head and tongue to reach Tim's spluttering, mildly protesting face.

Eventually Tim managed to tie Monty to the front bumper and it was time for Mungo to go solo, to keep to his request of his 'back up' to back off for now. He turned back from the door, having second, third, and fourth thoughts, but was met by the folded arms and tight lipped stares of the other three. Even Monty seemed to be glaring at Mungo trying to back out, or more likely sizing him up for a meal he had been denied for too long ...

Mungo took a deep breath and pushed the nearest wooden swinging door just avoiding its return swing as he had a sudden fifth thought about this potential folly. But he was in.

Chapter 27

My old friend, the booze

'So there you have it, Mr Laird... I've layered my cards on the table.' Albie laughed at his wee joke. 'What do *you* suggest?'

(For the eagle-eyed, the earlier speech pattern of Albie has not been overlooked (unlike the CCHHRR) but Albie spoke many languages, especially fluent was he in sucker-speak i.e. he used the language of the sucker, remember he is a bookie: synonyms: 'chameleon' or 'fly lizard'.)

'Call me Mungo, please, everyone else does.' Despite himself, Mungo remained as ever polite.

'Okay, Mungo I'll summarise where we've got to. Me – no *oof*. Me got business. You due mucho *oof*. Me give you the business instead of *oof*. '

'*Oof*?' Mungo asked, his eyes scoping the premises in the hope of espying the lovely creature who had been behind the counter on his first visit. His heart sank – the money he could do without – no he couldn't, silly man – but the thought of seeing whatsername (*we* know it's Raylene) has given him courage to confront the monster that was Albie. But he had even been wrong about that – Albie was a deeply sincere man, just like he was, Mungo judged. And Mungo had got where he was today by trusting his judgement of other men.

'Oof, Mungo. Sorry, Mungo, in times of stress like this I lapse into slang Yiddish... '

'Right. Sorry, right ... *Oof* is money, cash, whatever?' Mungo wondered if there was a dictionary of Yiddish slang to hand, but he had not noticed a library in the vicinity. Not even an outreach of the British Library. He made a mental note to gee them up on this.

'Oh I know everybody and their maiden aunt's budgie think bookie's are loaded and we're always looking to diddle the client. Not so. You'll have read the recent government White Paper on... '

'Of course. White Paper, yes, Mr...

'Albie. Call me Albie. And may I...? Mungo.'

'Albie. Of course. Mungo, yes. Why not, Albie?' They shook hands and Albie said quickly,

'So it's a deal then. Who needs lawyers when a man has a handshake on him?'

'Really?' Mungo played for time. What was this new friend saying? And the manly handshake?' (Thankfully, no huggy-wuggies, shudder-shudder.) 'And what was that bit about lawyers?'

While Mungo was digesting the contents of what Albie had said, Albie was coming to the end of his spiel:

'The truth is, Mungo, a couple of years ago, I changed my 'terms and conditions' from 'official result' with all that hanging about for weigh-ins, steward enquiries that seemed to plague the last races particularly, and me desperate to get out of here...' He paused and taking Mungo's hand swept the room with an arm – it badly needed sweeping and Mungo wondered if Idris would be interested in another job. He made a mental note of this and promptly forgot it.

'You are one lucky g*y, I mean guy, Mungo.' So: this is a First Past The Post shop, for my sins... my conditions, my obligation to you. Lucky g ...fellow that you are.'

Mungo's steel-trap mind raced through the possibilities then gave up: he didn't have a clue as to what Albie was saying and then, like... something seeping really slowly to the surface it came to him: he, Mungo, had hit the real jackpot with his line – whereas he, still Mungo, thought one final part of his line had failed because his last horse had been objected to and eventually disqualified... Albie was saying that he, Albie this time, paid out on 'first past the post'. Mungo had cracked it. And from the froth-laden syllables coming from Albie's tongue (all those cccchrrrrooows), it appeared that he was offering his bookies business to Mungo in lieu of money – or *oof* as his yiddisher mama might have said if he had had one.

And just at that sweetest of moments – perhaps the sweetest since he had first been pinned to the sheets by Ethel five decades and more ago... no! dash it, it was as sweet as that moment burned into his steel-trap brain – YES, WE SAY, just at that sweetest moment, the back-up cleaved through the mephitic air. Led by the sledgehammer-wielding Uncle Richard – whose tendency to aggressive behaviour can be put down to the fact that there was a tendency, possibly inherited or due to nurture (is there a difference?), that the ventrolateral part of his ventromedial hypothalamus (in the brain of course) of his got pure-dead excited at times. Which should get him off any charges, we submit.

Summing up the situation in the blink of an eye – okay a bit of poetic licences – Mungo took charge of the situation and by force of personality and the natural air of authority he exuded (a bit more poetic licence), his 'team' calmed down immediately. Whether that was due to the aforementioned 'air of authority' exuded by Mungo, or was in part due to the Tannoy announcing. *'And they're off at…* '. never became a matter of serious discussion among the chattering classes. Perhaps there was another reason, unseen by the all-seeing Mungo: Uncle Richard lowered his raised sledgehammer and almost shamefacedly tried to hide it behind his broad back in the light of a brief remonstration by, and altercation with, one of the punters, a tiny woman whom he seemed to refer to as 'Aunty Binty'. When the race was run, the sucker-punters had gone home – and so did Mungo's team (should that be Team Mungo?).

(Where was the divine Raylene during all of this kerfuffle? Why there she was, high up behind her grille. Those eyes had seen it all and more. She remained unmoved by the high emotions, for she had other matters on her mind, which we will reveal anon.)

Chapter 28

Reflections in a golden puddle (or on the back of a shiny coat

[NO COMMENTARY:
Tattoo parlour
Nail bar
Turkish barber
Tattoo removal parlour
Tanning salon
Scottish barber
Whitening salon
Charity shop(s).
Cash Convertors
Electronic cigarette information centre
Eyebrow plaiting
Hair extension]

Wending homeward Mungo, (the team had dispersed) who had sought solitude for reflective purposes, cast his mind back to a time in which he had been Mungo Usher Ballantyne Laird, Master Brewer and sole proprietor of Laird's Lager. In this previous life Mungo had been a captain of industry – oh that he had only been a little corporal (just obeying orders, sir, yes, sir!) – for a time then he might have conquered all but for an unlucky combination of poor judgement and crass incompetence in the selection of his junior officers. For a time, he had blamed it on the perfidy of his invisible enemies, but once the paranoia had cleared up thanks to a cream and a little tincture bought at a Chinese Medicine Shoap, he faced the facts of his own role. And so his empire had crashed about him.

Once the dust had settled, Mungo and Ethel were living in virtual poverty, and all the time with the burden of living in Villa Laird, a shuge rambling mansion that looked down augustly (and every other month) on the little town below. However, thanks to Ethel's background – despite her airs and heirs, she was not from the same social class as Mungo – they had squirreled away a substantial little pile, 'a little crock of gold', and Her Majesty's servant Hector the tax inspector, knew nothing of it.

Entrusted by Ethel, Mungo took that little crock to an 'independent financial advisor'. He charged her to turn it into a large crock of gold. She was regulated by the FSA (now calling itself (for this week only?) the Financial Conduct Authority) so you can probably guess what is coming next. When the time came to purchase their annuity and use the surplus to get a new roof on Villa Laird (today the property of Mrs Idris Watters and Tim – we've seen the deeds), and buy their little place in the sun, it had all been eaten up in 'expenses'. (Motto: *Qui prosit? Facio, ha, ha, ha;* Who will benefit? Me, I do, ha, ha, ha – incidentally, another example, if it is needed, of the personal cost to Mungo of having been excluded from Latin at St Kent's.)

To be fair to her, the independent financial advisor suffered such stress at the plight of her elderly couple that her doctor (BUPA) prescribed a ninety-day round-the-world-cruise (we hope it was Royal Caribbean – Wolf Blass@$35 a bottle – hell mend her). She did send a card from Aruba, the location of which is known only to the Dutch, opulent migrants or vacationing Venezuelans and the drivers of cruise boats – those big ones that are basically Benidorm on sea and where you get charged $35 for Wolf Blass's cheapest range of wines – Pirates o' the Royal Caribbean and every other sea. (See TripAdvisor.)

The very thought of all of this – not just W-B @$35 a bottle – caused Mungo to pause on his wend...

With a grim determination to face Ethel and narrate his coup de finance and that he had The Project that would seal their fortunes, he transported himself back to ~~the Queen Mary~~ the Queen Margaret, where, after checking on the progress of his fiancée in the Violent Patients Ward (*holding space*), he slipped in beside Ethel who was snoring gently.

For a moment he thought he must be in the wrong room, then seeing the tip of ~~Laddie's pink-and-white mottled scrotum~~ the water bottle protruding from the pillow slip he regained his composure. While his mistress slept, he engaged in what other great thinkers have called 'a thought experiment'. He had gained and completed The Project – but with that capacity for all great and mediocre thinkers ~~to go beyond the curve~~ to push the envelope, he saw the possibilities for an empire to be founded on that single stroke of luck that had seen him become the proprietor of Albie's business. Had he (Mungo) not espied that, adjoining Albie's in that little pocket of urban decay that had been cut adrift from burgeoning metropolitan Borrfoot, a whole set (*a full house* even) of perfectly complementary commercial premises: a chippie, a ladies hairdresser's (where the women can wait while their men get on with the business of investing in horses), and a derelict pub (with planning permission for conversion to sheltered housing). NOT A PROJECT, BUT A SET OF PROJECTS! he exclaimed (silently, he hoped), looking around guiltily; there was no sudden charge of burly security folk (gender-neutral), and so he continued with his reflection, having slipped the water bottle from the pillow slip, and having sipped a sip of the tonic wine that the slumbering Ethel had been good enough to leave for him.

PROJECTS! That was it. He would make Ethel happy. But first things first – one at a time. He slipped his entrepreneurial mind into first gear and engaged the clutch: Capital? Where would the capital come from? Okay he had landed Albie's business by dint of luck; but even he could see that the place needed sprucing up to give it a patina of credibility if it was to compete with those ruthless capitalistic beasts of betting, Hillbrokes, Packie Power and others of that glossy ilk. Yes, Capital! Once problem was solved, then next would be the... chippie or hairdresser... that was a hard one. His investment bankers could deal with that once the window dressing of Albie's had been completed.

He took another sip of his favourite cordial and with the help of the nurse with the lovely coral ears – she blushed and nipped his arm when he thought that thought – yes with her help, he slipped the water bottle back into the pillow slip without disturbing Ethel.

EUREKA! ~~a body immersed in a fluid is buoyed up by a force equal to the weight of the displaced fluid~~ forget that: this was more important. Mungo sent his disembodied mind, out of the hospital window on a recce to confirm what it had subliminally noted earlier; and it came back and told that it had indeed espied a billboard advertising... MONEY FOR NOTHING – PAYDAY AND RETIREMENT DAY LENDERS.

If Mungo had learned one lesson in his life it was to forget about the last lesson, the last mistake, prepare for the next one. In this respect he was the living embodiment of the aphorism of Santayana:[55]'Those who cannot remember the past are condemned to repeat it.'

It was a eureka moment; a flashbulb moment; a *blue sky thinking* chimera-like thought soft-landing right in front of the flag pole where Mungo now saluted the idea he had run up and now unfurled; another cliché in similar vein moment; and at that his mind swooped back into the hospital, narrowly missing banging into the window which Mungo's corporeal self had closed because Ethel had murmured something about a draught as she rose upwards through several strata of unconsciousness.

But before Ethel awoke, Mungo's mind found its way back onto the shoulder of the very attractive nurse with the delightful coral-tipped ears, (if that is not too explicit an allusion). This time she only wagged a finger at him. He was pushing his luck, she seemed to be implying, so he strove to wrestle his mind back on to more mundane matters and with that Ethel awoke and gave him the sweetest of smiles. Must be good stuff they're giving her, Mungo thought to himself.

'Mungo, you have no idea how good,' Ethel almost drooled. 'Must ask for repeat prescription.' She reached for his hand, and Mungo wondered if both she and he were dreaming separate dreams. Nevertheless, he liked what he saw: a pacific Ethel. But he had more pressing issues to deal with and as he wallowed in the seductive effect of Ethel's hand

---

[55] *No, not the lead guitarist of Grateful Dead. That was Jerry Garcia; you're thinking of Carlos Santana (no relation).*

caressing him, he fought the urge to jump in beside her and take advantage of her vulnerable state of mind.

I'm out of here as soon as it's decent to do so. Or should I wait and share Ethel's supper which must be due? he wondered.

'Yes, Mungo, stay for supper, why don't you?' Ethel giggled girlishly. 'Then we'll see when it's decent for you to leave.' This was a definite promise, if ever there was one, Mungo attested to himself.

'Indeed it is, Mungo, you devilish rogue, you.'

All of which cast the scales from Mungo's eyes regarding his *cogitative-vocalisation* syndrome: it had its good points as well as its bad.

He stayed for supper and afterwards, those lovely medical staff turned discreet eyes away as we will. (Well if those felons can access their *human rights* in this respect, is it too much to ask for equity of treatment for septuagenarians? A letter to the *Mature Times* is perhaps called for.) Later that same night – after a decent post-coital interval – and in what might be termed a defining moment, Mungo rose and after making himself presentable to civilised society, stooped to kiss Ethel. In an excess of what he thought at first was renewed passion, she grabbed him by the tie (*College of Pulmonologists*, Oxfam, Byres Road) and gasped in a hoarse whisper:

'Project Mungo. You need a project to keep you out of mischief. Where's the Buckie, Mungo?'

Relieved that she had returned to a semblance of normality – though he still wanted some of whatever they had pumped into her – he thought to himself, 'Now I'm for it. What will I tell the lovely old dear? It breaks my heart to see her like this. She'll never forgive this oversight.'

'Oh yes, I will, Mungo. Come here and give your one true Ethel a big smacker.' Which he then did. Mungo was now very careful not to think that he had been very clever and had double-fooled Ethel with his… for if he did…

He bade her goodbye and just as he was leaving he saw the computer thing at the bottom of the bed and thought he would just login to Packie Power for the next day's racing card, when the nurse with the lovely coral ears skelped him on the head.

'Don't bother,' she said. 'Packie Power is banned in here.' Then, as he was going out the door she whispered, 'Thanks about the ears.' She touched them touchingly.

As he staggered down the corridors he wondered how the devil that lovely young lady (with the pink coral ears) could have guessed his intentions. One of those unfathomable mysteries of the universe that is perhaps not within the grasp of mortals to comprehend.

Makes you think, though, so it does, by the way…

Chapter 29

Men and manopause

At the Queen Margaret (no relation) they had not been able to find all of the bunting that had been used for the opening ceremony by P******* A**e (It's no' use trying to fill in the asterisks: you wouldn't know him). So instead the staff of the unit who had been ~~landed with~~ ~~sorry~~ *allocated to care for* Ethel were asked to bring in pots and pans and spoons with which to strike them, as they formed a guard of honour for her leave-taking. Many a tear-filled eye glittered that day – there had been an incident in the Elderly Care Unit and Mace had been deployed.

As if on cue by a celestial ringmaster (we're not suggesting that hospital is like a circus or heaven), the sun broke through the thin layer of cirrocumulus (*'a relatively rare cloud forming ripples which may resemble honeycomb'* according to the Met Office (?)), and as the heat rose up from the petal-strewn red carpet, Ethel paused and beamed and with the support of Idris in her role as Lady of the Bedpan, became semi-conscious as Idris, now in her role as taxi driver, levered Ethel into the back seat of her cab, secured her seatbelt (Ethel's – Idris being a cabbie never bothers with hers), and moved off. Miraculously, it seemed to Ethel, those myriads of weeping nurses, doctors, jannies, porters and cohorts of uncelebrated support-staff who had a few seconds before been cheering Ethel, all of them seemed to have evaporated in the blazing morning sun.

When she was fully conscious, there was a brief moment of panic as she scrabbled through her ~~sack~~ bag and thought she had left behind her hot water bottle and its contents. Idris, with a glance in her mirror – the only time she would use her mirror that day – saw Ethel's anxiety and with that instinct that all good cabbies have, called Ethel's attention to the water bottle that swung from that very same mirror, where it had pride of place as a mascot.

The only thing missing that day was Mungo's presence; it rendered the occasion something akin to Romeo without Juliet, Banquo without his ghost, or Hamlet without the cigar. But apart from that there were more people happy than were unhappy and that must have kept Jeremy Bentham, fiddling with his felicific calculus, relatively happy as he looked down or, up, on the scene.

And so among the things other than her gall bladder that she had left behind, Ethel remembered that she had forgotten to ask the ward sister for that little present for Mungo: a Jubilee flask of Methadone (or even a commemorative mug of the stuff would have sufficed). Nevertheless, she had during her stay been treated like royalty (high on drugs) and she in turn had responded with a graciousness she had never been noted for (the drugs again).

Chapter 30

Philosophy versus common sense

So. And so, so later that same afternoon, Idris and Ethel were having a pleasant chat, at the heart of which was the whole business about the need for Mungo to have a **PROJECT** – to keep him out of mischief and make them some money, Ethel added. But first they dealt with the usual desultory small-talk that inevitably arises whenever two or more women are gathered together over a teapot and a plate of digestives (Lidl: 39p and money back[56] if you can tell the difference between them and McVittie's at 89p in Tesco), with a bottle of gin on a side table (Lidl do these as well – gin and wee tables; there's even a vodka called *Putinoff*, about which we pass no comment since Vlad has opened a free-speech media centre (and a speech-free non-media centre) less than fifty miles from us, and we do not want to incur his wrath; no' that we're saying he is or has ever been wrathful)…

'Aye, mine's like that as well,' Idris said as she pushed a plate of digestives towards the invalid who was propped up in bed in what had once been her own bedroom – though she had shared it now and then with Mungo. Ethel had asked Idris what Tim would say when he discovered that she, Ethel, had been given her old room back *pro tem.*

'Oh Tim disnae speak Latin.' And that was that taken care of. Now they were dealing with those issues that arise whenever two women… tea, cake, then MEN.

'Does yours scratch his arse for ten minutes once the lights are off?'

'Ten minutes? Twenty at least, Idris. I hate to think what it does to his pyjamas. And he cups his balls.'

'And does he jiggle them as well? I bet he does. They all do.'

---

[56] *Terms and conditions apply.* Cheques may not be honoured.

'Cups, jiggles, juggles the blighters. If he could he would throw them over his shoulder, shouldn't wonder and catch them behind his back... and do you know what: when he gets out a car he roars with pain and says...'

Idris completed the sentence, 'that his balls are too big. That he's *snecked* them.'

'Exactly. That they've tumbled out his Y-fronts,' Ethel trilled melodiously.

Both women stared off into the middle distance – doubtless recalling a precious moment in which Y-fronts featured large. After a moment both opined simultaneously almost:

'*Too big*? Can never be too big, balls. Balls!'

There was a lull in the conversation while they stuffed their faces, broken when Idris raised the matter that Ethel had largely forgotten about.

'I'm no' happy with this project business, Ethel. Tim is awfy secretive about it. Did Mungo say anything to yourself about it?'

'Project? What project? Mungo? Whatever it is, he'll well and truly bugger it up. All I had in mind was for him to keep himself busy. Out from under your feet until I was back to control him. You know that he buggered up the family brewery, although we don't ever mention that.'

'Oh aye, Ethel. The whole town knows. No that anyone ever mentions it, as you say. He's a bit sensitive about it. Just the other day, there it was brung up at a cooncil meeting – I mean, after how many years ...?'

And just at that, almost unheard – and certainly unseen – Mungo and Tim entered, perhaps to inquire after the invalid or to ask if anyone had seen the digestive biscuits, only to listen in awe to the conversation they had been about to interrupt, as Idris said to Ethel,

'And as for yon Nietzsche – excuse my pronunciation – you can never underestimate the influence of his ideas on the individual's conquest of, and transcendence beyond, structure and context.' (This sounds like an unattributed quotation to us.)

165

'Exactly my point, Idris. Especially with those Jerry philosophers. Prefer the Austrian meself... Oh there you are, Mungo, my dear.'

[Idris is now cleaning for a professor of philosophy – while it would be too obvious (though true) to state that their relationship is purely Platonic, Idris for her part preferred to think of it as being more Aristotelian in that she aspired to the characteristic virtue of Aristotelianism, *phronesis (φρόνῄσή)* – that is 'practical wisdom and prudence'. Something that she had to sharply remind the old fella (client) more than once in the early days of their cash-nexused relationship. ANYWAY, but, an' that, the old fella follows her about with her duster (sounds a bit like Mungo) and while he drones on about his research and his teaching she inadvertently is absorbing the concepts and ideas while he is absorbing the play of the motes of stoor on her skin that always has a sheen on it – not composed of normal sweat, ye ken – one of the consequences is that from time to time, Idris, if called upon, will switch to discussions of various philosophers, chosen for her judgement as to how their concepts will appeal to the listener. For her part, Ethel listened to Idris and absorbed much from her discourses – though in the past she would have dismissed all philosophers as a bunch of tossers. Which is a point of view best expressed in the works of yon ...]

ANYWAY,

[Mungo's own ideas on Nietzschean (excuse our spelling) philosophy had been arrived at when he saw the start of yon film where these monkey creatures batter the lights out of each other with bones and then dance around a big black slab thing.[57] But even he would be the first to admit his perspective was not fully formed as when yon music that Nietzsche wrote started and he was ejected from the GFT – or was it GTF? – along with Ethel before they even had time to finish the Buckie.]

---

[57] *It would appear that he has in mind thon 2001 A Space Odyssey; according to Imdb, yon Nietsche has no credits listed. Mungo must be confusing it with something else... not like him.*

ANYWAY: discovering the digestive biscuits had just been scoffed by Idris and Ethel, Mungo and Tim mumbled their excuses and left as they did not want to appear unable to fully engage in the debate.

Once they were gone – both women listened for the tell-tale sound of the front door having to be pulled off its hinges and levered up before it would close properly – Idris pronounced that this little discussion on gender differences had made her feel much better. And Ethel reciprocated with: 'a pain shared is a pain relieved.' If Idris would maybe give her a wee hand up, she was ready to face the day.

Idris cautioned her, 'But Ethel, you'll need to take it easy. Your legs might no' work right after all that time in hospital.'

'Legs have not worked for years, Idris. But the buggers are just going to have to lump it.'

She held out her arms to Idris who – though not built like Betty the Stoker – put her arms around Ethel's shoulders and heaved her up and on to the carpet in one fluid motion (the teapot fell over).

This was a very emotional moment for Ethel – for apart from the all too infrequent moments of affection from Mungo, when he was trying to get aboard, this was the first cuddle Ethel had had since her mother mistook her for a wardrobe that needed shifting. (Ethel's mother had been big-boned as well and equally myopic.) Her eyes brimmed with tears as did Idris's as she popped that troublesome third disc (Tim would re-insert it later. He was good for that, when he wasn't scratching his arse or juggling or snecking his balls).

Twenty-nine downward steps later, Idris, if she had ever read Buchan's work, would surely have read most of its thirty-nine faster than the time taken by the tortuous painful journey from ex-mistress bedroom to ex-mistress main room. A second 'purely restorative' Buckfast later had removed some of the colour from Ethel's cheeks and osmotically injected some into Idris's. They were both a bit cheery if not fully restored, Idris being considerably fuller of 'cheer'.

'Ah should dae this mair often, but,' Idris giggled. 'Ah mean it's no' gone whitever-time-it-is-yet. Ah'm glad Tim talked me intae takin' a half-day.' She drained her glass of wine and in such condition they thought they would speak of trivial matters having already exhausted the topic of man *qua* man or something.

And so Ethel expanded on her belief that what was wrong with Mungo – apart from the usual man thing of scratching and jiggling intimate parts – was that he was insufficiently intellectually challenged. Or too smart for anyone else's good… and not smart enough for the Laird's… which brought them by a circuitous route to the issue of The Project.

To which Idris said, 'Aye, well that's what he gets for teaming up with Tim,' reaching for the Buckie to calm her nerves, then remembered just in time that, as a plebeian, she was not entitled to have nerves that were ever jangled. That was close. It would be existential *angst* next, or even *ennui*. See the middle-class, they've got a right hard time o' it, so they have, she nearly thought.

'A project. That's what he needs. Mungo needs something challenging to keep his mind off his concerns. Until such times as we are safely re-ensconced in the Algarve,' Ethel pronounced (using received pronunciation). 'Got that from the telly in hospital. These people all over England – too much money, too much time on their hands. Half a million available to buy a second home; a place in the country, location, location, place in the sun and what have you and the house they see is too good. Need a project. Put own stamp on it. Blank canvas. Knock all those bloody walls down.' Ethel was beginning to recover, it sounded like, as the Buckie lubricated her tongue and her concern that Mungo never got bored.

To which, Idris this time reached for the Buckie – not because her nerves were a little Bo-Jangled, but because she needed to try and get her brain round the idea of Mungo knocking walls down, putting his own stamp on things and with her Tim as his project manager. But then, what harm could it do? It would keep them from under her feet. Tim would be so tired after a day's work with Mungo that he would not be able to scratch his arse or jiggle his balls in bed, let alone cup them. She would need to think about this one. (And she did and decided that she would buy a triple pack of yon men's pants that are not Y-front and which have wee short legs making it impossible for him to sneck his balls when he next got out the motor. She might even buy a pack for Ethel to give to Mungo. And with those warm thoughts she drifted off. (We think she has in mind the Asda Three-pack A-frame trunks, £8 atow. Lidl don't seem to be in this market, though their peanut butter is recommended.)

And so we will leave them where we found them – for just as we left whatever room they were having this discussion in, we caught one or other of them saying,

'Here, does yours never replace the lavvy paper when it's run oot as well?' Over which comment we will draw a Nietzschean hand-washed veil.

LATER:

Thinking not to disturb the tranquillity of the great house, Tim and Mungo – ever-sensitive to the latent neurasthenia of their respective and respected wives (Tim could not bring himself to say 'partner'; whereas in Mungo's case the term would always be associated with a professional who was about to bilk him), YES, seeing that all was at peace they climbed the stairs in the darkness – in Mungo's case because his bunnet (Homburg obtained from a charity shoap that very day in lieu of nicked one) yes, his bunnet had slipped down over his ears (which is counter-intuitive given that for men of a certain age the only thing that grows is their ears and hair in inappropriate places…like ears); while the darkness that befell Tim, not used to hard drink, was occasioned by him being blind drunk.

But lo! there in their path was the Behemoth (Job 40:15–24. KJV), and Mungo was sore afraid. But lo again! It was all right, for it was the snoring form of Ethel on the second landing and the peacefully snoring and silently wind-passing Simba or Rajah or whatever the Doberman's name is. And thus it came to pass that Mungo found his strength is in his loins, and his force is in the navel of his belly, and he tip-toed over the recumbently positioned Ethel and left Tim to his own devices. But Tim being Tim stood on Rajah or Simba or one of the other Dobermans and there was again a great racket throughout the land to which was added that of Ethel who bit one of the dogs.

169

And so Idris, disturbed in her dwam summoned all of her recently acquired philosophical skills, and packed everyone off to bed, then she went down into the scullery and made herself some tea and toast and had thick full-fat, heavily salted butter (*Lurpak*) that dripped down her chin as she ate the toast, (Simba or Rajah or Tim could lick it from her later); and with her feet on the old back-to-back range, roasting nicely she said to what might be the dawn that seeped in the window, 'Ramorra's anither day. F*ck it.'

PART TWO

The not so gentle touch

Chapter 31

The whims of the father.

Raylene McMaster was walking the short walk from her council flat on the edge of The Park to her work at the bookies. As she stepped across the boundary that marked her entry to Borrfoot proper, she abandoned the struggle with her umbrella (£1 Poundstretcher; can double as crotchet needles; safety-glasses recommended) in the horizontal drizzle, pulled up the hood of her parka, and smiled to herself. Then she smiled at herself smiling to herself. It's been a long time since I've done that on my way into work, she said to herself.

Probably the thought of this being her last week, the joy of escape; but deep down she knew it was more than that: she was actually *looking forward* to today and the rest of her last week, more than curious to see what this strange old guy Mungo or Mingo, (or MugNo as this keyboard sometimes hsa it), her new boss, would make of his new business.

Of course, as usual with those types new to a business – any business – they have to bring in the family. No matter how *otiose* that family member may be. Ray had first used that particular word in earnest to her last boyfriend – an assistant to the local MP. When he – the boyfriend – had preened himself when she told him, 'Hutton, you know when it comes down to it, you and your boss are really otiose.' He had blushed and thanked her, for he knew that Ray was stinting in her praise. And that was the moment she knew it was time to dump the chump. Anyway, Mingo's or Mungo's boy was starting today, and she had a bet with herself he would turn out to be a right warrmer.[58] But so what? She was offski in a week.

---

[58] *Dolt, eedjit, otiose in extremis. (slang).*

173

She had been introduced to Mungo by Albie – during which introduction, something hinted to her that Albie was in a hurry to be gone: there was the suitcase, then the wee case on wheels; the Hawaiian shirt; the sunglasses and the silly wee hat with the donkey ears. But anyway, more importantly was the impression she had got of Mungo – and with Ray, first impressions took a long time to be modified or even mollified. She had been prepared to dislike him from the off; but it would have been like disliking a child before it had been born. Mungo Laird, in her seasoned opinion, was not born for this world, let alone born to be a bookie – sorry, *turf accountant*, as he termed it. In fact, it was her unstated opinion that the elderly gentleman was not born for this or any world known over her lifetime of thirty plus (just). His best bet was one of yon exo-planets that astronomers and other doomsayers were wetting themselves about every other week.

There was a touching innocence to him, that in a younger man – men of her age bracket – she would have characterised as 'gormless'. And she had known plenty of those. She would never have used that expression of Albie who was like a shark circling his clients (from the safe waters of the counter-grille) and picking them off; and just before he swallows them, commiserating with their bad fortune of the day.

She had watched Albie groan aloud, as if in the throes of childbirth – oh that he had tried that one – in sympathy with his clients as a stream of 'bad' results came in over the tannoy; bad for them, good for Albie. He would shake his head, pencil in his mouth as the sucker-fish came up to the grille for one last time (Aye, heard that yin before) having found a twenty pence coin in the lining of their jacket.

'Some days are like that,' Albie would sympathise with his victim/client, adding, 'it's got to get better for you. Oh, I see you're on *Bent Banana*. Fancy that myself.'

And they're off! (Heh, heh, heh, snigger, snigger, ccchorrrtle, etc.)

No' that Ray really, deep-down disliked Albie. He had been not a bad boss. Money was above the minimum wage. A wee bonus at Christmas – in cash; he had tried to give it to her in 'free' bets but she had given him the chewing gum-stare, had taken off one of her stilettos (Peacocks – no apostrophe, Black Ghillie, Slim Heel, ~~£22~~ £17.60 atow), had examined the heel with the tip of her finger, wondering aloud if she needed to re-hone it. At which point Albie revealed that he had only been jesting.

What sort of man used the word: 'jesting', she had asked herself? She had been collecting words associated with specific men for most of her adult life. The faither of her wean was 'coitus'; if only she had interrupted him seconds before he had screeched that one … but that was another story.

Ray never carried a copy of DSM-5 (or IV for that matter), but had she done so, she might have designated the term *abulia* to Mungo for he had a *pathological need never to act decisively.* Although commonly associated with schizophrenia, this could never be said of Mungo. Never, for he only had one personality and he was perfectly comfortable in it. So, Ray, in ignorance of such a term to describe Mungo took the simple approach: he was pretty useless but harmless… either Abulia or Dysphoria – maybe she would have hyphenated these as Mungo had the bearing of a hyphenated-gent (who had a *pathological aversion to making a decision* while always appearing somewhat ill at ease underneath his see-through carapace of *sans souci.*) Yes *Aboulia-Dysphoria* (Or *AD*) he would or could have been in Ray's eyes from now on. But she settled for, Distinguished and Slightly 'Furrin'. And probably otiose – but in a harmless way.

On the other hand, Ray herself had no problems about decision-making and *time management.* Did our mothers know they were good at *time management*; how could they have been when the term had not been invented by some ~~tosser~~ jargon-inventing sociologist – don't answer that one.

Ray, without the benefit of higher education, juggled everything effortlessly: the wean and the joab through the auspices of her mother (maw) and sister who was in a similar position to Ray, with her own wee, now fatherless, wean. Between the three of them – the two sisters and their mother – the wee yin(s) (cousins) were at nursery, were picked up on time, were clean when they set out in the morning, were well-fed and healthy. Ray, like her sister, looked for no help from outside agencies – it wasn't the government or the social work department that had prised her legs apart. If she needed help, then it was to her sister she turned and she reciprocated. If the two sisters needed help at the same time, then it was their mother. Is that no whit grannies are fur?

When she had applied for the job on the executive training scheme at Hillbrokes, Ray had waited for the inevitable bit: the interview panel (does it really take three executives to spot talent?! she asked herself when shown into the 'interview-space'). BUT ANYWAY, Ray waited for the question that would seal the deal for her: one of the palookas on the 'panel' raised the question of the wean and how it might… Ray gave the chewing gumless stare and waited until there was complete silence in the 'interview-space'.

Ray said 'Is it because I is wuman?'[59] in an accent redolent of palm trees, surf on beaches, *Lilt*, Rastafarian dreadlocks, the words and phrases *Rhyrie* and *Yay Man,* the heavy scent of ganja (not the city in Azerbaijan) in the hot air, delivered in a beat that looks like this,

'When can you start?' the chairman said, keeping the beat – he fancied Raylene, but he was onto plums.

Ray took strength from the frailties of others, those around her, especially men. She rarely laughed aloud, but inside was a permanent smile of … well almost of superiority bordering on omniscience. She looked at the men she worked with and the men she had 'made love to', and all she saw was

---

[59] *With no apologies to Lewis Hamilton.*

weakness after weakness. She could see the traps they were making for themselves and watched as they approached them blindly. She rarely intervened – especially with those who were cocksure (dick-certain) of themselves, bathing herself in the anticipated pleasure of their fall and how they would run to some woman for sympathy and… a bail-out: either financial or emotional, mostly both.

Once she was to meet a man she had been seeing for a few weeks. On the way as she walked up Sauchiehall Street – they planned to go to the movies to see the most recent piece of romantic/thriller nonsense – when, a few hundred yards from the cinema she decided enough was enough: she didn't particularly like the guy.

She turned up a street and found herself outside another cinema she had never noticed before. On a whim she went in, bought a ticket and went into the auditorium just as the film started. *Scheißen*, she might have groaned aloud: it was in German (Jerry) with subtitles. On a point of principle, she hated subtitles. On a point of prejudice, she laughed at Germans and their need to be loved and respected and to be the bail-out kitty for all the feckless other countries of Europe; and for the fixed smile (rictus really) they collectively affected when they opened their arms to the asylum-seekers and economic migrants of the troubled parts of the world. And she wondered: what is the half-life of collective guilt? Oh, and they had bombed her Great Granny in Clydebank. Ray took that personally.

Anyway: *Scheißen*, she might have said to herself as she settled into her seat. The film was *Der Himmel über Berlin* (*Wings of Desire*) and it left her in a strange state of mind as she walked back down into the city centre. There was something about the main character, an angel called Damiel that she identified with. She couldn't think clearly. But that night in bed she thought and thought and she got the solution: she was the angel Damiel, who observes (unobserved) the follies of mankind, until the fool, Damiel himself, fell in love with a mortal. No chance of Ray doing that, unless she was 'mortal' (hammered) she consoled herself and fell asleep, resolved never again to watch a film with sub-titles. So there! And what's your point? Well, she was once more Damiel with a secret smile when she first clapped eyes on Mungo Laird as he agreed to 'buy out' Albie.

Ray still had reservations about quitting Albie's, now Mungo's, and joining Hillbrokes. Sure she could do with the extra cash but the hitherto easy balancing logistics of a single mammy with a four-year-old would become a little more problematic as soon as the wee yin began going to school; there would be no more easy stroll from her flat or her mother's to her work, for Hillbrokes was in the New Town and the one-way system…

ENOUGH, we all know the difficulties women have – they tell us often enough! (Not that we're complaining like, and we do believe you, honestly). And anyway, Ray'll manage something. She always does.

On the way to the 'working space', she as usual collected the day's essentials: scones and cakes from the Home Bakery; the racing papers from what used to be and still was called 'The Paki's' as well as digestive biscuits and milk. (These latter she could have got much cheaper at Lidl,[60] but she wasn't paying for them – Albie had been, but now Mingo-Mungo was.)

Then she went to open the shoap and lo, it stood agape.

---

[60] *39p in Lidl and we defy anyone to tell the difference between them and McVittie's @ 89p in Tesco at time of writing. (They do dark chocolate at the same price - thought you'd like to know.) Previous offer of money back no longer applies. Offer open to one per family (traditional definition – legal documentation (marriage certificate etc.) needs to be provided. Photocopies will not be accepted. Calls from landlines at £3.64 pm.*

Chapter 32

Then she went to open the shoap and lo, it stood agape

Then she went to open the shoap and lo, it stood agape.

Ray spat her chewdie out (into a nearby receptacle we hasten to add) and entered. And there he stood, scratching his napper. If they ever built or carved or whatever it is they do to make a statue (apart from sculpting), if they ever did whatever it takes and made a statue of Mungo, that would be the signature pose – one hand on hip, the other scratching the back of his head – a sort of inverted Thinker. (We do not use the word 'invert' in any way that might cause offence – unless you've something you're ashamed of? Mmh?)

She tried to break the mighty Mung's reverie by slapping the papers and other things down on the nearest surface.

He started, then started the comptometer (no, we do not mean *computer*!) again and made as if he had been up all night working. After a hearty amiably-gruff greeting, he began to think aloud. This time he meant it – it was complicated and he did some of his best reasoning *au dehors* so to speak, and he did that now. In his hand he held a betting slip, while punching the comp.

'Let me see… that's a third at seven-to-four, so one-quarter of seven over four plus. No, times a second at five-to-four. Now is that a treble or a four timer? Oh Christmas, let's start all over. Stop damn you blasted infernal comptometer!'

The comptometer squeaked, burped, vibrated then farted, objecting and inchoately rejecting its relatively recent transplant of 240-volt electricity.

'What the? Mungo. Mungo! Switch that damn thing off. Mungo! Right!' Ray strode to join Mungo behind the grille at the counter that fronted the back shop.

'Oh! How did that… Ah, Raylene. Just in the nick. Thought the beggar was going to swallow me.'

Ray stopped before the work table where the betting slips were organised. This was the equivalent of Mission Control at Cape Canaveral/Kennedy/Johnson/Nixon/Paul Revere (or whatever they are calling it this week). For a moment Ray almost forgot she was the Angel Damiel and she snorted through her nose – both nostrils, septum intact – then she controlled her emotions.

'Mungo. Tell me. What are you doing?' She gestured to the table then placed her hands on her hips (and very nice too, Mungo almost thought aloud). We forgot to say that Ray is wearing a slim-fit pencil-skirt in charcoal grey (Welt-pocket, £17.50, £14.99 M&S Outlet) a crisply starched white blouse (with lots of pointy-bits in the right places – you know the one: *The Premier Short-sleeve Pilot Blouse* – Workwear Express, £13.60 inc. vat; the one with the two strategically situated pockets and those wee belt things on the shoulders; all nipped-in at her narrow waist by a broad, shiny-black belt with a very big silver buckle (provenance unknown).

'Damned machine has life of its own, Raylene.'

'Mungo, what are these? What was the last thing I said last night? Two piles of betting slips, not three. Is that really so hard to remember? *Winners* and *losers*. It's just a mirror of life. As a rough rule-of-thumb for telling you how you're doing business-wise, one of those piles should be much higher than the other. I'll leave you to work out which.'

She turned away to take off her jacket – no details available as she had picked up her sisters by mistake at the child-handover that morning; suffice to say the sister must be a cracker as well, if that is not too sexist a comment. YES, she turned away to take off her jacket when she noticed something on the table.

'Mungo, what's this?' She rifled through a third pile of betting slips on the table. 'A third pile? What is it supposed to be?' She slapped the table for emphasis, shook her head and was about to purse her lips into a prune when she decided she would save that for another time; and anyway, she felt that to do so transformed her instantly into her own mother, yon time she had given her '*that news*' four years before. God forbid.

'Two piles. Yes. You did say, but thought it would be more interesting if we had a pile with intriguing, educative names. Look, this one here. *One pound win: John of Gaunt, 2.30 Newmarket.* If memory serves, *John of Gaunt* never made it to Newmarket. Born in Ghent, Belgium.'

'Loser.' Ray grabbed the slip.

'Another one Ray: *Bent Banana.* Bent Banana. Don't you see? All bananas are.'

'Loser,' Ray gently started to prise the slip from Mungo, then released it into his hand. 'Tell you what, Mungo, you do it your way. Because, another week it's all yours. You can work on your little piles and when some psycho comes in for their pay-out, you can explain all these interesting little facts. I'll go check the fire insurance.'

'You're angry with me, Ray. Say you're not. Oh Ray, not easy for me adjusting to this. So new. So different this side of the counter. Did not expect it. All so complicated. Not like the brewery at all.'

'The brewery. Oh aye, Laird's Lager. We've all heard about that one,' she said, not under her breath.

Despite her determination to remain professionally indifferent to Mungo, she was beginning to feel sorry for him. But she steeled herself – that type preyed on your humanity, she reminded herself, and tried to remember what that Jerry film was all about. There had to be a hidden message in it: it was Furrin.

'*Complicated?* The punters come in. If they can read, they lift tips from the *Daily Skitter,*' she waved one of the racing papers under his nose. 'If they can think, they study form. The rest? They've had a dream or a cat ran in front of them. It doesn't matter. In the end they pick losers. *Losers.*' She looked at her wrist…

Mungo thought it very attractive, a certain delicacy of bone structure, the way those two freckles seemed to mirror the twin points of her …

'Mungo, your slevering! Are you all right?!' Ray demanded, then seeing he was just coming out of another dwam, she returned to business. 'Look at the time and the front shop hasn't got the racing papers up yet. You just sit there, I'll do everything.' Ray went out into the front shop. She stopped to sniff the air. There was something strange, alien. The air was almost clean. No smell. Clear visibility. Eventually she realised. She had *never* been in here without the miasma of nicotine and punter. She shook her head at the wonderment and resumed her gentle chastisement of Mungo and his bumbling nonsense. She ripped the last of yesterday's newspaper racing sheets from the wall and shouted over at Mungo.

'*Complicated?*! This game?! Try psychoprophylactics when you are in the middle of dropping your first wean!'

Mungo who didn't do medical, shuddered then changed the subject ever so slightly. 'But why? Why do it? The punters?'

'Why?' Ray had returned behind the grille and stood by Mungo, looking over his shoulder unaware of the frisson she was causing as she continued, 'To dream. Tomorrow. Next week. That that winner will come in for them.'

'Ah. I like that. We're trading in *dreams*.' Mungo looked into the middle distance and started a dream in which Ray, for some unfathomable reason, was kitted out in biker's leather, a veritable Suzi Quatro in her tannery-treated prime… he riding pillion, like a bat out of hell (though if asked, it is unlikely that he would have known who Meatloaf was).

'And nightmares… and Mungo, you were right about one thing: a third pile. That comes later: the Tax People. Make it look like you didn't win.'

Chapter 33

'L'enfer, c'est les autres'... family members
particularly

Somehow, as if by magic, the rest of the day went pretty much without any major crisis. Well, it was not by magic – it was Ray's skills as an organiser, manager, pacifier (of irate punters) and general dogsbody that won the day, just as she had so many times before, under the previous regime. But like the angel she was, she foresaw weeping and smashing (no not gnashing, *smashing*) of teeth once she was gone. For it did not take a team from Anderson Consulting (now defunct – how good were they?) or PriceWaterhouse (not saying a word against them, milud till the jury's *in*) to identify the managerial catastrophe that was Mungo.

Mungo kept assuring Ray that things would be all right, for his boy was returning from a very successful sojourn somewhere with an unpronounceable name – Mungo couldn't pronounce it – and all the skills that he, Mungo, did not have (and there were a few, he conceded) were embodied in his son. Ray had never read a great deal on genetics – she did not even have some vague memory of Gregor Mendel and 'trait inheritance' – as a girl it was okay to slit a frog in the classroom, but leave the hard stuff to the boys – which was fine by her, because just from observing the people who had lived around her all her life and from listening to her mother complain about this one and that one, and from working with stumours (aka *stumers* aka *bampots*) who employed their own sons and daughters, she knew that very rarely did crass idiocy, unlike baldness, skip a generation.

Her position on the *nature versus nurture* controversy was simple: there was no controversy – feed an eedjit as much as you like and he'll still be an eedjit. End of.

And so she waited, with a tranquillity of the soul, to be proved wrong by Mungo's boy. Anyways, she was leaving, sure she wuz.

Chapter 34

Here comes the son

'Raylene, he's here. Eh… my boy, this charming young lady is Raylene…'

The heir to Mungo's debt mountain was out of breath. He had jogged by a circuitous route to his father's new 'secret' project. He was wearing a black UnderArmour top (*Moisture Transport System wicks sweat away from the body*; and if that wasn't reason enough to buy it, why, it's *Anti-odour technology prevents the growth of odour-causing microbes* – wee stinkies). His tree-trunk legs – Ray was paying attention – were swathed in red UnderArmour Raid International Shorts (*Think incredibly light, loose, quick-drying & very breathable. It's your new favourite'*)

As he looked about him with awe, and tried not to laugh aloud, his manly chest heaved and he began to do some Canadian Airforce exercises against the door jamb, which began to give way and so he took from his backpack (Yep: *UA Worldwide Mesh Backpack*) a towel[61] and wiped himself down.

Ray ignored the display as being too obvious and far too early. She waited for Mungo to do the introductions, which he sort of did: 'Well eh… my boy, this delightful young woman is Raylene. She'll be keeping a weather eye on you until you are up to speed.' And with that Mungo walked away into the back office where he might have done some pelvic-floor exercises or the one-legged dance of you-know-what for all the good he was in personal situations.

Ray waited, one hand on hip while this finely honed specimen of mankind ensured there was not a drop of

---

[61] *You'd think that with all that UA technology, he wouldn't have sweated? No criticism intended or implied of Under Armour, Inc., no way, honestly m'lud. It must just be that the young man is abnormally sweaty having run only 14k.*

moisture on him before offering his hand which Ray took, all the time wondering: could this really have been the fruit of the loin of Mungo? Then perhaps the explanation lies in the mother, of whom she had not yet had the pleasure.

'And do you have a name?'

'Oh, sorry. Thought the old boy had said. At school I sometimes got Mingo or Mango, sometimes Mongo. St Kentigern's. That kind of school, you know.' He looked about the room, and with that almost imperceptible shake of his head, and a look of disbelief on his face, he had made the second good impression on Ray, though he might never know it.

'So, is it Mingo or Mango or Mongo?'

'Oh, no. That was school.' He perused the racing papers tacked to the wall; picked up a grubby pencil stub glanced briefly at Ray then scribbled on a blank betting slip before peeking inside the door to the toilet – from which he quickly shrunk back.

Ray waited until he faced her again. 'You tell me, you have to kill me, that it? A state secret?'

'State secret? I don't... '

'Your name, for godsake.' She turned away.

'Cosmo.'

Ray stopped, her back to *Cosmo!* She turned slowly, both hands on hips.

'It's Cosmo.'

'And that's short for ... Davie, Rab... Universe?

'*Cosmogenous,*' Cosmo said.

Ray waited.

'You know, Ray... from an extraterrestrial source.'

'I'd just been thinking that. No quite in those terms. Do you know Johnny Cash?'

'Johnny Cash. Is that our rival on the next street?'

Later, when Cosmo had changed into clothing more consonant with the job in hand – it's amazing what that *UA Worldwide Mesh Backpack* holds – Ray was issuing instructions to her boss and his heir and watched both flounder – especially Cosmo.

She shook her head. 'Extraterrestrial indeed,' she mused, then issued some instructions and set about getting things in order. Later that day she heard Cosmo humming a tune that was vaguely familiar. She listened until she had identified it: the smart-arse she said to herself – he was humming *'A boy named Sue'*. Johnny Cash 'our nearest rival', my arse. As she passed Cosmo, she gave him a good punch on the arm.

Over a coffee in a nearby greasy (aka filthy) spoon, Cosmo told the story of the name with which he had been registered at birth. Mungo had charged his brother Torquil to do the necessary form-filling – Mungo having partaken of fine wines (pre-Buckfast) in celebration of fatherhood. Torquil, who himself had had a few goldies in celebration of unclehood, forgot the name that Mungo had mentioned. After discussion with the Registrar – who was pissed for some known reason – the Registrar (a graduate of Edinburgh Uni who had managed to turn his life around), came up with *Cosmogenous.*

Seemed fair enough, Ray said, wiping her mouth and rising. When Cosmo went to pay, she brushed him aside – 'exes'. She explained. Expenses.

Back at the office, Ray was fixing the racing papers and generally tidying up when she picked up a stray betting slip and made to place it into the little tray that held them for the punters. She glanced at it. Was this the one Cosmo had scribbled on?

'You do this, then?' she held the slip out to him.

Cosmo took it, looked at it, crumpled it saying, 'Sorry Ray, a little habit of mine. Hope it didn't offend you.' Before he could chuck it into a waste bucket, Ray prised it from his grasp, flattened it out, saying,

'You've gone and spoiled it.'

'I'll do another if you like it. Just a little pen-portrait.'

'You draw people. Just like that. It's brilliant. I've never been drawn before. It's actually… quite good. In fact, better than that.'

'If you want, I'll do a full-size portrait.'

'Would I need to take my clothes off?'

'For a portrait... normally yes, but I suppose I could work around the clothes. But usually...'

Ray punched him on the arm. The second sign of affection she had shown to a man for quite a long time – though Cosmo could not have known this; that blow, like the earlier one, gave him a frisson along with the momentary pain; except the frisson lasted much, much longer, holding out as it did, a subtle promise of another punch to be earned.

ANYWAY

Cosmo had been schooled at St Kentigern's, where mention of his father, Mungo, continued to raise smiles and multi head-nodding reminiscent of an oil field in Texas – even after all those who had actually known Mungo, had gone to meet their Maker or to Largs (the latter being a sort of prep-school come waiting-room for the former). Not noted for his academic qualities – in this one respect Cosmo was like his father – he was teased mercilessly by his peers and by some staff, until a perceptive art teacher discovered by accident that the young Laird was a dab hand with pen, pencil, chalk, etc. That art master revealed the secrets of caricature to Cosmo and how to use it with the potency of a Gerald Scarfe.

Cosmo's final years at St Kent's were distinguished by their uneventfulness and when he left – actually he was kicked out when Mungo could no longer pay the fees – and with no A-levels – there was a collective sigh of relief. [St Kent's was nominally Scottish; it aped the pretensions of its English counterparts and refused to countenance the Scottish Schools Certificates of Ordinary and Highers Grades. So there.] After which his skill with pen or pencil served him well in various fraught situations when he engaged in voluntary work in some of the more benighted regions of the world.

'Now Cosmo, you can tell me all about it, your trip and that, while your lifting the grille ... No, that's the microwave, Cosmo. The grille is this rusting roller-shutter that serves no purpose other than to keep out the natives.'

'Yes, allow me, Ray. Just off the African Queen and straight into manual labour. Father, never mentioned this. *Cerebral*, he said. Should have known. No matter.' Cosmo struggled manfully, even boyfully, eventually succeeding in raising the heavy, rusted grille. He sucked on a throbbing thumb then checked for blood. 'There we go. How did I do, father? First day in the job? Feel quite fulfilled. Quite fatigued... I'll be off now.' He glanced at Ray who studiously ignored him – she was in management mode now; personal feelings and life beyond the job in hand were quarantined. Realising this after a bit, Cosmo mucked in and did what he was told and substituted his natural inclination for otiose banter, with a readiness to learn.

The next day, when the only slip-up was when Cosmo raised the shutter and it crashed down after a few minutes. Ray folded her arms over her crisp, starchy blouse (the Tesco Back-to-school range; well it's cheaper for there's no VAT.) ANYWAY, RAY, arms over starchy white blouse, gave Cosmo the look. Again he raised the shutter – again it duly crashed down.

Cosmo jumped back. 'Oops. Meant to do that, is it, Ray? Chop off the punters' paws?'

She ignored his attempt at wit, for he was trying too hard. Neither had mentioned the little portrait of yesterday, nor the prospect of her sitting for Cosmo.

'The pole'll fix that. Mungo, did you change the bulb in the lavvy?'

'Ah Poland. Marvellous people, Poles. Do anything – drive buses, clean cars. Play piano...' Mungo was in full musing mode, praising Poland and its countrymen, for all the experiences he had had in recent days convinced him that if for no other reason than the defence of that country against Vlad's hordes, Nato was worth every zloty otherwise wasted on useless weapons and worse than useless Secretaries General who tended to be ex-prime ministers of upstart countries like Norway or... or ex-defence ministers with Scottish-sounding names or ... ENOUGH POLITICS!

SETTING HIS POLITICAL ANALYSIS TO ONE SIDE, it had not gone beyond Mungo's notice that a certain *rapport* seemed to have sprung up between Cosmo and Raylene – *Cosmo:* yes, he would have to learn to call his son that now;

in the past he had managed somehow never to address him by his given name.

'Goalies,' Cosmo offered with a quick look at Ray. 'Goalkeepers. Poles'

'*The pole*, Cosmo. In the cupboard behind the microwave. Jam it under the shutter.'

'Ah, that pole. The treachery of the language of the bard,' Mungo pondered on, as Cosmo quickly found the pole, slowly raised the shutter then rapidly rammed and jammed the pole into its supporting role. Cosmo stood back to warily regard the raised grille.

'From bard to worse. From Baden-Baden to Warsaw and worser, eh, Ray? There we are. Second job finished and it's not yet...' Cosmo's voice trailed off. He knew he was trying too hard to impress and with each effort he was making an arse of it (though he would never use that expression).

'Right, help Mr Laird now. That's your dad, by the way. Mungo, show him how to separate the slips. I'm staying in here for a quick smoke. I am indulging myself with decent nicotine, un-surrounded and unadulterated for once by Old Holborn or Golden Virginia or Marrakesh roll ups.'

'How on earth...?' Cosmo began, but Mungo put a finger to both their lips (two fingers actually, one to each of their lips and done with separate hands).

'Don't mention the smoking. Suffice to say that it is our USP,' Mungo whispered.

'Wilco,' Cosmo whispered back, puzzled but not surprised that he was puzzled by anything his father said. *USP*?

'*Unique Selling Proposition,* Ray called it... you know allowing indoor smoking... place would be empty otherwise, Ray claims. Grand lass that, Cosmo. Don't know what we'll do when she goes.'

Cosmo's face fell. 'Ray's going? But you said that you had this wonderful manager who would see us through until I learned the ropes.' He looked towards the door behind which Ray was now working on the accounts. (A multi-tasker *and* fast-worker. And even faster smoker – though she was only on the nasty-modern, three-draws-per-fag variety.)

'And so she will. And so you will. You've got until Friday. Now, my piles. Quite simple. You separate these slips into let's say, x number of piles where y is the unknown. My day X was the unknown. Now what did Ray say? Ah yes, three piles... these ones here, these are the interesting ones: John o' Gaunt. What does that speak of to you, Cosmo? And here's another... Bent Banana?'

'Are these the winners then?' Cosmo asked.

'Winners? Well I've not yet... '

'Seems to me father, that there should be two piles – both interesting in their own way: *winners* and *losers*? Or am I being naïve?' Cosmo said this rather too loudly.

[He's definitely trying too hard. He should stick to those wee sketches for he's in there if he plays it right. But then there is a touching naïveté about Cosmo. Wonder where that comes from?]

Mungo was astounded, pleased and a little displeased. It had been his intention to gently introduce his son into the arcana of the world of turf accountancy, and here was the young whippersnapper plunging headfirst into it without a by-your-leave. Still, he did show a hint of acuity in cutting through the chaff – even though that chaff (the curious nature of horse names) was already fermenting in Mungo's steel-trap brain as he felt a paper coming on. But acuity or no, time to put the young fella in his place (gently of course):

'You've passed the first test, my boy. Now to the serious business. Now remember, this is not a charitable enterprise. Not like that other nonsense. Trust that your ten months in Ethiopia made you see straight. This must seem like a weekend in Saltcoats?'

'*KwaZulu-Natal,* dad. Zululand. And three years.'

'Quite. *Heart of Darkness.* Mother had practically given up on... you. *Taken by the savages*, she ranted in her more lucid moments.'

'Dad, we don't use that term: *savages. Socially excluded.* We are talking Saltcoats?'

'To business: where were we? Two piles, Cosmo. If you learn nothing else about turf accountancy, learn that there are only ever two piles: a large one for the losers and a small one for the winners. Oh yes and a third one...'

'For the tax man!!' Ray shouted, shook her head and ground her dowt through an empty fag packet and into the dusty concrete floor.

[Social and tobacco comment: We are old enough to remember when a cigarette (*Churchman*) was actually advertised as 'the *fifteen minute*(!) cigarette. Mungo for his part could remember sitting on the barber's chair and reading '*Craven 'A'. Good for your throat*'. *O tempora o mores,*[62] he might have said or even thought had he not been excluded from yon Latin classes at St Kent's. The world would never know what it had missed by that eagerness to 'select' at an early age.]

'On you go, you try it.' Mungo encouraged his son, smiling, as once again he took pride in the perceived, admirable, inherited, now disinherited qualities he had passed on or more precisely, down.

'Like this, Dad?'

'Oh excellent, my boy. You were born to this. Oh look at this one. *Alexander Nevsky*, Kempton Park. Now if memory serves me, Alexander Nevsky ...'

Cosmo gently tugged the betting slip from his father's hand. 'Loser,[63] Dad.'

---

[62] *Note the absence of exclamation marks (!!); Latin did not offer such displays of uncalled for showiness!!!*

[63]*Here Cosmo is alluding to the horse of that name. In real life, of course Алекса́ндр Не́вский (Sandy Nevsky) was a winner against the Swedes and the Jerrys and had the nous to kow-tow to thon Mongol hordes (no offence intended, we celebrate diversity) and ended up a Saint. Not bad for someone who was the grandson of Vsevelov The Big Nest.*

Chapter 35

Cosmo's coat of one or two colours

While Mungo tended to worry over his son (and his daughter from time-to-time), on account of his, Cosmo's, tendency towards compassion for those less fortunate than himself, Cosmo in turn worried about his father. When he had abandoned the family pile (just before the crash of Mungo and Ethel's finances), Cosmo had headed for Africa to lose, or maybe find, himself.

Somehow, by a series of misunderstandings in which featured large a small lady who had won Cosmo's heart, he found himself one day sipping a medium-sized fruitjuice on the V & A Waterfront in Cape Town with that young lady. The next day she had arranged to meet up with him at a village in the north over the SA border where like-minded young folk would lay drains, build schools and avoid the local plagues. Alas the young woman never made it for reasons that were never satisfactorily explained – though we know she was the best recruiter of idealistic young men like Cosmo. SIGH.

For a number of years Cosmo toiled at drainage and building with mudbricks, with the occasional trip home to recover from some debilitating disease, then off he would go again. One day smiling men with guns came to the village and thanked Cosmo and his co-volunteers for their efforts and invited them to leave. Briefly, Cosmo considered showing them his sketch pad, thought better of it and that was that. By then Cosmo was in his thirties (Ethel would remind him as often as she could of his *difficult birth* at her *very difficult age*) and while he retained his idealistic urges, he was better able to control them – it's amazing what you can learn from men with guns. And so he had returned to find his father in a guddle that would have tested the patience and mental health of all the saintly volunteers in the heart of Africa.

TO THE PRESENT: and now as he looked with bright-eyed wonder at his father, Mungo, Cosmo thought to boost his morale – with perhaps more than one eye on the lovely Raylene.

'You know, Dad, as I look around me… with wonder and… I think this might be just the thing for you. And I think about all of those naysayers that fabricated a litany of travesties in your commercial enterprises and… other ventures. They claimed that you made a right royal fiasco of the family brewery, but where are they now?'

'Six feet and more under,' Mungo mumbled, as he did not like to talk of death and other semi-serious matters in front of the boy. There'd be time enough for that stuff when the boy reached an age where… zounds, what age was Cosmo? Mungo's steel-trap whatsit went to work and reckoned, without the aid of a calculator or ready-reckoner or even that blasted comptometer that young Cosmo must be all of ….? Can't be right. He'd leave it for later.

'One of the lessons I've taken from life is that it's a mistake to try and learn from past errors or… Each venture has its unique stamp. As will this one. Mark my words, Cosmo, this is your heritage we're building. Doing it together. Man and boy; father and son. Like bleak tales from the Yorkshire moors or even bleaker tales from… somewhere equally drab.'

'Mother will be fascinated by this project, I dare say.' Cosmo said, restraining a smile in anticipation of the obfuscatory merde that his father was likely to produce from his steel-trap brain in response.

'God, look at the time. Can't stand about here all day nattering much as would like to. Bulb to change in lavvy, Raylene said.'

[Parenthetically re the 'episodes' in Mungo's chequered career as captain of industry, pater familias, etc., it is all too easy to lay the blame at his feet (today encased in Loake's Cadogan; Byres Rd, British Heart Foundation; £215 new – no-way!). In fact, Mungo had constructed a new 'narrative' (a method of re-writing history based upon the Foucaultian[64] method whereby there is no truth independent of power relations – note this is a controversial view known as the *Mungonian Interpretation* and will not work for just anybody so don't try it at home especially not with the wife/partner/bidey-in). The essence of it is that Mungo was able to blame others for taking the family brewery down the stank. He was fighting back and he had a mind to set to rights this alternative and derogatory view of his history – this would take the form of something or other, once it turned up. (Mungo's position falls somewhere between the post-structuralist and the post-modernist tradition; though of course Mungo, if given the chance, would reject these labels. So there.]

'And the person that is providing the capital for the refurbishment you were speaking of... adventure capitalist, is he?'

'She, Cosmo. And I think you'll find the term is 'venture capitalist'.'

'Not in this case, Dad, I think you might find. Anyway, Mum will be delighted when she learns the nature of THE PROJECT. What a surprise it'll be. Why just this morning when I visited her... ' Cosmo began.

'Not the time to bother her with such trivia. Delicate state of health at the moment... let's just say for the moment – I'm not asking you to lie to your dear mother... and there is an element of truth in this,' he opened his long arms and embraced the 'betting space': 'this is all in lieu of capital that the previous owner did not possess... in lieu of my felicitous winnings... ' Mungo spread his arms further. 'And the chip shop through the wall don't forget, and... yes the erstwhile pub on the other corner... though those are for the future. Sparing you the detail, as I did your mother... yes, persuaded your mother we were establishing your legacy. Though do admit to running through the plan rather rapidly before she fully recovered from the recovery room anaesthetic... '

---

[64] *No, no that Foucault wi' the pendulum. It's the French guy, whose work, used properly, allows fiends and criminals to blame their victims with a clear conscience.*

'Anyway,' Mungo continued as the grille seemed stuck up and Cosmo seemed to be breathing again, 'we shall reside in the Algarve or somewhere equally sunny content in the knowledge that you will not forget us. What we've done to you. That is, what we've done for you. Make sense? You won't? Forget us?'

'As if. What you both have done to me – for me – is imprinted on my soul,' Cosmo said sweetly – for, if there was one fault with the lad, it was his infinite capacity for forgiveness. He'll never learn. Unless yon Raylene sorts him out.

But, from somewhere, some ancestral vestige of the brute that most of you spring from, Mungo's son tried to inject just a little, the tiniest amount of venom into the discourse, 'But to mother: when she sees this place – no offence, Dad, but this is a cowp.'

'None taken, Cosmo. The refurbishment will soon take care of that. Never fear. As to your dear mother, the mater, no matter… the thing is, she's practically not seen it.'

'*Practically* not seen it? You mean she's not seen it at all? She doesn't know about it! Well, Dad, that should be an interesting moment when you unveil it to her. Will you give me good notice of the unveiling? I'm sure to be doing something else that day. Will you promise that I can be here to see her when she arrives? Maybe I'll get a video camera. Post it on YouTube. Might make money when it goes viral.'

'Thing is, you know how she is about detail – gives her a headache and that on top of her jumpy legs and as yet unexplained liver malfunctions and well… wouldn't want to burden her with details, not during enforced convalescence, would we? Would you?'

'Ah, those jumpy legs again. Anyway, setting aside the matter of the *mater* for the moment,' Cosmo looked about the *shoap* (as he would have to learn to call it when communicating with the clients), 'just one question and I do not intend to interrogate your business acumen: why would anyone in their right mind use this place when they can go to Hillbrokes? The Ritz of bookies. Where they get tea or coffee and little dried biscuits and there are banks of TVs and colourful gaming machines and the toilets do not remind me of bad-stink town Kolkata or even Mpumulanga bus station. Anyway this is a cess-pit compared with that. Look we've only got radio commentary by the looks of things. Not one TV monitor do I see … Is it even legal?'

'Cosmo,' Mungo began, his steel-trap mind having discerned a worrying implication from the foregoing, 'how the daisy-cutter do you know what Hillbrokes is like? Hope you haven't learned bad habits from spending too long with those savages.'

'And which savages would those be, Dad? The ones in the dark continent or the ones that threw stones at me on the way here?'

'Setting aside your aspersions as to our neighbourhood and our clientele, Cosmo, I will riposte and raise you: can they go to Hillbrokes? Need to take the bus to Hillbrokes, you know. And it's only the halt and the lame and those sheltering from the rain that come in here.'

Cosmo looked about and saw the glum look he had inflicted on his pater. As previously diagnosed without recourse to DSM-IV or even DSM-5 , Mungo – 'suffered' is not the right word in this context, as he had another condition called panglossian-euphoriaxis (just coined and a candidate for DSM-6 when it comes out) – ANYWAY, Mungo's condition known as abulia (or aboulia, if you prefer), had long been recognised by his son, and now Cosmo thought he would try and point him in the direction of actually facing reality – but a reality that can be changed, and arriving at a decision on 'what is to be done?'[65]

And so in the time it took for these thoughts and books and things to flash through his mind, young Cosmo Laird evoked the spirit of praxis and said:

---

[65] *This is not an intentional quote from VI Lenin's work of the same name, 1902; incidentally and not totally or even relevant, VI Lenin, borrowed the title from a novel of the same name. No harm in that we say.*

'If we had time. And money. Suppose we could refurbish. The first thing to go, this counter. The Berlin Wall. Open it up. What does that say to your punt ... eh clients?'

'Ich bin ein ... eh .. oh, I give in.'

'Then the toilet.' Cosmo pointed out to the corner of the front shop with stiff finger and wrinkled nose. 'I mean that is a shocker. And I've only got within twenty metres to know... makes me quite nostalgic for Mpumalanga bus station, as it is marginally better. No snakes there.'

'Capital, Cosmo. Capital.'

'You agree then? Refurbish. Great. That's a start.'

'I mean *capital,* Cosmo. *Capital.* Everything we have. Look around you – it's all here. Loads of potential. Blank canvas. Tick boxes, all that location, location stuff. Put our own stamp on it. *Wow factor* and things. Blank canvas yes. *Tabula* whatsit?'

'A blank canvas, if only – could try and pass it off for the Turner Prize. And with Ray going, hopeless. Six thousand miles back for *this*?'

'I'm sorry, my boy. I've done it again. Put my own and your dear, unwell mother's interests and happiness before the... the whatdjacallem... natives. And she, we, were so pleased to see you after what was it, ten months?'

'Still three years, Dad.'

'The jungle does that to you – alters your sense of time. The myriad stars at night, the vast, immeasurable tracts of sand... '

'That's the desert, Dad, the sand.'

'The desert *and* the jungle!? We don't deserve a son like you. Your mother has said those very words several times, and with vehemence.'

Cosmo felt he had to decide between buggering off back to Africa and sanity, or trying seriously to see if he could contribute to his father's enterprise. But then on reflection, if the choice was between another dose of malaria, or lanka fever,[66] being confronted with genial men with guns inviting

---

[66] *This seems to be an aberration on Cosmo's part - unless he kens something that the compilers of The Oxford Handbook of Tropical Diseases don't. And we certainly do not wish to imply that he*

him to eff-off, or trying to see if there was any hope for his father, then it was, in the parlance he would need quickly to learn, 'a close run thing'. But then, there was Raylene...

'Look, Dad, if you – we – are to make a go of this, then we need to be able to compete. It's no use relying on what seemed to be good enough in the past. Today is the future. There is no present... like the future.' Cosmo had indeed inherited Mungo's ability for obfuscation... and seemingly apposite nonsense... if you ever thought about it. (Not recommended.)

Mungo interrupted his son as he had been inspired by his evident commitment: and to show that he had been listening and not thinking of that woman who had served him in Greggs this very morning – he suspected under that blue overall were... and the tuna baguette was excellent and they threw in a free bottled water – so he said:

'Today is the Future'. That can be our marketing campaign. Excellent start.' And he felt better already for what he believed to be his own contribution.

'How much is our marketing budget then? And what do you plan? TV, Radio? Bus shelters? Billboards? Free Sheets?'

'A mere detail, my boy. Now that, allied to our refurbishment...'

'Refurbishment from earnings? What's our turnover like?'

Mungo was in danger of getting a headache from all this technical detail...

---

is perhaps confusing his experience on Air Lanka with a chronic medical condition for which there is no known cure (if you exclude snake oil).

Chapter 36

Applied arithmetic and delegation

Mungo was in danger of getting a headache from all this technical detail and from assuming all of the burden of the enterprise so he decided to delegate like that fellow that bootlegged tapes of The Stones but now drove aeroplanes all over the world and the cabin crew – the female ones – in that very fetching uniform, probably wore… given the proclivities of that chap who bootlegged tapes of The Stones but now drove aeroplanes all over the world.

And anyway, since it had been a long time since he had contributed to the demise of the family brewery, he had forgotten what exactly was meant by the term 'turnover'; which was as good a reason as any for giving it a body swerve. Something would turn up. And as soon as that phrase entered his brain his headache lifted as if his brain was already full-to-brimming and it needed to get rid of the stuff that gave him headaches. Who needs aspirin?

And so, Mungo said, 'Well you obviously know what you're talking about Cosmo, so let's agree that will be your sphere of influence. Anyway, a person of your vision can afford to take the wider view. Think of it like when you were on the Serengeti, all those wildebeests and among them the jackal and lions. One does not count the individual wildebeest, one sees the panorama, the spectacle of it all.'

'You're saying we have no wildebeest in the kitty? The bank? You do have a banker?'

'Cosmo, Cosmo, you still have that measure of idealism, that makes me want to, well not hug you, but maybe put my arm about your shoulder. Just for the briefest of moments. And you have been away for too long. These days if you want a loan the last resort is to approach a bank. If you get past the Scylla at the door and the Charybdis at the counter and avoid surrendering the collateral of your abode, your whole caboodle including your offspring and all eighteen of the carats in your molars, banks may just agree to allow you to participate in their licensed usury. A bit like hospitals – the last place safe from infection.'

Cosmo moved from the counter and went out into the front 'shoap', strolled hands behind back then turned and spoke to his father, up and through the grille.

'Okay, let me reflect on some of the lessons I learned in the jungle – or was it the desert? Let's see: we have a dump that cannot compete with the big bookies, we need to refurbish but we have no money. No bank, not even an Icelandic, Indian or Irish one would touch us. And Ray, the only person around who appears to have an inkling about the business, is leaving at the end of the week. Maybe we should seek Mother's view on this. She has a way of dealing with crises.'

The impudence of the young rascal! To bring Ethel into it just as Mungo had been preparing his usual, 'You won't get any argument out of me, Cosmo' – which phrase Mungo found fitting for most occasions whenever he didn't have a scooby what someone was saying or if there was the merest hint of hostility or even the mildest disagreement in the words of others or if 'something will turn up' had abandoned him temporarily, leaking from his steel-trap mind. In this respect it was the verbal equivalent of Mungo engaging in the *one-legged dance of Yü*. And indeed we can say objectively if more of us reacted to hostility in this manner there would be less strife. On the other hand, there is a certain satisfaction to be gained from clobbering someone you don't like and who has upset you or simply looked at you the wrong way. But that is another story for another day and it is not in the Mungovian style.

During all of the above, Cosmo set his mind to the problem he had let himself in for by agreeing to help his old man out. His instinct for survival honed amidst the wild beasts of Africa was to take his chances with the wild beasts of Africa. However, some familial empathy if not sympathy kicked-in and he thought about the practicalities of getting this place up and running for his father to such an extent that he could take himself off back to Africa with the knowledge he had done his wee bit, and, if not face up to the men with guns, at least have a few refreshing drinks on The Waterfront at Cape Town, or among the lovely young students at Stellenbosch, or simply stand alone at Southern Point and enjoy the moment. Then it hit him: **Raylene**. That was his first thought, because among the beauties of Africa, he had not found a Raylene.

'Ray, you need Ray. If we can persuade her to stay a bit, she'll know what to do.'

'Would be nice, Cosmo. But what can we offer her? Look around you. Wait. Unless ...?'

'Unless? Yes?'

'Oh, was hoping you would fill that ellipses thing... you know, those three dots followed by a space then question mark.[67] I seem to be out of ideas at the moment.'

And in that response from Mungo, Cosmo took hope; for if his dad knew what ellipses were and how to use them properly, then that showed a mind that was not totally useless... or did it?

---

[67] *This can be done by pressing Ctrl and Alt and the period on the keyboard. You can use two hands if you're more comfortable that way...*

Chapter 37

And they're off!

'Two pounds each way at nine-to-four, placed is... let me see... quarter times nine over four divided by. No: take away thirty-two, multiply by five, then divide by nine. No wait: multiply by nine, divide by five and add thirty-two. Oh god, back where I started. Oh God.' Cosmo struggled and blamed his father and his creative rather than logical genes – although he was not that far out in that he was using the formula for converting Fahrenheit to Celsius and vice versa. Or was he?

At the root of the problem was that without warning, THEY had renamed Centigrade to Celsius without telling Cosmo. He was a sharp cookie – as they might have said on the streets, had he ever played on the streets; but Kentigernians tended to avoid the streets especially about that afternoon time of a weekday when the plebeian schools ('bog-standard' to quote a 'socialist' Prime Minister) were emptying.

Cosmo was not back in the classroom wrestling with Maths 4 problems. He was attempting to 'settle a line'; the problem was of a practical nature and if representative of those that would confront them in the coming days of Mungo's new venture, could be a harbinger of doom.

You see, a (wee) punter had placed a bet of two pounds (sterling) 'each way' on a horse whose odds were nine-to-four (9/4). The stake money is four pounds. In simple terms that meant that if the horse won (it did, the bastard!) that there was two pounds multiplied by 9/4, plus the two pounds, PLUS two pounds multiplied by one quarter of 9/4, plus two pounds. That sounds complicated to those who have never indulged – but see that wee fella over there in the corner, with the fag in his mouth, the ragged bunnet, the sandshoes without laces and the folded copy of the *Daily Record* in his pocket, he would have calculated the sum in a nano second without even knowing how he did it. Oh, and by the way, his arithmetic teacher (he wasn't allowed to do *mathematics*) had called him a *numpty* and his last year at school was not at school. So there.

ANYWAY, Cosmo Laird, product of the Scottish private school system,[68] was struggling. But don't worry, help in the delicious (judgemental language of sexists) form of Raylene is at hand. And she has such a sensitive manner with those who are a bit slow on the uptake. Especially if they are her titular bosses.

'Let me see that.' Ray and Cosmo were alone, Mungo had nipped out (well, called a taxi from the firm that had taken almost his last pennies for allowing a daily account to-and-from The Park) to check on Ethel abed at ex-Castle Laird as it was Tim's monthly disability check-up – they were now using a couple of ex-paras to put him through the hoops; and if that was not sufficiently degrading (and well-nigh impossible), one of them was of the female persuasion who had quickly demonstrated her thoughts on lily-livered men with limps (no pun intended).

Meantime, the always reliable Idris could not be relied upon as her job count threatened to relegate Tim – the one true love of her life (apart from Rabbie the rabid Rottweiler – now put down) – to secondary consequence, thus inadvertently lending credence to the forms *alienation*[69] may take under the capitalist system.

'Did they no' learn you to count at that school, your old man told me about. Whatdjacallit?'

'St Kentigern's. Counting? We had a whole day devoted to cheque signing and the division of heritable property under diverse jurisdictions.' Cosmo's eyes took on a glazed-over look (he had been licking the wrong end of the pencil which had been produced long before those awful EU bureaucrats

---

[68] *This remark has to be qualified: Cosmo was not a fully-formed product of the private school system; sure they had chucked him out in his final year because Mungo could not pay the fees and was behind with the payments for the previous year. Still, somebody has to be blamed.*

[69] *Who among us does not recall that for Marx, alienation was not rooted in the mind or in religion, as it was for Hegel and Feuerbach?*

and busybodies took it upon themselves to protect eejits from themselves). Then, when he realised that it could have been less to do with the pencil lead and more to do with the crisp white blouse that Ray was gracing with her form and that Ray was conscious of the effect she was having on this effete public schoolboy who was absolutely useless as a bookie, then he acted like an intelligent, sensate and animate pair of curtains and pulled himself together. And with that his steel-trap mind (inherited from his father, no matter what those nurturists say) brought him back to the present with the words,

'Ray, could we have a word about...?' He indicated the slip he was working on.

Ray, who knew a thing or three, and who treated Cosmo with the respect he had earned, ignored his question – it was as if all the capital he had accumulated with her with his little portrait sketch had gone out the window for he had not followed it up with sufficient alacrity – and with her hands on her hips, with her chewdie-gum neatly wedged in her lovely cheek said,

'One other thing: during racing, as the results come in, one of you has to skim through the slips. Any winners that are backed with others to come, you need to keep your eye on. Doubles, trebles, four-timers, accumulators, roll ups and the likes. Your daddy should know the consequences, seeing that's how you are here but somehow I think he has difficulty remembering important things. Or things that might cause him anxiety. That red phone there is a dedicated line to Benny Queen's head office. We lay off bets we don't want to risk.'

'Bets we don't want to risk? In what sense, Ray?' Cosmo said, wanting to appear as if he was interested in something other than currying favour with Ray.

'Bets that we think if they come up, might cause serious damage. So we punt them on to another bookie who could bear the loss.'

'But what if this other one thinks the same as us?'

'Then he'll punt it on to Ladbrokes or Hills or somebody else. The big boys like Hillbrokes.'

'So would the punter not be better going straight to the big boy?'

'Aye. But they don't and that's why we – well you and Mungo – are in business. We get the crumbs that the big sharks[70] let slip from their gobs. So, be careful – you never know one of these jokers – sorry, our clients – might just be the second comet after Mungo that hits the Earth again. Anything else?'

'Inside knowledge, kind of thing?'

'Not really. All common sense: don't look the punter in the eye cos he can reach into your soul and detect any weakness; don't give credit – it offends: our sensibilities. Simple stuff, like. And don't upset the Muslims.'

'Muslims. We get many of them?'

'Muslims? In here? Never. Just meant it as an observation on life.'

'Open the bag up a bit, or maybe you would prefer to shovel, with your background, Cosmo?' Ray had roped Cosmo into the late morning clean-up of the front shop. Cosmo was cold, glad of the exercise, and the heat of Ray's company. Like father like son, or the sins of the father and all that, Cosmo admired Ray for her efficiency, her grasp of detail and, yes, for her corporeal attributes. She, with her small, neat, compact frame, and her hair – chestnut brown with highlights that must have been acquired on the Cote d'Azur or perhaps that hairdressers at the end of the block – had skills disproportionate to the impression given by her exterior. Whatever, Cosmo was smitten.

In a different life, Cosmo would have been an artist – a Renoir, painting all those luscious bare-naked nudes when all the time his friends (Renoir's that is – for Cosmo had no friends (but we'll see what we can do for him before the end of this tale), WHEN ALL THE TIME HIS FRIENDS (Renoir's that is)

---

[70] *Ray's use of the word 'shark' is particularly unfortunate in this context and we judge it to be merely indicative of her restricted vocabulary, rather than being a fair comment on the practices of these companies who have been at the forefront of the campaign to Bet Responsibly. In this respect they are in good company with the Tobacco firms (Smoke Responsibly) and the drinks industry (Booze Responsibly). We should be thankful that we are being saved from ourselves by such public-spirited bodies.*

were wasting their oils on apples and pears and even less obscure edibles and non-edibles.[71] Had he had a whit of street-smarts, Cosmo would have latched on to the effect his rapid little sketch of Ray had had on her and used it to his own advantage. He'll just no learn, will he?

Later that day, when after all his efforts to pee-hee to Ray had come to naught, Cosmo decided to broach another subject that had been playing on his mind ever since he learned from Mungo about Ray's plans.

'Ray, we were thinking, you know how you are leaving at the end of the week, well... could you recommend anybody to sort of step-in and... '

'Sure, there's any number of people I could recommend. But I wouldn't recommend you to take them.'

Now while Cosmo (like Mungo before him) was an old Kentigernian (motto: effortless incompetence; *imperitiam, sine labore*), he had never read Wittgenstein on language[72] (or for that matter, on house renovation, cookery or valuing antiques); and yet his reaction to Ray's conundrum was precisely how he would have felt had he read the aforesaid Ludwig's *oeuvre*.

'Whit?' Cosmo said to himself, slipping easily into the patois, so eager was he to find favour with Ray of the crisp white blouse whose starchiness was wholly due to biology and her *Weltanschaung*. Upon which they were transported for a coffee break to Le Greasy Spoon just across the border.

'Three years, eh? Can't say it ever appealed to me. Living in a hut. Flies, creepy crawlies. The rain coming in.'

'Oh, it wasn't so bad, they let me back in the house in the winter.' The bold young brave expostulated in an attempt at levity, which was met by The Stare. 'Oh, sorry, Ray, you mean Africa? Well, living with Mungo and Ethel prepared me for that.

[71] *There is of course the Freudian argument that apples, pears and fings like that are symbolic of the male and female genitalia. Apart from that being a load of bollocks why no' just paint the tackle in situ? More fun, we conject.*

[72] *Philosophische Untersuchungen (1953) Not yet available on NetFlix.*

I was eleven before I learned that not all houses had buckets in the roof space.' (By the way, talking about living: Cosmo is not lodging at Villa Idris with Mungo and Ethel and Idris and Tim. Just saying like.)

'Buckets?! My God, you had buckets. Any photos? Oh let me see them, please, please, please.'

Even sarcasm became her, Cosmo smiled. Ray was more than *all right*.

'I was simply trying to say that people thought we were rich because we lived in a big house on top of Snob Hill, 'Cosmo said, a tear in his eye as he recalled life as a child, occasioned not by a shaft of nostalgia but by the proprietor of Le Greasy Spoon brushing the floor by their table which caused the stoor to head for his nose; this in turn caused him to sneeze which raised even more stoor, and like the *Bhava chakra* or even the *wheel of the dharma* this cycle could have continued indefinitely except they ran out of stoor.

When he had settled down and the sneezing had eased off to a mild asthma attack, Raylene said, 'No, Cosmo. People knew you were rich because you had that big house, acres of land and a gardener, a huge motor and a driver, and you went to a snotty boy's school and… '

'… we had buckets. Probably should have been rich, if it hadn't been for Mungo.' Cosmo sat down and thought back to life under Mungo – a memory that reminded him as to why he had chosen ~~The Heart of Darkness~~ (better not use that term today, but you know where we mean) in preference to shovelling mountains of barley at a brewery that was, like its product, quickly going down the stank. But now he was back having survived several mentionable tropical diseases, the amorous attentions of a large guerrilla (no, the spelling is taken under advisement) as well as a Ryanair flight from a tiny airfield complete with un-weeded tarmac (better fun than Prestwick even though the latter will surely have more weeds soon). And now it might just be time to buckle-down and help the old fella and fellette out of the hole they were in and digging with all their might.

Of course these good intentions, apart from being the stuff that paves the road to Auld Nick's domain, had no effect on

Raylene who was insufficiently interested in reading his thoughts – that could or might come later – and also because Cosmo had not yet contracted that thought-speak syndrome whose name we invented but which we have forgotten.[73] ANYWAY, the point is, Raylene has her own thoughts and here are a few of them…

'I went camping once. *T-in-the Park.* Don't suppose that counts? I could see the orange glow in the sky. Quite haunting. Romantic even. I think it was Grangemouth. Often wondered what it would be like, Africa and that. That vast dark sky, no lights for miles around? The sounds of wild animals snuffling in the brush, the low muttering of marauding hunters searching for their prey. The hot, rancid smells. The steamy …'

'Sounds like Grangemouth. No really, Africa was not so different. Less flies and better roads. Got me away from Mother and Father – especially Mother. When Mungo drained the family brewery, Ethel became quite unbearable. All his dreams for the business – we would discuss in letters – how he would market Laird's Ales in ways never thought of before. Sacked all the marketing people and took it on himself. Made quite an impact – just not in the way expected. *Laird's Draught: drink 'til you droop.'*

'That was Mungo?! I remember now. My favourite was. Let me see… Gottit! *Laird's Light: sees you home…'*

'… *when no one else will.'* Cosmo and Ray finished in tandem.

'Mentioned in despatches in the *Harvard Business Review.'*

Ray glanced at her wrist – which is delicate and fine-boned, even though she does pack a punch,

'Cosmo, the time.' They headed back across the border and after Ray had a few words with Mungo, had checked that everything was in place – racing newspapers on the walls; blank betting slips in their places; little blue, red, green and yellow pens purloined from Hillbrokes and other places that wrote them off against tax – satisfied that all was as well as it ever could be, she indicated the clock above the door – which

---

[73] *Cogitative-vocalisation is copyright of the Duignan-Hopkins corporation.*

was one of the few pieces of technology that actually did what it was intended to do, addressed Cosmo:

'Come on. Your first test. Ready for the *tired, the poor, the huddled masses yearning to breathe free, the wretched refuse of your teeming shore.*'

'Why, Ray, you're a poetry-lover. Have you read the latest…?'

'Whit?! Poetry-lover!'

'The poetry. Quoting whoever…'

'I tried to get away from here to America. With the wee yin. Learnt that damn poem and cannot get it out my head. Then they wouldn't let me in. A record for minor assault, would you believe?' She shook her beautiful head and a sunbeam caught the sheen of a sheaf of her tresses and… not to mention the pointy blouse,

'You all right, Cosmo? Why are you dribbling? Your da' does that as well. Never mind.' She took him by the hand to the door, 'Stand clear for the deluge. And now: *I lift my lamp beside the golden door!*'

Ray removed the heavy metal bar that secured the front doors.

She was met with a croaking voice asking, 'This the Social then, hen?'

'Piss off!' replied the divine Raylene.

Chapter 38

Three wise Punters: well one, and Nearly, one other

[Who among us has not swooned over the Fermat-Pascal correspondence that laid the intellectual foundations for probability theory? Who among us is not familiar with its axiomatization with Kolmogorov's *Foundations of the Theory of Probability* (1933). Put simply:

Let Ω be a non-empty set; A field on Ω is a set $\mathbf{F}$ of subsets of Ω that has Ω as a member, and that is closed under complementation (with respect to Ω) and union.][74] HINT: THIS WILL NOT APPEAR IN THE FINAL EXAM.

But without intending to be intellectually snobbish about such matters, there is no irrefutable evidence that Bunty McAllister had not read Kolmogorov or even Fermat or Pascal on matters germane to her very existence; but we can be confident that if any of those three could be transported back to this century and if Fate should find them in Mungo's bettin' shoap, Bunty could have held her own in any discussion relating to chance and odds with sods.

Anyway, the shoap was open and when she had bade a good morning to her friend Raylene and had nodded and shaken her head at the two warrrmers (Mungo and Cosmo) that had taken over Albie's business, as she looked across the table at her two fellow punters, Bunty could bite her tongue no longer – this was not because her new false teeth (wallies) were ill-fitting and tended to click over a range that had

---

[74] *We don't know why he bothered to write a monograph to say the above – which many of you will ken under the title: Grundbegriffe derWahrscheinlichkeitsrechnung; which, when you think about it, gives the plot away.*

similarities to the G-Mixylodian scale; (though musical purists would perhaps argue that it was more akin to a *raga*, which would be unsurprising as Bunty tended to have a curried fish supper most days). In which case we must surmise that in this instance the phrase '*could bite her tongue no longer*' is being employed metaphorically – in other words it was time for her to give vent to her thoughts as she serenely looked across the big communal table in her bookie's at the two men she seemed to have inherited and had to keep apart on a daily basis (except Sundays). 'Argy' and 'Nearly'.

She had listened for long enough to the two of them unwittingly undermining the very foundations that Kolmogorov had laid in 1933 (does anyone among us think it a coincidence that it was that very year, that Winston S Churchill made his first public speech warning of the dangers of German rearmament? Did he know something the rest of you didn't? We exclude ourselves as we were not around at that time, so cannot be blamed for anything.) However, this was not what was concerning Bunty at that moment.

'A coin can land heads, tails or on its edge. Three possibilities. And that's hit,' Bunty said quietly.

'On the edge? C'mon. What are the chances o' that?!' Argy argued.

'Not zero. So the chance of it landing heads must be less than fifty per cent.' she said even more quietly than her first and definitive pronunciation.

'Horses are no' coins – that's my point. What are the chances of you getting a six-horse accumulator? Eh. Tell me that, Bunty. What are the odds?' the man called Argy – for some unfathomable reason – snarled and prepared for more reasoned discourse in this tone.

'Horses are no' coins. Coins are predictable over enough throws,' Bunty said, now in the tone of an old-school school marm that had obviously never worked in a Scottish inner-city school in the 1950s. She continued in a similar vein, as if speaking to an effing moron, (no offence intended to either our moron or effing community – we celebrate diversity after all), which in many senses she was as she addressed her remarks to Argy.

'The odds the bookie gives have nothing to do with real probabilities. They're a price to get you to bet. That's all. If they were real probabilities, then we would all back favourites like you Argy, and be no better off. Or really skint mair like. Either way the bookies win. An' that's hit!' Bunty drew her hands across the air in front of her in termination.

'What's your point, Bunty?' Argy asked, not knowing to quit when he was well behind.

And again in that quiet, tolerant but not quite patronising tone she proposed, 'Listen you moron, the point being the chances of my six-horse accumulator coming up are not computable by the bookies odds. Tosser!' And with that, she returned to the racing page before her and broke her pencil which greatly irritated her, and if she could have laid her hands on the jawbone of an ass, she would have smote the arsehole who had mightily got up her nostrils (septum fully intact).

Argy turned to the old man sitting beside him, a stranger he had never seen before or if he had, he didn't remember him nor did he know this man's name for 'a stranger is just a friend you do not know.' (Cf: Jim Reeves.)

'You see what I mean?' Argy said to Mungo (for it was he, and really he had no right to be mixing with the punters). 'Women and horses don't mix. They're a different species entirely. You cannot reason with them.'

And the stranger nodded his head vigorously and when he went to speak, Argy continued, 'Shush... We're live!' And he pointed to the tannoy with a nail that had not recently seen the inside of a nailsalon, of which many had sprung up in the new Borrfoot.

VOICE OF TANNOY ANNOUNCER (PROBABLY AUSTRALIAN)

... with the favourite Barney Rubble on the outside! But Lucky Lenny just holds on. First, Lucky Lenny at 6 to 1. Second Barney Rubble, 5 to 4 favourite, third...

'Bunty! See what you did?!' Argy exploded and tore up his betting slip.

Bunty smiled blandly and said to herself, *'One up, five to go... ramorra.'*

Mungo slipped away behind the counter where a heated pie awaited, and such an impact had his presence made that no one noticed him come or go. He was like the shadow that rides the wind, the snowflake on an unknown Everest (not the double-glazing), the desultory fluff on a macaroon bar.

'Where you been then, Mungo?' Ray said, demolishing his self-image at a stroke and whipping off his cloak of invisibility.

Chapter 41

Mungo's muddled mingling

Mungo, from before and from behind the grille, had been listening with keen interest to Bunty's disquisition on probability. Ever eager to increase his understanding in the areas of arcane knowledge, he left behind the grille and did, what, to the uninitiated, seemed like the *one-legged dance of Yü* until he collapsed unseen at the table next to the man who had been introduced as the local moron Argy. And as he listened to Bunty's disquisition he had already framed within his head the opening paragraph of a paper on probability which we will conceal until a later time.

This had been a subject with which he had been wrestling with for many years – well, actually since he had received a couple of weeks before, a letter from a lawyer acting on behalf of a body called the Legal Defence Union (or something similarly dodgy-sounding) asserting that an article he had sent to the *Legal Times* would *probably* be viewed in a court of law, *on the balance of probabilities*, as slanderous of the entire legal profession not excluding the Supreme Court – whose writ extended to Scotland, the baistarts – which now assumed the judicial function of the House of Lords removing the Lords of Appeal in Ordinary from the legislature (an' no' afore time, in the considered opinion of one of us. No, both, on reflection).

And so, at the first opportunity – when there was a lull in race commentary, Mungo slipped out from behind the counter – on two legs: the *one-legged dance of Yü* should never be performed more than once per day, and even then, it is dangerous to dancer and worshippers alike. And so with a winning smile he went to Bunty and bade her a good day'nthat. (He was learning what he thought of as being 'the Vulgate'[75]

---

[75] *Why Tim should know the fourth century Latin translation of the Bible and why he would want to teach it to (learn it to) Mungo is*

from Tim. The basic rule being that at the end of any clause – principal or subordinate – you tack on 'nthat', if you are uncertain as to the class of person you are addressing. Supplementary rule is to sprinkle your offerings with 'by the way', thus suggesting that you are not an over-confident posing *flaneur*.

ANYWAY, having greeted her and not having elicited any obviously hostile intent, Mungo posed his question to Bunty, without once wondering if she was wearing sussies.

'Couldn't help but overhear your masterful account and I was wondering whether the use of *probably* and *probabilities* in two adjacent subordinate clauses rendered both of them redundant? You know – I mean, you ken, something along the same lines as when you multiply a negative by a positive you get a positive... no... a negative. Anyway, would be interested in your take on that one. Bit trickier than the old tossing-coin-trick, what?' Perhaps just a fraction too late, he appended, ''nthat by the way.'

To which Bunty, hardly taking the time to digest the question riposted in a manner that demonstrated that her polymathic abilities stretched beyond the mathematical to the linguistic by inviting him to,

'Awa'anf*ckyerselfahvemairtaedaewi'matime!'

Not nonplussed by this rejoinder, Mungo switched tack smoothly and segued himself on both legs back behind the grille. At which point he broached a broader cultural thesis which he thought might be of interest to Cosmo and perhaps even to Raylene, as it was germane to their prospects of business success.

'Been thinking, people. Drawing upon my time in the Far East – way, way, way beyond Coatbridge – Malays, Chinese. Orientals. That's what we need. Stuff the place with them. buggers for gambling. And not averse to tipple. At least the more right-thinking Malays – those 'not of the Book', to put it sensitively or sensibly, calling to mind Ray's advice on not

---

neither here nor there. Suffice it to say, that Mungo was trying to mimic the speech patterns of Tim – in terms of syntactic structures as well as favoured vocabulary and modes of phraseology. 'n that, by the way...

upsetting the you-know-who's. If we can get away with the smoking, why not drinking and you can trust folks that keep their elbows loose. The other sort? Don't give them season of year.' Mungo sipped from his hip flask, mused further then remembered his manners and offered the flask first to Ray, then Cosmo. Both shook their heads. Cosmo looked up again from the 'discard/loser' pile of paper slips in front of him.

'What do you propose, Dad? We import them as if they were going to work in the paddy fields of Shettleston?'

Mungo did not immediately reply – though he had stored that question of his first born in his … the part of the brain that generally ignores awkward questions. For more than a little time he had been observing a little bit of banter between Raylene and Cosmo. It reminded him of his courtship of Ethel which had been nothing like that.

Although Mungo and Ethel were not 'people of the book' – no offence meant, honestly; and we really mean this so sincerely – their marriage had elements of having been arranged with just a wee hint of compulsion. And just like many such arrangements contracted on the south-side of the city ('the Soothside') it had turned out more than tolerably well, and had the added advantage of never having to have been checked out by a visit *à deux* to the family (tribe) in the Punjab or similar environs. [There are some advantages in being Scottish, it would seem.]

BUT ANYWAY, after that cultural commentary of dubious rumination (by Mungo, and not one of the authors) he snapped back into the present, with 'Shettleston, you say, Cosmo, my boy. Tank country.'

Ray, who had no intention of ever visiting the Punjab or even Govanhill if she could help it, muttered to herself, as she arranged the small pile of winners in order of risk, 'God give me strength'. She had learned this, not from the *real Guid Buik*, but from listening to her mother welcoming her dad home on Friday nights – nights when wages were properly paid: wee broon envelopes with notes and coins.

[We wonder: is Ray perhaps being economical with her age? Still a cracker though, and thon Cosmo should be hammering that sketching business. It worked for whatisface, Picasso. Might have a go ourselves.]

MEANTIME AT LEAST MUNGO REMEMBERS WHERE THIS IS GOING: 'No, no, Cosmo. Comes of living among foreigners for too long. Since you left, all those months ago, this town has been swarming with all sorts of what we have to call *ethnics*. Chinese, Roumanians, damned Russian reds and the likes. What they need is to be catered for in their carnal needs.'

'The Shona have a word for that, Father: *yepfambi*– translates as *brothel'*.

'Not too fast, Cosmo. Let's limp before we can run. One of us – have to be you, Cosmo – nips over to Partick or Clydebank – bound to be a Chinatown there now it's been partially rebuilt... the Chink... eh chinesessses themselves probably did all the hard work – wherever these beggars live. Bus them down for a day's honest gambling. Advertise in the local *Strait Times*. Gottit. Even better! Chink ...Eh Chinese and soup. Explosive cocktail. Heavens – or maybe that should be the Celestial Vault – Soup. Served personally by our own lovely geisha.'

And with that he looked at Raylene who took it with relative equanimity, for she had found another betting slip with a 'scribble' of Cosmo's that clearly was a group caricature of Bunty, Argy and Nearly – and she thought: that lad has talent. Whyfur is he wasting it here? Then she forced herself back to the mundane – Cosmo was like his old man: likeable but not one to pin hopes on, or even one hope... Time, Ray, to be cynical again – get back in character: working-class, hard-nosed, chippy and... oh forget that salt-of-the-earth shite, [patronising bastards, she might have added but had seen the square brackets looming and had given them a right body-swerve, and re-entered the dialogue with]

'Aye, right.' Ray snorted, thinking that the job with Hillbrokes was looking increasingly attractive by the second. She wondered if she should treat herself to a nice new business suit then remembered that the posh bookie had these sexless uniforms. Still, the money was better, the clientele – she looked at Bunty and Argy and the ither wan – would be different.

'Well, perhaps not. Not right away. But personalised services.' Mungo blustered.

'*Noodles,* Father. Call the soup *noodles.* To show you are ethnically sensitive. And why not involve Mother. Ray, Mother has a special way of treating foreigners – which term she interprets generously.'

As he spoke, Cosmo was scribbling on a piece of paper – yup: another pencil portrait; but the eedjit is doing it of Mungo now. Has the lad no sense? He was wasting his time as Ray was thinking how she could get her new company to change its uniform policy.

Mungo spluttered, 'Ethel? Not sure that the time is yet right to... '

'Father, at some soon stage Mother is going to insist on seeing the... business. Then as the Xhosa might put it, if they weren't so damn polite: *ilindle will hit the fan.'*

'This is not the time to worry about that. Something will turn up.' And with those words, as if it was needed, Freud's *Civilization and its Discontents* was consigned to the dustbin of History along with other fantastic creations.

And so we return to the immortal words of Mungo (plus other middle names) Laird in which he adopted an alternative, but equally effective strategy to adopting the *One-legged dance of Yü,* and that was to assert, sure in the knowledge that it had always worked in the past at times of crisis:

'Something will turn up.' (We recommend that approach as cheaper than going to a psychiatrist, every time.)

'Just as long as it is not Mother, eh?' Cosmo somewhat cruel for him, interposed. For a moment Mungo almost retrieved his well-thumbed (metaphorically) copy of *Civilization and its wee irritating things* (very loosely translated from the original *Das Unbehagen in der Kultur* (1929)); but he was made of sterner stuff than he or anyone else could have imagined. And anyway, he had other troubles to deal with for at that very moment...

FOR AT THAT VERY MOMENT - At that very moment a small reddish fist banged on the counter. It was accompanied by a snarl from Argy.

'Nae commentary. Kind of shoap is this? Pure shite.'

'I'm sorry. Didn't quite catch that,' Mungo said, then quickly added, ''nthat', which he hoped may have given him a tinge of street cred.

'The Radio, father. Silent films yes. Silent radio no.' Cosmo was taking very quickly to this environment, it appeared to Mungo.

'Ah. Ray? I say Ray?' Then he looked at Cosmo who also looked at Ray who seemed to be on a different planet.

'The Pole'll fix it.' She said dreamily as she came out of her dwam – she is thinking about… her new job and things. (She's given up on Cosmo – for the eedjit did not followup in the sketch hint. He's a warrmer – but likeable, but.)

'Oh, well… ' Cosmo said and grabbed the pole supporting the grille. It dislodged. The grille crashed down nearly removing Argy's middle finger that he now raised to accompany:

'F*ck'ssake. You no' content with the shirt off my back?!' Argy trilled then fluted almost harmonically, despite the size and range of his mouth organ.

'Oh well done, Cosmo. What do you think you're doing?' Ray struggled not to laugh, such was the extent of her affection for Argy.

'The Radio. Fixing it. With the pole. I take it I just give them a tap, or what?' Cosmo asked.

'No' the pole. *The Pole*. He kips in the wrecked pub on the other corner. Get him to come and fix it. Give him a fiver from the till. The Pole can fix anything. Cheap. Never mind, time for my lunch/dinner/supper break, anyway I'll send him round if he's there.'

Chapter 39

Poleaxed

'The Pole. The Pole. As Captain Scott would have said if he'd ever managed to find it. The Pole: Dad, could this be the answer to our refurb conundrum? Fixes anything and cheap?' Was there just a whisper of scepticism in Cosmo's words, though his tone was encouraging to Mungo?

'And if we could do it without Ray knowing, as a surprise for her, she might just hang around a bit longer? Tomorrow's her day off. Brilliant. Did she not say, that this place needed gutting?' Mungo let his second foot touch the floor.

'*Burnt to the ground*, I thought she murmured.' And with that Cosmo surveyed this emporium of dreams and in the blink of an eye – a bit of flaking paint had been working its way into his superior lacrimal punctum – he said, 'Somehow I think it'll take more than tarting this place up to get her to stay one minute more than she needs to.' And with that thought, he almost fell into a slough (sluff) of despond without for a moment worrying how to pronounce 'slough'. But having seen peoples with much worse to worry about in Africa, he cast aside all thoughts of Ray – for about another minute until he realised that Mungo was singing her praises so he tuned in.

'Yes. There's something of your dear mother in Ray. Women of mettle. We Lairds always go for women of mettle.'

'Okay, Mum's dad, dear departed Papa, was a scrappy – not a commodities trader on the metal exchange. I've known it for some time.'

'Just don't mention it to Ethel. She has her dignity to retain. And not much more if this,' his arm swept the room and knocked a mug of tea of the counter, 'if this project goes under.'

'Ah, Mum's dignity. That will be the last thing to go.' Cosmo said quietly, as if he was speaking to himself – which he was, because Mungo had stopped listening some time ago as a

221

natural defence mechanism; another of his strategies that defeated the whole corpus of psychiatric literature on *Anxiety: its causes and consequences* (which again sounds better in Jerry: *Angst: seine Ursachen und Folgen.*)[76]

'And this Pole fellow. Think he could do it, my boy?'

'*The Pole can fix anything.* If he can mend a radio, then minor carpentry and shop fitting: a bagatelle.' Cosmo said in a tone that a normal person might take to be tinged with the merest soupçon of sarcasm.

'Bagatelle. And cheap. Let's go for it. Radio and counter today. Tomorrow – that bog of a toilet, if he passes muster.'

And with that Mungo felt much better – though he had been feeling pretty good all day, so a marginal increase in well-being was no big deal; nevertheless, he began to hum; for he had tried to fix the tannoy and got a very mild electric shock. Another no big deal. This all had the portents of a good day ahead. Maybe after all, he *would* let Ethel see their new venture – after the Pole had fixed all.

---

[76] *But have a gander at Karin Schertler, (2004) who makes a convincing case for something.*

Chapter 40

Polish entry – pre-Brexit.

'Cosmo, sure he understands what we want? Nine thousand seems very reasonable? Ask him again, my boy, just in case you've missed a nought at the end or something. Tricky language Ingerlish for foreign types.'

'Nine thousand? Dad, we haven't got nine pence, it would seem. Oh what the hell. My father was wondering… '

'Okay, you tough negotiator. What the Dudek…? For you, special Free Polish price. I take zilch off end. What you think?'

The bull of a man seemed ill at ease with his stub of a pencil and his dirty little note book. He licked the less blunt end of the pencil, scribbled with it, scored out hastily, clumsily and rewrote slowly all the while his lips mouthing the written words. The Pole handed the paper to Mungo.

'Nine hundred pounds the whole works? My god, Cosmo, it's incredible.'

'Mother of Boruc. Okay, best price.'

The Pole licked, scribbled, re-licked and re-scribbled as Mungo spoke what he thought was softly in Cosmo's ear.

'The toilet, Cosmo. Ask him.'

'Good to ask, I'm in comfort zone. No need. Bladdey good bladder,' The Pole smiled, revealing a half set of teeth. (The other half was 'a work in progress', but one of many in his 'to do' portfolio.)

'My father, he means, would you like to look at our toilet?'

'Sure, no Dudek in that.'

The Pole headed for the indicated door with an air of a man who for whom nothing can disturb his equilibrium, while whistling tunelessly the introduction to Henryk Górecki's Symphony Number 3, which, little did he know was most apposite to what lay ahead, for as we all recall, this piece is also known as *Symphony of Sorrowful Songs*. (In the unlikely case that a few of you have not heard this work, stay clear of open razors when you sample it.)

And so the Pole returned unsmiling, holding his breath. He exploded his words, 'Most interesting. Very most interesting,' while thinking what old Henryk would have made of that toilet had he been alive today.

'Well, what do you think? Can you do it?' Mungo asked eagerly.

'Ah, you mean. You want me to. Sure. No Dudek. My brother. He do it. He come. He complete bottom hole. Then...'

'Your brother complete bottomhole?' Cosmo queried. 'We say *complete arsehole.'*

'Ah, you know my brother? Complete arsehole but okay plumbering. He complete bottomhole, priority number one. Then he complete face and hand hole. Toilet as good as whatever. Wash your feet in it. No more M.A.R.S.'

'*M.A.R.S?* What the Dudek he talking about, Cosmo?' Mungo said, slipping effortlessly into the lingua franca of the moment.

'I think he means *MRSA.'* (Authorial intrusion: at the time of writing (17.19; evening sunshine, going, sofa and brain and EMERGENCIES-ONLY Mars Bar, good-to-soft) MRSA has been absent from the headlines having been elbowed aside by other IDs; we predict that it will re-emerge within a twelvemonth. An outside bet to appear, but worth an eachway, would be yon ~~necrophilly~~... ~~necromansingphiltitis~~... the flesh-eating bugger. You heard it here first.)

'Your boy, he got dose of that slysdexia. He puts the words elbow to arse. I can fix that. All inclusive price.'

Chapter 41

More work in progress...

The day after Cosmo had been installed as Office Manager Extraordinaire was Ray's day off. She spent the morning shopping for gear for her management course with Hillbrokes. After a fruitless search, she chose a trouser suit in charcoal to try on. The assistant complimented the fit when she reappeared from the changing room, running her hand down Ray's back and looking at Ray in the mirror before tugging just a little bit on the buttocks before smoothing down a crease that seemed to be so stubborn that she just had to pat it a few times. Ray did a couple of turns then said:

'What do you think? A bit too lezzie?' The assistant met Ray's gaze – she was a better man than Ray had given her credit for – and said, 'Can you ever be too lezzie?' And with that she had made a sale, for Ray liked people who stood up for what they believed in. At the door the assistant put a hand on Ray's arm and said,

'Doing anything tonight?' (She was confident this one.)

'F*ck off.' Ray fluted and, with a whirl on the pavement, she was gone, while the friendly shop assistant blushed to the tips of her Valentino Rockstud 100 burgundy leather ankle boot (£395 atow).

Once she had picked up a few other items, Ray made for her mother's flat where the wee yin was. Her route took her past The Shoap and as she approached it she saw a crowd milling about and cries and cheers and laughter were carried her way on the prevailing wind – most of which came from the crowd she judged, because there were fish suppers and pie suppers and of course, too much curry in the air.

Her instinct was to cross over to the same side of the road and pretend she did not see what was going on. But her stronger instinct was that those two warrmers, Mungo and

Cosmo of the Jungle, were doing something that not even she could have foretold.

And so as the crowd parted with a murmur as she approached and made a path for her to the door…

A voice called out, 'I'm Spartacus.'

Then from another part of the crowd it came, 'I'm Spartacus.

And a third time, 'I'm Spartacus.'

'Ur ye f*ck. I'm Spartacus!'

And a great melee ensued unto the end of time – well, the next paragraph.

Meantime, those of the crowd that hadn't parted for Ray and who were not engaged in the mêlée had to be moved on by some sharp elbow work; thus she approached the door and looked in. Then putting a paper hanky to her mouth (Tesco Basics DINE, 30cm, 100 pk, £0.50 ATOW; Lidl had run out) she ventured in and thought: if ever there was a need for a different kind of Jerry helmet it's now.

Ray could not believe her eyes.

'Mungo, Cosmo. What the bloody hell are you thinking about?!' She had to shout over the demolition by the Pole's sledgehammer. 'And while the racing's on. The radio, I said. Just the wire service. He's doing it for nothing, isn't he?'

'Competitive pricing, Ray,' Cosmo said.

'He's only good for mending wee things like radios and tellies, tinkling pianos, or performing keyhole surgery on the side. Look at him! Loving it. Like a pig in shite!' Ray shouted above the din.

'Didn't expect you today, Raylene,' Mungo said. 'But we did it for you, Ray. In a manner of speaking … '

'Hoping you would change your mind and stay,' Cosmo continued. 'I told him, no chance, but … '

'And there's some that says private education doesn't work… ' Ray started to say but Cosmo interrupted with,

'Oh, oh, Dad. Mother at twelve o'clock high!'

'What?! Remain cool, Cosmo. Pretend we don't see her. Sometimes works with Ethel, if she's forgotten her medication. Strong stuff.

Mungo's plan, for what it was, was apparently working but due not to medication (we don't count Buckie) but to Ethel's myopia symbiotically tied to her vanity re wearing eyeglasses.

'You there. Yes, you with the pickaxe or whatever. Where the devil is this address? I was told that this was where..'

'What the Boruc keep you? I say one-clock start. Man at burro he give me the gip. You community service felons, bunch of no-gooders. Jail too good. Kick down the arses you need,' said The Pole whose name was... unspellable.

'What language is that?! Do you speak English? I said, where is this address?' Ethel trilled while the Pole drilled.

'Address is here. You too... Okay for your semmity vest but where the Dudek you head? Your arms? Bit flabby, wee bitty speckled, I feel ... but strong ... oh yes! Here you take hammer of sledges. You smash this and this. I take break. Go fix telly somewhere far. Remove kidney stone or two. Then tinkle piano. Yeah, piano. All we Poles great pianoers. Sh*te goalies. I come back, I give you Jerry Helmet.'

The Pole left abruptly leaving Ethel swathed in ambivalence, holding the sledgehammer.

'We've not even been introduced,' she mumbled to herself, but to an extent her temper tempered by his effortless charm. Then she spotted the vague outline of her two male family members despite Cosmo crouching behind the high grille and Mungo crouching behind his son.

'Mungo! Cosmo! What the blazes?! Explain, Cosmo!' She trumpeted like a hoarse tuba, having decided it was mostly a waste of her time to ask Mungo to explain anything with which he was involved.

'Mother, is that really you? You've been accessorizing again.'

If anyone ever doubted the efficacy of a private education (viz Ray above a few paragraphs ago) then here was the demonstration of what could be attained for just a few thousand pounds per month: disarming charm, while the rest of us from bog-standard comps blush and scratch our arses, clutch our groins or... and ... Cosmo – no fault of him – has one advantage over us, so in the same vein he continued, 'Most fetching. Lime green with a hint of verdigris on the cardigan. Quite this season's combo for the chic road worker. Ray, you must meet my mother.'

Ethel found herself for the second time in a minute preening then she got a grip of herself and got back into character:

'Mungo Laird! That strange little fellow? Who in damnation was he?!' she guttered, pointing in the direction the odd but interesting little chap had gone.

'Ethel my dear. How lovely to see you. I see no little fellow. And may I join with our son in congratulating you on your ensemble this morning? Why just the other day I… '

'Father – it's too late for that: Mother met The Pole. Got on famously at first, then there were words, and he left in a dudgeon.'

'Left did he? In a dudgeon?' Mungo was saved from wondering for Cosmo quickly explained:

'Dudgeon. Latest Polish car – sewing machine under the bonnet, piano in the boot.' He looked at Ray for evidence that she was in the least bit taken with his effortless wit to go with his effortless charm.

She wasn't.

'I say, he's really done quite a bit in such a short time,' said Mungo displaying his keen powers of observation despite the still all-enveloping stoor.

'Yes, seems to like his work. Got stuck into it with gusto,' said Cosmo.

'Ah. Gusto. That'll be his brother.' Mungo displayed his inside ignorance of the workings of the Pole's extended family.

'Say goodnight, Mungo,' Ray said.

'Enough of this nonsense, Cosmo. Mungo, what is the meaning of this war zone? This surely can't be. You told me *the little betting shop* was *cosy and fit for purpose*.' As she said this, Ethel did a quick recce of the shoap.

'And so it was my dear. In my opinion. Our son thought otherwise and insisted on refurbishing to the highest standards. Cosmo, show your dear mother the plans you have. Much as I would like to, 'fraid can't take the credit this time.'

'Plans? Thanks, Dad.'

Ray decided it was time to take a hand in this farrago, 'Mrs Laird, Ray McMaster. You've made a great job of raising that fine boy, Mrs Laird, speaking as one single-parent to another.'

'I've always said that I was the original single-parent – being married to Mungo, you know.' Ethel surveyed the young girl sitting up high beside her two 'boys'. Ray was not yet 'guilty' as the jury was still out in Ethel's mind.

'Oh, I can imagine. And you must give me the name of your make-over stylist.'

Cosmo whispered, 'Laying it on, a bit thick, aren't we, Ray?'

'A bit like her facial, would you say?' Ray whispered back out of the side of her mouth.

The jury pronounced at worst 'admonished'... 'You mean it's not as bad as I think, my dear?'

'How bad do you think it is, Mrs Laird?' This was as close as Ray had ever got to curtseying and she was beginning to feel bad in herself for she did not need these people.

'It's just that in the middle of my first Scottish perm in nearly ten months the damn dryer exploded... (Two disasters in less than a year (see Skelp the Aged) in *Salon Shug*... we know, we know, stretching poetic licence you might think Dear Reader, but you have never visited the SS have you – we hope, for both our sakes.)

'... but if you think it is not so bad, well. I feel so much better, my dear. You must call me Ethel. Mungo, if I know you, and I do, you won't know how lucky you are to have such a discerning employee. Thank goodness there's someone who seems to know what is what. Hold on to her, Mungo. Tightly. Metaphorically, mind you. Got to spell everything out for him. Now! Where were we? Ah, yes; these plans, Mungo...?'

'Such class. Such breeding,' Ray said flatly to Cosmo.

'A Laird sired by Laird, dammed by Turner. A McNiven sired by Sharp damned by everyone she has come across ... Mother's version of our family tree: her father made the family fortune from coal and steel. Except it was stealing coal.' [Cosmo should have known that this line can only be effective if delivered 'live'. Still, no' bad for an artist manqué. But would Ray crack a light – that is the question.]

229

'Mungo, as I said, I don't have time for this nonsense. House keys, Mungo, and a little something from the till. I have an infernally expensive taxi running, and an extraordinarily intense migraine pending.'

Bunty rose from her punter's table, wrapping her old, threadbare, puce overcoat tighter and addressed Ethel:

'Here, you, do I no' know you? It'll come to me. Ethel? Ethel? The accent's gone bools in mooth but I never forget a face... Gotcha! Ethel McNiven. Or as you used to insist. Ethel Sharpe-McNiven. Go on deny it.'

'Madam – and I use the term loosely – you have me confused with someone else.'

'That nose. The way you look all the way down it. I'm telling you I know it. The voice as well.'

'Mungo. Is there not some law against soliciting or something in these establishments? My dear woman, I have no idea what you are talking about. Now step aside. Mungo, unless this crashing shambles of a gambling parlour is rendered unrecognisable from its present derelict condition and up and running by the time I return this evening, funding will be no more. Remember the little we have left is all in my name... You buggered the brewery. Now you are well on way to trashing the turf accountancy. What next? Fu*king up a fish and chip shop?! ...'

Bunty interrupted Ethel's diatribe. 'And your old man was done for lifting wood from the ...'

'That's a damn lie! Was my granddad. And it was coal from the trains. Only when it fell off, of course. And he was admonished. Ah, I remember you now. You've had your venerean strabismus fixed. And you've learned to breathe with your mouth closed. The wonders of modern medicine. I think I'll get my tear ducts seen to. Mungo, you've been warned!'

Ethel made to, what she thought was, 'leave'.

'No, Ethel, wait! That's the... *toilet*. Oh... ' Mungo held his head in both hands.

'Shall I fetch the smelling salts?' Ray asked.

'Grand idea. And an extra-large sherry for mother.'

Chapter 42

Pontificating punters

When things had settled down somewhat later that day, and the stoor had been dampened down by the rain coming in through a hole in the roof – that made Mungo feel really at home – business was quiet and Mungo had a quiet read of the *Racing Post* to while away his ennui. Cosmo was pretending to be leafing through the betting slips purposefully – in fact he was making quick-draw sketches of Ray as he did not have the courage to ask if he could take a snap of her, while Ray was on the phone speaking to Benny Queen about laying off and giving him gentle assurances in her inimical style, as to how he could trust her new boss.

Mungo, with a purposeful stride (actually he tripped over the kettle on the floor and this gave his stride a sense of purpose) left his position behind what was left of the counter, went into the front shoap, took a betting slip and wrote on it with his paper by his side. Then he went up to where the grille had been where Cosmo ignored him for a bit (he was a quick study, young Cosmo).

Eventually Mungo handed over his betting slip and his cash. Just as Cosmo was about to stamp the slip Ray grabbed the betting slip and looked at it.

'Mungo, what the bloody hell do you think you're at?'

'Don't you accept three-cross bets across the card, Ray? What kind of bookies do you call this?'

'Mungo, you cannae bet against yourself. It's your bookies. Where's the sense in that?'

'But if I win, I win. And if I lose I win.'

Ray took the stamper from Cosmo – who for a moment imagined he was back in the jungle and wondered how the West had ever cleared *some* of it – and triple stamped Mungo's line and just refrained from leaning over and stamping his father's forehead.

Later still – though not really that much later …

Not much later that same afternoon, Bunty McCall was trying to contain her excitement. That lucky feeling she had had when she had got up that morning was still with her. Her 'method' for horse selection of choosing two trainers and sticking with them through thin and thinner and thinnest if need be, she was sure would pay off sometime. Sometime very soon she felt. (Her first winner in a six horse roll up was already 'up' and the other five were to run today.)

The most immediate assistance to subduing and concealing her emotions stared her in the face. For once she would actually listen to Argy who was declaiming on a theme familiar to all who dream of the big line coming up.

'Would the Big Win change me? No. I'd remain fundamentally unchanged. The same hard-working, honest, salt-of-the earth type who would not shun those people who've depended on me over the years and to whom I am closest.'

'Like the bookie, the Social and the publican.' Bunty couldn't help herself. She went on, 'Me? First move. That would be my first move. Move to somewhere there are no dugs. See the dugs round my place. They are fuc*ing animals. Nearly as bad as their owners… You know the truth of it, I think I come in here just to get out the road of they dugs. First thing in the morning to last thing at night, barking growling snarling howling…you can hardly hear the neighbours arguing for they dugs.' (If only she knew it, help was at hand for during the writing of this paragraph, The Cooncil had given outline planning permission to a Korean Delicatessen and Exotic Burger Takeaway Shoap. An' no afore time!')

'And they are off at Doncaster. Five furlongs… only three runners… A fast first out the stalls is the odds-on favourite Tequila Sunset, followed by Hard to Bear with first timer Baby Boomerang a close third on the stands rails…'

'Come on Tequila ya beauty!' Argy was on his feet, arms in the air, his Denis Law victory salute already assumed. 'Stonewaller. Certainty. A Stick on. Like buying money! Go on Spencer, bring her home!'

... and with half a furlong to go. The outsider Hard to Bear has edged in front of the odds on Tequila Sunset, the favourite is beaten, but here comes Baby Boomerang with a late rally... and they go past together. It'll take a photograph...'

'A photograph. Don't bother.' Argy slumped, the veins on his neck subsided in collusion with his crumpling body. For although he was generally thought to be of the moron (Complete Eedjit Provisional) tendency, there was a certain visceral intelligence located somewhere within him – probably his pancreas – that told him he was doomed to failure again. 'Why do ah come in here...?' he might have said, but no one, not even himself, bothered to listen.

'It's the milieu that best matches your aspirations to your resources, perhaps?' Cosmo said *en passant*. Whit! Cosmo is new and has not learned to ignore the whines of Argy.

'You can always tell when they've gone to a posh school,' Bunty said to Nearly, 'you never know whether they're taking the pish or jeest talking it. It's what they call *manners*. Never got that from his mother, I can tell you that.' Bunty kept the tremor from her voice as to contain the excitement that was bubbling up within. *Baby Boomerang* was her third winner in her six horse roll up. The second that day.

Meanwhile Ray was talking to Mungo, the two of them behind what the Pole had left of the counter. The grille was long gone, sold and now on its way to Krakow aboard a Hebridean trawler via a marginally off-white Transit van out of Nullson.

'Mungo. I've thought it over. Again. But I'm finished. I'm going to a better place.'

'You're ill, my dear?'

'Listen to me: the better place is Hillbrokes; better conditions, more money, clients with both ears. Toilets that flush. You cannot compete with that. As for all your talk of Chinese and modernisation? Do you think any self-respecting Chinese punter would mix with this lot?' Ray stared down into the front shop at the threesome at their one big table. She knew them well. Despite the all-enveloping cigarette (and Nearly's pipe) and non-tobacco smoke their outlines were in exactly the same spots around the table that they had been for the last too many years since Ray had started in here straight from school.

Bunty was counting to herself. 'Twos, seven-to-two, and eleven-to-four. Seventy-six, fifty on to *Faraday's Lamp*.' Nearly started to speak. Bunty would listen to Nearly. Unlike Argy Bargy, auld Nearly sometimes made a kind of sense. Nearly.

'The first thing I'd buy, Bunty? A boat ah think. You know like that one in the Deacon Blue song.'

Nearly sang, '*And I'll sail her up the west coast, Through villages and towns, I'll be on my holidays, They'll be doing their rounds, A Ship Called Dignity.*' His voice was reedy but strangely pitch-perfect; a kind of in-tune Scottish voice flute. 'Just think, Bunty, he was just a bin man, tae.'

'Street sweeper, actually. But still: he did it. You can do it, Nearly.'

'You think so, Bunty?'

Argy barged in as ever. 'What the fffffurcoat are you talking about. Street sweeper. Boat. It's a song, for CCChristmas sake.'

'Just a song to you, Argy. To some a source of inspiration.' Bunty was matter of fact as always with Argy. 'That's *hit!*'

'But he didn't get the boat by wasting his time in the bookies backing no-hopers, did he? He got it by saving. *Saving.*' Argy argued.

'Saving? A street sweeper? Enough for a boat? No way? That's no' credible.' Nearly was nearly unconvinced.

'It tells you in the bloody song. It's in the words.'

'Aye, right.' Bunty sometimes used this more sardonic Glasgow assertion with its nod in the general direction of litotes.

Argy leaned back on his stool. 'Let me see: *I'll be on my holidays, They'll be doing their rounds, They'll ask me how I got her I'll say, I saved my money*. There. Told youse: *I saved my money!* He saved his money. Where in the song does it say...' He started to sing, very badly, off key... *I got up from my pit, went for ma Giro, cashed it at the bookies and threw it all away. Then I bought my wee boat and sailed up the West Coast.* Eh, tell me that!'

Bunty was listening to the next race but managed to say 'It's only a song.'

'Aw would you look at that. Missed the bloody race! Who won? Oh no – see what you've done you two. That was a cert. *Faraday's* bloody *Lamp*. Six tae wan tae!'

Nearly tore up his slip. 'Damn. Nearly! Just missed my double. Bang goes my deposit.'

Bunty despite her fourth consecutive winner coming in just managed to speak,

'Deposit? Deposit? You buying your council house at last, Nearly?'

'The last person to buy their house in our street was trashed before the ink was dry on the ASBO order. No, it's my winter plan: Benidorm. You know, Bunty, it's half as cheap to stay in Spain in the winter than it is here. And that's before they put up the gas and electricity again. And they'll post you your Winter Fuel Allowance out to you as well, straight up. And the heat. It'll do wonders for my sciatica. Getting there's the problem. They cramped cheap bucket aeroplane seats would kill me and my sciatica way before I landed.'

'So the deposit is for…?'

'*Business Class.*' Bunty and Nearly concluded in harmony. Nearly.

Chapter 43
Short commoners

'The princely sum of two hundred pounds. All that sweat and grime and excitement for two hundred pounds. One day's take. We can't survive on that. Ray, is it always like this?' Cosmo looked bleakly from the tallying-up sheet that was now his task at the end of each day. For a moment – one of those nano-sec things – he saw the map of Africa on the wall; but it was merely that the ceiling's heavily nicotined damp 'spot' had spread seriously overnight. As he waited for Ray to swivel her hips he scribbled idly on a pad before him, alert to the sound of her chair doing what it did. It did and he chucked the sketch of her back to the side.

Ray swivelled her commendable hips (encased in the charcoal-grey pencil skirt) off her stool and lifted the comptometer. 'Over the last couple of years or so. Sure. Why do you think Albie was so keen to sell to Mungo? To anyone. God he even spoke of getting Bunty, Argy and Nearly to form a consortium to buy him out. When he raised it with Bunty, she gave him a stare that I've tried to copy since. And that was that. And as for Benny King, he laughed in Albie's face. And then – what *you* might call serendipitously – your dad came along. I wanted to scream at him. Bar him from the place, but too late. He was hooked.'

Mungo had apparently gone for a wander in The Park, probably on a suicide mission by the look on his face, Cosmo thought, unless someone did him a favour and murdered him first.

'What am I going to do? He's poured his soul into this. No he hasn't. He's poured mine into it.' Cosmo said to himself (he thought).

'Have you ever thought about telling him straight, about anything?'

'Why yes of course I have. There was the time. No. That was someone else. You're right of course. I don't have the heart to tell him… I don't suppose you would consider…?'

'Oh no. Family affairs, Cosmo. Time to grow up.' Ray slipped into her jacket, and lifted her bag. 'Well, see you in the morning.' She made to leave.

'Less than two hundred quid. It doesn't come near to covering our costs?'

'Cosmo, there's people ken that their whole life – their relationship between their incomes and their needs – is summed up in what you just said. They just get on with it and do the best they can.'

'Ah, what was it Mister Micawber said…'

'Something will turn up,' Ray said and began to leave.

'Annual income… result misery, etc.' Cosmo tried to remember his Dickens.

Ray's head reappeared, this time under the remnants of the grille, 'Something will turn up. So much simpler, believe me.'

'But Ray, less than two hundred pounds,' Cosmo could think of nothing else to keep the conversation going and Ray from going.

'What's less than two hundred, my boy?' said Mungo who had entered unseen.

'What's that, Dad? Oh, just saying to Ray here, eh… A pair of trainers.'

'And under two hundred, Cosmo?' Ray interjected theatrically, 'Now that is a bargain, limited edition as well.'

'For a pair of shoes? Two hundred quid? How things have changed. Takes me all the way back. You know your mother and I didn't spend that much on our first car. And it lasted near on twenty years.'

'Yes, Dad. I know. Why do you think I told you, when you visited the school, to park round the corner? Behind the mountain.'

'The car. You never told me. All those years and you never told me you were…' Mungo's voice began to crack – the stoor again after being out in the freshly curried air of The Park.

'Dad, it's no big deal. Didn't last long. After the rector saw the vehicle that first time, he arranged counselling for me. Got me off lacrosse.'

Mungo bowed his head – he thought he had seen the glint of a florin down by the skirting board, 'Is there anything else you'd like to tell me, Cosmo. That made you ashamed. Or maybe still does?' *Let it all stick out* as they say I believe ...' And then, with an almost superhuman effort – though normal for him – he prepared to filter out anything that Cosmo might say that would upset one or other of them. [We have provided a redacted account below – due thanks are given to the CIA for this approach to open government.]

'Nothing that immediately springs to mind, Dad. Tell you what, though, I was wondering: whatever happened to that camel coat? The one with the maroon velvet collar and velour elbow patches?' [The rest is too disturbing to be even redacted.]

As Ray was leaving, Cosmo said, 'Are you going via The Park?'

She shook her head. 'No, round the long way.'

'I'll get you then. I'm off to... to... eh, pick up Mother's prescription. Father, you'll be all right for a bit? I'll come back...'

Well done, Cosmo, thought Mungo. His son had the one and only character flaw that he, Mungo had: shyness. He reflected on his, Cosmo's, facility with a pen – excluding doing sums – was, if he only realised it, a honey trap for women.

He, Mungo, had had a similar facility for hand shadows in his youth: girls from all around the county flocked to the annual shire fayre just to see Mungo's camel neck (no relation to the aforementioned coat). But such was his shyness, he waited until the parochial hall lights were out and made his escape. It was a wonder he had ever managed to snare Ethel, for all the young farmers in the country were after her. Indeed, so lauded was she that a cut of beef was named after her and every year, on January 24, at a secretive rural gathering, a *Shoulder of Ethel* was piped in by McGlashan of McGlashan; and a few hours later it was piped out by Armitage-Shanks.

But enough, we will follow the young people and leave Mungo to do whatever it is he does when Raylene is not standing over him guiding him (most likely hee-haw).

Later in Le Greasy Cuillère, Ray smoked a cigarette over the coffee (a friend of her mother's runs it – so Ray can smoke if she likes, so there) and surveyed Cosmo. She was having difficulty figuring this one out – he was good looking, athletic, artistic (at which thought she thought: why the hell is he no laying that on thick to me; ah'd tipple over at the wave of his pen), and didn't seem to have a love interest. She made a mental note to ask him if any of those exotic diseases Mungo had mentioned were STDs. Could make a difference. Would make a difference. She'd approach it obliquely, she said to herself, then, said to Cosmo,

'Mungo says you've had all sorts of tropical diseases. Right? Simple question: any of them STDs?'

Cosmo breathed heavily, 'Straight answer is, no. But, some of them if still in the bloodstream could be transmitted by… you know… engaging in relations of a carnal nature.'

'Damn,' Ray said to herself – or maybe she said it aloud, for Cosmo perked up.

'Ray, in my case, I've had the all clear for more than a year. So… if you want that portrait you were talking about.'

He broke off when Ray broke off a piece of her French bread and hit him on the head. She'd really need to stop being so obviously affectionate to this man. Where would it all end? She was leaving at the end of the week. She decided to go for safer ground and steer the conversation to the less provocative:

'That exclusive boys' school. Bit cruel, was it?' Ray asked with just a hint of hope in her voice, as she stirred in her sugar and that of Cosmo's into her coffee.

'Oh, it wasn't so bad for me. My best friend, now, take him,' Cosmo said. 'His father, a Marquis, met his mother on a Virgin Atlantic flight. She was cabin crew. Even the teachers called my chum *Doors-to-Manual*. He adapted all right. Learned to live with it. Was happy enough. I can still see his smile the day he was joined at the school by his young brother, *Cross-*

check.' He offered Ray his biscuit which she took and dipped daintily into her coffee before nibbling it (also quite daintily – she could when she wanted; a bit of a chameleon, is Ray).

'I went to a normal school. It was the making of me. If it had a Latin motto – it would have roughly translated as '*You talking to me ...again?*'

'They say your school friends are your best friends. Maybe because one never sees them again? What about you, Ray, I imagine most of them will still live around here where you went to school...' He blushed and added quickly, 'Not that I mean they would not be able to move elsewhere. I mean if that came out as ... '

'Snobby? Presumptuous. Aye it did. But you're right. Most are still around. Some of us meet up every month or so. It's good to see them.' She paused and added more sugar. 'Just wish they'd stop offering me their dinner money every time.' Cosmo gaped at her. 'A joke, Cosmo, a joke. *Acting to type* it's called. Anyway, there was a wee bit of truth in it. I could be a mean cow when I was younger. Could still be if called upon. But I've changed. I'm a mother. No a ned burd wi' a sharp steel comb.' She looked at Cosmo with a twinkle in her eyes – he just couldn't decide what he preferred to believe of her as a schoolie: the steel comb image appealed to something atavistic that had never been given the slightest bit of accommodation in his words or deeds.

[Where did this all end – for the moment nothing happened. Ray had to go and pick up her wee lassie and her sister's. No that anything would have happened anyway – it was the afternoon after all, and they're no' French.]

Chapter 44
A Wish called Fonda

The second meeting with Meg had gone better than even Mungo with his panglossian *weltanschauung* (Jerry) could have anticipated – had he ever bothered to anticipate anything. The brother that ran the tally restaurant was swimming with the fishes – on holiday in Florida at Dolphin Park with all the little fatlettes, and one wishes them all well.

Mungo had no need to worry about that little problem of speaking his mind – which some people do anyway: Meg Dalgliesh, as a for instance, who Mungo was meeting for the second time in … just a few days. Not because the 'walking-about-money' she had subbed him had run out – it had – but because his steel-trap brain/mind had espied a way in which they could help each other while helping themselves.

'Mungo. You look … different. From the last time. More alive,' she effused, giving him an air-shot on both cheeks. And though he checked his pockets later in the toilet after he had sluiced his face with cold water and rinsed his mouth out with what turned out to be anti-bacterial hand wash (quite pleasant on the palate as well), the abiding memory of that embrace with Meg was the merest brush – a *whisper* even – of her right breast-pocket (the one with the steel comb) almost touching his sternum (if that is not too low down for before the watershed). And the thing about Meg, compared with their last meeting, was that she seemed to have come to terms with her vulnerability within the new ethical framework that her employers – bloody furriners – were determined to pursue.

When last Mungo had seen her, she was deflated, almost in despair – so distracted had she been then that she subbed him without the usual penalty clauses, so he was certain she was either insane or being ill-treated by her new bosses. But he, Mungo, Usher, etc. Laird was here and he could rescue this damsel (who might have been still using sussies).

The rest of the lunch went in a blur – *grâce à* anti-bacterial mouth wash. He remembered to pocket one of the little green bottles before he left. Indeed, so much was he taken with the product, he scoffed a whole bottle during frequent visits to the gents, prompting Meg to ask if he had not yet seen to that troublesome prostate[77] – for which her company were now offering to advance funds that had to be hypothecated for use in a clinic in India (cataracts thrown in as a bonus, and a guarantee that the surgeons (man and wife) will not permit their children below the age of eighteen to assist in the theatre[78]).

But anyway – the lunch had gone well, despite the cellar still not catering for the Buckie connoisseur (Mungo made a mental note to pen a letter to the proprietor, (*il padrone*), which he promptly forgot); he scoffed a basin of pasta with tomato paste (the parameters of Italian cuisine are encompassed in that recipe); all washed down with the rudest valpolli (enhanced by the handwash) while Meg nibbled at what looked like seaweed and which in fact was … kelp, she said, gently laved with water from a bottle.

Mungo was quite taken with this latter: he had never seen water in a bottle (except a hot water bottle, which reminded him: whatever happened to that one from Ethel's hospital bed, for the nights were getting colder and had not been for Ethel's immense body heat he would have floundered if not froze.

Anyway, when he made his pitch for THE PROJECT, Meg had reacted favourably and he inked a few papers put in front of him by Meg (he liked that expression, 'inked', so New World, so expressive, so much easier to spell than '*singed*' after he had had a few. She left, with a *moue* across the table. His eyes followed her as she elegantly clumped across the floor (no loose heels – Stella Mac, Black Vanessa, £525 atow,

---

[77] *This is an error on Meg's part: Mung's prostate has never been better – thanks to the one-legged dance of you-know-what and the pelvic-floor exercises. She's clearly muddled – perhaps she was on the anti-bacterial mouthwash as well.*
[78]

http://www.theguardian.com/world/2007/jun/22/india.international - it's ok, it was only a caesarean and he was fifteen.

honestly!); and all about was a loud clattering and cursing: it was the sound of Mungo's teeth striking against each other, and the people at the next table covered the ears of their little ones – why were they not at school is not germane to the narrative – as Mungo's cogitative-vocalisation kicked-in again. Bugger!

Anyway, the deed was done – he had the finance for the refurbishment of what had been Albie's Bookmakers Emporium, and all that was required now was to get cracking to it. Or get someone who had a scooby to get cracking on it. At which thought, he wondered if the Polish roofer who had taken the slates (Welsh blues) was available – at which thought the couple at the next table said, 'Don't even think about it.'

'That bad?' Mungo asked.

'Booked-up for the rest of the season. And don't go for his cousin.'

Somehow he made it back to Villa Idris, and his hostess who in the past had always been so understanding of his little irritating foibles and nonsenses – which got really up her nose – gave him a look that could have been cloned from Ethel.

'You're pished, Mungo,' she susurrated loftily – she was up in the loft helping Tim with the buckets in Mungo's absence.

'I may be pished,' he said, playing for time while trying frantically to think of a riposte that had not been uttered by his hero, Winston S whatsisface... he slurred internally. 'But I can spell it, and I will probably be so again tomorrow, but you, dear lady whatsyerface, are beautiful and tomorrow is another day, and we're off to see the wizard.' He stopped at that point for he was up against a brick wall – a yellow one. He turned on his heel with great dignity and promptly fell over, the spare heel having dug its heel in refusing to turn.

When he woke he found himself at the kitchen table and across from him was... *Tim*! That's it... Tim. He knew he would get his name. Mungo bathed in the glow of his rapid powers of recovery. He reached into his jacket pocket and offered Tim a slug of his anti-bacterial whatsit. Following Tim's example, Mungo tried it on his hands and when he was done Idris served a repast that the French and the Tallies would kill for: pan-fried haggis fritters in a batter made from Idris's own recipe (copied from *The Sunday Post:* Healthy Lifestyle Supplement.) And all washed down with stewed tea – the pot had been on the stove for two hours while the Wattersssses had been up, up aloft and the landlubber was lying down below, below, below. And very pleasant it was too, as was the desultory talk.

Later that same evening – although it could have been a different day as far as Mungo was concerned, because he had achieved so much in such a short space of time, and anyway the handwash has that effect of compressing time and then expanding it (in this respect it is a bit like crack-cocaine consumed in a London Hackney Cab between Antibes and Tina Turner's villa above Nice – in the absence of Tina) – yes, later that same evening he sat in the little living-room (lounge-space) with Tim, the one that Ethel used to use for taking pot-shots at passing fauna, he explained what he had in mind.

Chapter 45

Roll up, up (not for smoking)

Among certain sections of the betting fraternity, there is a superstition that if you even begin to calculate your potential winnings after your first horse has come up, then as sure as Hell, you have put the hex on yourself.

Bunty was not of that persuasion – she had no superstitions; perhaps because she had had little luck in her life, thus nothing to associate with winning; while losing was in the nature of the beast. This day she was determined not to count her potential winnings should her sixth horse come in – not from superstition, but merely to postpone the moment of dreaming of what might be; or more likely, of what might have been. But despite her resolve – and she had plenty of that; not for nothing was she generally alluded to (out of her earshot) as a stubborn, pig-headed wee wumman – and yet despite her resolve, Bunty could not help counting her potential winnings if her sixth horse obliged in the day's last race.

As she silently assessed, (without need of a pencil and paper and certainly no need for a calculator or even one of those old-fashioned ready-reckoners that the settler in a bookies of the old school depended on), had she spoken aloud it would have sounded something like this, 'Three grand, four hunner an'… C'mon *Doomwatch*.'

Argy it was who ruined her concentration, a not unusual occurrence.

'No, no, no. The point is, probability is a science, just like… like…'

'Astrology. Or is it astronomy? Always get them two mixed up. Nearly always… ' Nearly said as he nearly finished.

'I'm like that with paediatrics and paedophiles, Nearly,' Bunty said, her precise calculations now abandoned.

'Feet and weans and funny looking bicycles…' Nearly, nearly concluded.

'Funny looking bicycles? What the fff...? Argy nearly asked.

'A cruise. Where would you go, Nearly? Benidorm again? You could lie out on the deck. You with a bad back,' Bunty stated, her ear on the race that was close to the off.

'I would be as well talking to myself. I'm trying to put scientific investment on a logical basis and it's like preaching to the missing link and his sister.'

'*Missing Link*. Look. The last race, Argy.' Nearly said.

'Oh... could be a sign... ' Argy jumped up and shot to the counter.

But he was too late. The *off* was called. He cursed and easily overlooked the fact that things could have been worse as the grille was gone and could well have been slammed down in his face or at least his fingers if that 'wee bitch Ray' could have had her way.

Chapter 46

The evening of reckoning

'Let's pay the lady.' Mungo beamed from on high down to the diminutive Bunty and then added a bit of whimsy, 'Do you accept cash?' He turned to Cosmo – 'What does the lady's little return come to?' He felt he was getting the hang of opening up a rapport with the clients. He was beginning to enjoy himself, and if he had not been so euphoric he would have remembered something that Ethel always said at such moments, 'Mungo, you're beginning to enjoy yourself. Time you went home.'

Cosmo made a frantic mime show and opened the cash drawer to show two sandwiches and about fourteen pounds and some odd change (not including a Chiang Kai Shek $100-dollar note, and a 1965 Winston Churchill Commemorative Crown – worth $15 atow on E-bay).

In a whisper he said, 'Stall her. We need to wait till your… eh… Benny Queen delivers on our lay-off bets? Did Ray say what the protocol is? Do we go round or does he deliver or do we send our punters round? Is there a hint of panic in my voice?'

'What did he say when you called him with the lay-offs? What did you agree?'

'Agree? Me call him? But it was you, Dad, who spoke to him.' Young Cosmo had known fear in the jungle – but it did not smell like this. '*I* lay it off? Father, we agreed – you operate the telephone, I do everything else? You did lay-off Bunty's bet? Remember, Ray said that any slip with a winner crossing on to another runner should be … you didn't, tell me you did. No don't.'

'I thought that you …'

'Mr Mingo, is there a problem? Do you wish for me to come back? Say in… oh two minutes? Or if you prefer, in ten with my three brothers and Annabel.'

'Annabel?' Father and son asked in unison.

'Our latest Social Cohesion Officer. She's from Kilmacolm. She's never seen a bookies burn down.'

'Problem, Bunny? Not in the slightest. Just the… Cosmo?'

'The time-lock!' Cosmo almost screeched.

'Time-lock?' Mungo did not wish to know.

'The time-lock on the safe. It's acting up.'

'We have a safe? Of course we have a safe. And the damned time-lock is always running late.' Mungo looked at his wrist and noticed that his three freckles were now merging into one large one, making a forgettable mental note to have it checked out for incipient melanoma.

CHAPTER 47

Coma toes

It was the best of times, it was the worst of times, it was the age of wisdom, it was the age of foolishness.

There is no strong evidence against Charles Dickens ever having lectured in Borrfoot, though the great scribbler and pundit had spent two very successful sojourns in Boston (giving a brilliant lecture at the Tremont Temple – not far from the Beantown Pub; recommended), so it would not have been surprising had he done so, given the literary turmoil the town was going through at the time: should an Alexandrine be used only when asking the butcher for a hambone? Anyway, Dickens used Little Nell's (gawdluv'er) grandfather's obsession with trying to win at cards to give us all a warning, which to this day, most of us have never taken to heart. But in a reversal of fortune, taking the old adage that only the bookie wins, Mungo was intent in showing that old adages are just a hill o' beans.

Ethel took the news with less than her usual equanimity.

'Eight thousand pounds?!' She bassooned. Mungo had asked her to be present. Mungo almost always resorted to the truth in times of real crises, when his back was to the wall and his baggy pants were no longer baggy enough in the face of possible accidents and after all Ethel knew Bunty (from way back).

'It's eight thousand one hundred and fifty-seven pounds and sixty-two pence, by the way,' Bunty sniffed across the table.

In the long silence around the front shop table all three Lairds and Bunty considered their respective next moves. On a positive note, there was no sign of Bunty's brothers. And as for Annabel from Kilmalcolm... her day would come.

'Eight grand, one hunner and fifty-seven pound. Stick the sixty-two pee in yer Xmas boax,' Bunty murmured.

During the next long silence Ray quietly half-entered and stood unseen behind one swing door. She is become the Angel Damiel again.

Ethel broke the silence: 'You, Busty, as far as I am concerned are what philosophers call, *The elephant in the corner.* You do not exist. This little matter is between you and for want of a better word, my spouse. I bid you adieu. And if you can squeeze even eight pence out of him, well, you'll have my grudging admiration.'

'Oh no you don't! You're not walking away just like that. See this wee pink slip?!... It's your family, but it's my business now...or it will be my business, once I get the Gambling Commissioners to hand it over to me. Seeing yer skint. And cannae pay up. Must be murder for ye. You having tae listen tae the like o' me. Assuming of course that I do actually ... oh ... ya... exist... And you stole my bike... You're nothing but ...Ohhhhhhh......'

And with that Bunty clutched her left arm, then the area of her chest where her heart should or could have been, and with not so much as a by-your-leave, keeled over. Fortunately, her fall was broken by Nearly who had been trying to extract with a Stanley Knife (very sharp) a coin from between the floor boards. (Yes it had indeed defied conventional wisdom's 50:50 probability) The Stanley Knife took off the tips of two fingers (we did warn him – and no fault lies with The Stanley Corporation), both of which at the time of amputation had just managed to grasp the coin (denomination unknown due to blood-spatter).

We will leave the coin and Nearly's finger tips (as he did in his haste to get to the A&E; let's hope it's still open) and return to Bunty and her 'condition'.

Mungo, who had a wealth of medical knowledge in his steel-trap brain, sat in a corner wondering whether it would be in bad taste to resort to the *one-legged dance of Yu*-know-who or go for the full syncope? Cosmo, who had had more jags (vaccinations/inoculations) and tropical diseases than anyone in Kilmalcolm or Nullson for that matter scoped the situation and for a moment, the appeal of those men with guns on the dark continent was almost irresistible.

But setting aside his personal preferences, he took command and begged Ray to take charge. Ray, who had already searched for Bunty's vital signs, had telephoned an ambulance and was administering *cardiopulmonary resuscitation* (though without the 'rescue breaths' – we note that without prejudice against Ray, who in every other respect is a paragon of womanhood (from a man's perspective, that is)).

Ethel, meantime had sat back, arms folded determined to immerse herself empirically for once in the latest Mungo cock-up, but cognisant (in the loosest sense) of the follies of the Heisenberg Principle (human error) she was determined to SAY NOTHING and purely (as far as Heisenberg with his principles would allow) OBSERVE.

Bunty, for her part, was not participating noticeably in the panic that – apart from Ray – had pervaded the shoap. Instead the wee ordinary wumman-punter lay prostrate on the floor, where she looked even tinier than she had when alive – not that we are saying she is dead, yet. That is for someone more competent than us to determine.

Anyway, she must be breathing for Ray stopped with the CPR, and placed Bunty in the recovery position. Whew, that's a relief.

Cosmo approached Ray tentatively and asked if he could do anything.

Argy was in a deep moral dilemma that he did not recognise for what it was: there was an evening race coming over the tannoy, all the way from Western Australia and… and without the benefit of yon moral philosopher that was on the telly (too often in the opinion of one of us), they just knew that Bunty would have wanted him to pay attention to the result.

Ray was happy that he should do so, for hadn't she told him not to step over Bunty, but to go round her lifeless form (we're still not saying she's dead or deid). Ray looked into Cosmo's face with a withering look that again made the idea of those gunmen in the chic-military uniforms very appealing.

'That's as comfy as I can make her. Her breathing's very shallow. She should never have chucked the smoking… if it was me I'd rather go out like a light and with wan,' Ray shuddered. 'Not a coma. Poor auld wumman… my heart bleeds for ye, Bunty. Cosmo, under the sink in the back-office, there's some brandy. Quick.'

Cosmo was back in a jiffy and handed the bottle to Ray who took a quick slug, wiped her beautiful mouth – there was no smearing of lipstick; if ever an 'upper or lower fleshy margin of the mouth' did not need artificially enhanced, it was those of the Divine Raylene – and handed the bottle back to Cosmo.

The post-Doppler Effect was somewhat skewed by the ambiance of The Park but it was unmistakably the sounds of an ambulance (no cop cars allowed in The Park – too noisy… and dangerous) drawing up outside, just past the bookie's. The two ambulance men who had never been called to The Park before, were sensibly in a hurry. One spoke, the other made a grab for Mungo.

'This the patient?!'

'Hands off… ' Mungo spluttered in protest.

Ray grabbed the hand of one of the paramedics – who responded favourably, but quickly realised that she was not Ray's type when Ray using a little known thumbblock (it's actually better-known as 'Fairbairn's Thumb Hold',) lowered the paramedic towards the form of Bunty. Immediately her training kicked-in (the paramedic's, that is; Bunty, had she had any training, is not in a condition to exercise it).

We will leave them to do their professional best and for the moment, wish all the best for Bunty (or her heirs).

Chapter 48

How Mungo met Mourinho

Mungo's faithful manservant Mourinho was looking after their welfare back in Algarvia. Before they had left, Mungo had had a discussion with Mourinho and taking very subtle hints and nudges and winks from the faithful retainer – so subtle that Mungo thought he had come up with the idea himself – it was agreed that Mourinho would find tenants for their place in the sun during their enforced absence. And with that peace of mind that Mungo was noted for, he and his beloved left that wee corner of Iberia on a sojourn, confident that their little love nest would be safe from the predations of the State (Portuguese and/or British) and illegal immigrants and diverse foreigners not excluding Portugueezers.

Mungo would have been doubly assured had he known that Keith (Keef) Mourinho was and remains a cousin of Dave Ashley-Cole-Cole (see *Skelp the Aged*) and a kissing cousin (and once upon a time, more than that) of Dave's present trophy partner, the bewitching Chelsea.

Although born in Kings Lynn, (Keith 'Keef' Paxman) there had been no successful prosecutions against Keef, and that remained the case even after he changed his name by going to a little kebab shop somewhere in Middle England (called Middle Walloper) where he obtained a driving licence, a pukka (try those pies, a Scouser delicacy) passport, and a bus pass that unfortunately was not valid in Middle England or any other part thereof. The TV licence was similarly useless for Portugal, but Keef (or *Mourinho 2* as he now preferred to be called, in order to be consistent with passport, tv licence etc.), was raised in adversity and ever one to turn his back on it, he hotfooted it to the new land of his birth just as the sirens were heard in the distance.

In that wonderful wee green country full of wee dark and friendly folk – we exclude the Brits (Ingerlish) on both counts

– Keef Mourinho was feted wherever he showed his passport or his TV licence. His bus pass – or *Entitlement Card* to give it its pompous designation of the 'Scotch' issuers of said handy piece of plastic – worked on the local bus services despite there being no extant government system. So popular did it become that Mourinho imported a batch from Middle Walloper, and helped the transport ministry recover the cost from the 'Scotch' government, thus proving that the European Union works. But all of this was before our tale begins and so we leave the two governments to thrash out the legality of the scheme at the European Court which should solve the unemployment problem among lawyers of all 27/26 and counting-backwards countries.

Anyway: Keef Mourinho found himself with time on one of his hands after release and in one of those damascene (not the breed of fancy pigeon) moments he decided it was time to find a good gaff with nosh and no worries. And just at that very moment – or a few months later – he was passing time in a hostelry when he heard two voices that sounded pretty much as if they came from Brent or its environs and they were discussing a roof job they were doing for some old Scotch geezer and his pachydermal wife (they actually used that phrase: we blame *Countdown*). At present rates the pair of blaggers reckoned they could get through to spring on the back of it. The trouble was there was not enough rain, one of them moaned to the other. The other one knew a plumber – well, self-employed builder with dirty-white van – who could rig up a watering system from the pool next door that would sprinkle the roof during the night and frighten the piss out of the Scotch geezer and geezeress. But the other one objected that the people next door might not like that. 'Simple', his co-defendant of a lifetime said, 'we gas them while their sleeping. You know, nitrous wotsit? Whatdyacallit… give them a right good laugh. Oxide innit?'

Mourinho had enough of this and he rushed pell and mell from the hostelry silently miming (see later) to the padrone: 'He'll pay,' indicating a small dark chappie who was sleeping in the corner while his dog ate the house speciality (sardines and chips with a tin of peeled plum tomatoes splattered over the pile - Lidl 52p atow; 15.08 in the afternoon). And so he hot-footed it (the pavement was scalding and he had sold his flip-flops) to the address of the old Scotch geezer.

That fateful moment when Mungo met Mourinho is not recorded on any type of recording medium, however it is imprinted in that steel-trap of a brain that Mungo Laird sometimes uses (despite the inexorable rusting). His first words when Mourinho vaulted the wall – he had gone to the house next door in error and the Rottweiler had not taken well to being disturbed while his mistress and her lover (who perversely was her husband) were preparing the meal of the day (sardines and chips etc.), and the dog was really wanting a big tin of Whiskas (not some ersatz shit from Lidl no matter what the f*cking price was), the dog said in canine equivalent as the buckets of saliva that it shed from its chops at the sight of Mourinho turned the water in the pool into a quite nasty looking foamy stuff that hinted of excess carnality by the husband and wife, which they were not impartial to, even after forty-seven years of such carnality, though to be fair they had only started doing it in the pool when they moved out to Portugal the previous week from Alloa.

ANYWAY as we say the first words Mungo said to Mourinho as he dropped down the Laird side of the wall were…

'I say, you're not with the perfectly lovely Angela Merkel (he pronounced it 'Angela") because Mungo in those days, like everybody else except the Greeks, the Spanish and the Eyeties, (and a few Jerries) loved Ankela (the Ironing Maiden).

How this came about is quite straightforward: a swarm of Jerries had been (legally this time and for once) swarming all over southern Europe and while they did not leave a mess like the previous time, what they did leave was ph*cquing towels everywhere. In point of fact, an advance swarm left the towels for the main advance. Like the weather, many people had remarked upon this bad state of affairs but not a single ph*cquer had done a thing about it.

Enter Mourinho who made his way down through southern Europe between the advance party and the main army, scooping up the towels and selling them off in the diverse market places. Now this caused an international stushie and the divine Ankela Merkel threatened to stop paying the bills at Strasbourg and that other place unless the constabulary of these little countries buckedup and put a stop to this scandalous behaviour. And so Mourinho had to turn his attention to other sources of income. And thus by a different route he entered the walled garden of Mungo and Ethel's little paradise, and there we leave him for a wee while playing his role of dumb mute (yes, honestly – you shall see later as we said above... we now *promise*). This self-afflicted affliction suited Ethel in particular down to a green or jasmine tea. A servant who could not talk (back)!

Chapter 47(B)

A vow of atoning silence

M2 with Jose Mourinho as his idol and role model had quickly learned seven European languages (including Brazil's version of Portuguese) and had begun his soccer career also as a translator/go-between for a non-speaking Portuguese, Italian, the old manager of Sporting Lisbon. M2 was a quick study and soon exercised his own big ambitions and bigger ego becoming a football manager of a minor Portuguese football club, taking them to a Europa League semi-final after placing third in the Portuguese league in only his second season.

M2 went on to minor successes with many European clubs (including Turkey) always fairly successful but as always guided by his role model (M1); staying less than three years with any one club. But the constant media spotlight (because of his relative successes, his personal charisma and above all his consistently coruscating, controversial soundbites imitating his idol and milking his adopted surname) took its toll. During his second spell in the Finnish Championship League (Division 2 in old money) he suffered a complete mental breakdown, was hospitalised (private nursing home) and under cover left to begin his rehabilitation back in his adopted-native Portugal after the epiphany he underwent – the self-realisation about his ego, his ruthlessness, his solipsism, his hubris. (And it will ensure that he tries to do the right thing by the Lairds and the 'sale' of *Casa Laird* later.)

Unable even to speak now (even his native tongue, never mind seven other easier languages) and as a first step on the road to recovery he wanted to find work in as menial a position as he could. In his condition as a mute, he felt himself fortunate indeed to be employed as a houseboy in the casa in the Algarve by the elderly Scottish Lairds.

Mungo and Ethel felt doubly lucky paying a pittance to a servant who never talked back. They would have paid double without quibble, if they could have afforded it.

Chapter 48

The heavy squad

[While we all recall that it was Proudhon who said, 'property is theft', more pertinent to the circumstance in which Mungo is about to find himself, is that there is a strong Judeo-Christian tradition by which gambling is a form of theft.[79] Maimonides (1135-1204) and Northbrook (1577) – and to save you time translating from the Hebrew and Latin – characterised as a type of 'robbery by mutual agreement'; an attempt to obtain property without paying the price for it. Now if only Mungo had known this he would have been quids-in with the moral torture that is about to envelope him].

With Bunty gone to a better place, Ray hitched a lift from her new paramedic friend – she had to pickup the wee yin from her maw's; in leaving, she turfed Argy out into the street and left the shop and the Lairds to it.

Ethel had had enough of her role as silent observer of Laird Financial Disaster and waved a pink betting-slip dramatically. It took only a matter of seconds for Cosmo to realise what it was and to whom it belonged. Mungo had thought that perhaps Ethel, in a gesture of solidarity had taken to betting; and where better than at Mungo and Son, Turf Accountant. It would be one way of getting some cash out of her after all those years. He was quickly disabused of this.

Waving Bunty's betting-slip, Ethel assumed a grand manner, 'Mungo! Pay attention! There are some people that would say we – the Laird family – are faced with some sort of moral dilemma in the shape of this 'wee pink betting-slip'. I say that as long as we pull together, act in a concerted manner,

---

[79] *We thank P Binde for pointing this out for us timeously; Journal of Gambling Studies, 2005, vol.21(4): 445-479 (apologies if we did not get this Harvard System quite right. It's a real bugger).*

agree what we are going to do and what will be said, should anyone raise the matter, I say that it is a form of kismet, that has struck down my dearly-about-to-be-missed school friend. Little orphan if memory serves… and eternal spinster… '

'School friend, Ethel. Bunty? But she accused you of … '

'Mungo, I will say this once: I did not nick her bike. Her idiot father traded it for a cooking pot. They were always indigent. Nothing to eat and nothing to cook it in.'

'Well,' Mungo said after a respectful pause, 'poor she is no longer. And even if she should pass away – heaven forbid – we'll be able to give her a send-off that she could never have imagined with her winnings and … '

'Mungo! What winnings? As far as I'm aware, she had not submitted her claim – for indeed she was in no fit state to do so. And what we have here… ' She brandished the betting-slip then made as if to tear it up until it was taken from her grasp by Cosmo. Her son did that to her?!

'A moral dilemma, Mother, that's what we have here. But one easily resolved.'

Ethel looked at her son as if he was speaking Xhosa – in fact it was the clicking of the old comptometer that was making a remarkable fist of reciting the Lord's Prayer in that language. Then she decided on a different tack.

'Perfectly correct, Cosmo. As her closest friend she would have wanted me to be her executor (we still don't know if she's deid, yet). And … '

'What about her three brothers?' Mungo said having just tuned in.

'That crew? Bunty despised them.' Ethel said. 'She would have nothing to do with them. She felt that they brought shame on her. They were recidivists.'

'Recidivists? Oh, like those Jehovah Johnnies who don't imbibe or gamble?'

'Dad, recidivists are… '

'Cosmo! Don't burden your father with new information. It only pushes out what little useful knowledge he has left.'

'Very true, my dear. Remember we did the bicycle tour of Islay and learned all about whisky? By the end I had forgotten how to ride a bike.'

'No, Mungo. You kept falling off because you were drunk.'

'Main thing is, these recidivists Johnnies, they've solved the ethical dilemma: they would not want this money, given its source. Any proposals what to do?'

Somewhere from the deepest darkest recesses of his brain (steel-trap or no'), Mungo remembered a learned article that he had come across that averred that gambling is robbery. And there it was. If they paid out to this robber Bunty, the business would be bust before it had even been inflated. And it would throw people out of work; and peace-loving citizens like Argy and Nearly would take to the streets having no alternative shelter; and riots might ensue; and the Russians under yon Putin would feel emboldened and march on Paris which could not be defended and – or at least, no one had ever tried ... this was beginning to look like the gravest decision that would have to be taken by the electorate – Remain or Leave; and god alone knows what the Scottish Nationalists would do...

(We apologise for the loss of sound above – we seem to have some cross-channel interference. Normal service continues below... Now the ferries are back on.)

Anyway, Mungo quickly summarised Binde's 2005 article from the Journal of Gambling Studies,[80] and convinced Ethel – who needed no convincing – that gambling was robbery.

Cosmo started to protest 'Oh come on you can't just... ' but was drowned out by the unilateral unanimity of Ethel and the silent nodding acquiescence of his father.

'We Lairds have lain down too, too often. It is time to strike back at the iniquities that have descended upon since Antiquity. Cosmo, what are you doing?'

Cosmo was shrugging himself into his jacket – (Next: Fire Sale – a blazer come smoking jacket). 'Include me out, Mother. I've seen sights that you could never imagine and... '

Just at that moment – while they and we were all waiting for Cosmo to tell us about these sights, in burst the Pole.

'Aha just in Dudek, you one smooth operator old yin, Mango. You knock my one best worker.' He turned from Mungo to Ethel. 'This keech-hole not for you, my ugly, this one big Boruc. I show you better place. You come with Jerszey I

---

[80] *Totally useless, by the way, for tips.*

show you Airdrie. That big hoot of yours fix that. Laser. Give you nose job.'

'He just won't give up. The man's besotted.' Ethel's ambivalence shone brightly for the second time in the presence of The Pole.

'We go piano bar. Grand piano bar. Class act, just you to the abc.'

'Oh, really now. Mungo, shouldn't you, you know? Show outrage or something?'

'You won't get any argument out of me, m'dear…'

'Grand piano bar six floors above ground, with no piano. No lift. We pick up piano. I drive bus. You carry piano.'

Chapter 49

Uncle Richard and Great Aunty Binty and the great big hickory-shafted sledgehammer

Not even the greatest minds of our generation (not excluding 'Dr' Stephen Fry and 'Dame-to-be' Fiona Brus – you heard it here first; betting has now closed) know what causes the ~~awrrora borreall~~ the ~~orrorrea balllearics~~ ... the Northern Lights. WE SAY NO ONE KNOWS THEIR CAUSE, but they are the result of collisions (*crashes* in scientific terms) between electrically charged particles emitted by the sun with gaseous particles in the Earth's atmosphere.

Bunty had resolved this unresolved question of astrophysics just as she was coming out of the ~~annasttsht~~ ... the ~~annnaprosthe~~... used to be ether... the stuff that she had snoaked (tr. *inhaled*) but as she reached the surface, as usual when you have the answer to profound questions the f*cking thing faded away without even those wind chime things to warn you that ...

'Bunty, breakfast. You up to it, dear?' The charge nurse leaned over her and pressed the wee button thing that raised her bed ever so gently, ever so slowly.

Bunty opened her eyes and tried to get the answer to the f*cking borealis thingy. It was there, just beyond her consciousness, but as she reached for it, it slipped away and she was reminded of Tantalus (she had bet it at 8-1 and leading by twa lengths in the final furlong it too faded awa').

'F*ck it!' she thought – and maybe even said aloud, thus shocking the charge nurse who was from Ashgill. 'Ah'll have the full Scottish. White bread, full strength butter. Three sugars... demerara oan the toast. Tetley's: nain o' that poofy Earl Grey shite... '

The nurse smiled, plumped her pillows and as he tripped away he skirted the entourage of Professor (Mr) Kimball... the consultant cardiologist in whose care Bunty was.

(Mr Professor whatsisname has a wee psychological whatsit like all other consultants – they want to be called Doctor (well who wouldn't) rather than *Mister.* Their psychosis - not yet in DSM% (sorry wrong shift key used) is matched by those of university principals that give themselves the title of Professor when all they are is a bunch of failed accountants who have ~~serendipipit~~ by chance wandered into academic management and by a combination of Sod's Law and Buggin's Turn reached the 'top', the otiose baistarts. (Apologies for authorial intrusion: another psychological condition.)

Where were we...?

Actually Mr (Dr) Kimball was one of the more human of the sub-species: he was youngish, had never seen a film in which either James Robertson Justice or Dirk Bogarde appeared (what would (his) Bogarde's even more precious (but much less precious in another sense) brer Humphy have thought of him acting, sorry, *appearing* in such a genre we leave to posterity to judge), and did not feel the need to drive a car that was far too young for him, which was just as well as he was banned; something to do with ... something or other.

And so he addressed Bunty as if she was a sensate human being (which was a wee bit presumptuous at that precise moment in time as she was still trying to resolve that Northern Lights conundrum and wondering whether the Full Scottish Breakfast came with a sweet or pudding, preferably a sweet pudding). But anyway he said:

'We'll have you out in a very few days, Ms Bunty.' Mr Kimball (who was not one-armed) said with a nicely nuanced tone.

'An' Whitfur. Ah jeest love it here.' She said this even though her conscious experience of the Queen Mary/Margaret/Pippa – *Peace be upon her* – Hospital was limited to the previous thirty or so seconds and counting.

'Bed-blocking, dear Ms Bunty. It's all the rage.' And he tapped away at his little tab thingy (a wee handy computer) and expressed himself happy with her vital statistics (though he did not use that term as it is so easy to be on a charge of sexual harassment or racism or ... ageism or something else ending in -*ism* yet to find exploitation then indignation, finally legislation).

'But whit aboot ma heart attack?' Bunty expostulated.

'Fraid not this time, Bunty. *Vasovagal syncope.*'

'Whitsthatthenwhenit'sathame?' Bunty asked.

'It's a name we give to something that we don't have a clue about. Medicine's like that Ms Bunty. When we don't know what causes something we give it a medical-sounding name to make us appear important... and *knowledgeable* to be fairer... '

At which Mr Kimball turned to his team – students: '*Vasovagal syncope* – and switch those damn wee computers and phones off.' He rapped the nearest student on the napper with his knuckles, saying, 'From in here. *Alla prima.*' (Which actually is a term that refers to a painting technique but we'll let him off with it seeing as he is a doctor... well, a mister.)

And one of the students, we would say 'a pretty redhead with lovely green eyes' but that would be sexist, (as he was a male as far as we can tell) said in a lilting Irish accent (we're guessing from about ten miles south of Cobh), 'fainting caused by something triggering the vagal nerve.'

Which was correct and it sounded as if (s)he was as clever as (s)he was (allegedly) pretty or handsome, we'll settle for *pretty handsome*; but as readers will have spotted the answer lay in the question, *syncope* being a medical word for fainting and we all have heard of the *vagal nerve*. Gold stars all round.

'So ah fainted again. Fine. But could you no' put me down for one of those 'we'll keep an eye on you for... say five days things, Doctor?'

But before he could reply just at that moment that nice charge nurse came in with Bunty's Full Scottish Breakfast and in medical language told Mr Kimball and his entourage to get to ph*cque out the way.

Earlier that day the same nurse decided that he was not paid to argue with hard men speaking softly. He had seen enough Taggart episodes (he's quite young but he's got thon Freesat with *Yesterday* on it). He gave a token final tug at the old woman's taut bedsheets and made to slope off.

'Pull the screens,, cherub, wull ye, there's a good girl?' Bunty's favourite (only) nephew Richard whispered. The nurse pulled the screens and left for a safer ward, the one ten minutes away on his WD40'd roller blades.

Richard sat and looked at the tiny figure in the bed, a sad smile forming, twisting his long facial scar into the start of a 'Z'. He wondered what if anything the wee wumman he regarded was thinking and thought back to the best two years of his childhood when he went to live with his great, Great Aunty Binty. Great in both senses, just magic. (Sadly for the rest of humanity these all too short two years to him were not 'formative' in any permanent or civilising sense.)

And now look at her, Richard thought. In a coma. *'Sno' right'.* He spoke softly over his Aunty Binty's comatose body. Things like this were always somebody's fault to Richard. Somebody was to blame. Somebody has to pay *Someone wull pay Aunty Binty* he whispered as he reached into his inside jacket pocket.

In the relative cocoon of the screens and over the suddenly subdued hub-bub of hospital noise – it was as if the rest of the Queen Thingummy were as cowed as the recently departed nurse – Richard began what he hoped would be communication with the only person he had ever respected or listened to – at least for those two years.

From his best leather jacket, reserved for weddings, funerals and Big Jobs like this one. He took out a small metal object, aimed it at Aunty Binty and hit the button.

'Oh-ho-ho-yes, I'm the Great Pretender', Tony Williams of The Platters crooned silkily.

Richard was sure he saw a flicker of recognition behind Aunty Binty's right eye. This was going to work. It had to. Aunty Binty's all-time favourite song from 1955 would let Richard into what had really happened to her. And there it was again – the twitch. Even if her mortal coil was becoming completely un-sprung, there was spirit there somewhere... he was glad he had thought of this when he had last visited his Aunty in her coma.

There was another positive outcome of Richard's assiduity in visiting Bunty every day to play *The Great Pretender* – from that day forward until the end of time, he could not get the fu*king song out of his head. Ever.

The next day, like sleeping beauty (well no' exactly) Bunty came completely out of her coma. And after swearing because she had just been about to solve that business about the Northern Lights when she woke up, the first thing that she remembered was her line. HER WINNINGS!!! Had it been collected? Then she saw this hulk sitting morosely at the side of her bed making a complete djuck of a song she had hated almost it seemed, the whole of her life: *The Great Pretender*.

Using her time compression powers, Bunty told that great hulk Richard about her line and asked did he know what had happened to it, meantime she weaned herself off of all those tubes and drugs and got dressed and … made her way poste-haste to Laird and Son Turf Accountant.

When she (and he, the big fella) arrived, she almost fainted (syncope, remember?) for the whole effing shebang was done up like as if it was a Hillbrokes or even a LadHills, and way far better than yon Packie Power shoaps.

'Right!' she expostulated. 'That's hit. They've used my money - my winnings! - to tart this place up.' She turned to Richard who went to the car – which we forgot to mention – from where he took one of his favourite sledgehammers (he had got a whole set of them one Christmas – a traditionalist, Richard had not taken to the Wickes Powastrike 10lb Sledge, (£26.49 atow); I mean, who could blame him: it has a fibreglass handle – whit if his mates saw him wi' it? Nuff said. And so, instead electing for the hickory-handled ten-pounder: the weapon of choice).

As soon as she entered the music started to fade down; the lights became softer; she noticed Nearly and Argy smiling shyly at her – the pair o' baistarts hadn't visited her once but they had reasoned that since she was comatose, she would never ken. Seems fair enough.

From behind the grille – which had in fact been replaced with customer friendly glass – Mungo came towards her holding out one hand to clasp hers. She stepped back and Richard made to move in. Raising his sledge-hammer (hickory shaft; none of your fibreglass here), he prepared to smite the newly refurbished counter.

But before Richard could strike a blow, the Pole burst out the toilet.

The Pole had been on an underwater swimming course and, having beaten the all-comers western Polish record for swimming underwater while holding a sledgehammer in your teeth, had finally come up with the confidence to take on that bookie's toilet. His brother-in-law, the bottom-hole Pole, had said 'no way' (in Polish) until the Pole had first done his preliminary, preparatory, indelicate bit with the sledgie.

'The Donald Ducking Dudek you playing at?!' demanded the Pole of a nonplussed Richard. 'You Stone-chucking Boruc you?! Bronco Bucking amateur... Me ah got ze Franchise on the hammering of sledges in this *shoap*! (The Pole's one proper Scottish word, albeit vulgar, vernacularish and distinctly argottish, but Scottish nevertheless.)

But he should have known better than to address Richard with the words 'amateur and 'sledgehammererer' inferring a derogatory accusation, if not a 'put-down' thereof.

Richard struck a blow for (amateur) Scotland. On the nearest wall.

The Pole retaliated for all professional, franchised and unfranchised non-indigenous tradesman (pre-Brexit, just, remember). On the opposite wall.

AND so it went on. Mungo, Cosmo, and Raylene watched in helpless shock as the shoap was reduced to even less than its former non-glory in less than forty blows, none of which unfortunately landed on either sledge hammerer.

Mungo mused on his apparent but fairly evident ruin.

'Something will turn up,' he may have said out loud as the dust refused to settle.

Epilogue 1

The explanation explained

Mungo and Ethel's faithful myrmidon, Mourinho – acting on his own initiative, and under instruction from his employers (which sort of contradicts calling him a 'myrmidon', but there you go), went into the casa-rental business while the Lairds were offski getting Ethel's wee internal unknown thing seen to, while giving Mungo an opportunity to try and raise more dosh to let them live a life back in Iberia that they had come to expect.

Mourinho's rehabilitation: A WEE REMINDER WHAT THIS WAS ABOUT – was further facilitated by a courtesy call from an outreach[81] branch of associates of owners of English fitba clubs and supporters of the London property market (Polonium wing). They made an offer he was not tempted or able to decline (mute remember) for the casa he had been instructed to rent out until the return of Mungo and Ethel. The offer was in hard cash (Swedish Krona – everybody thinks that country is perfect in every way, except the turnips (no offence meant, diversity, diversity, diversity) themselves; and who would even consider euros today – Toytown *and* Monopoly currency). It was generous given the circumstances (Vladimir et al were not to know that Mourinho would have settled for them just untying him and letting him scratch his arse. And so with the inevitable confusion that arises in international negotiations, the impatience of our friends from the Steppes (not the leafy outer suburb of Riddrie) was demonstrated by the rough push on M,

---

[81] *The outreach model used was not dissimilar to that of Scottish Opera – they turn up at the village hall in a wee braw toon in the Western Isles and the folks crowd in thinking there might be a ceilidh in the offing. The doors are locked and they sit for three hours listening to one of those pieces that everyone kens anyway from an advert for British Airways or, if they're really auld, for Esso Petrol. And they better enjoy it. It's 'Culture'. And no getting hame until the feedback form is **correctly** completed.*

out the front door, bulging satchel[82] in his hand, listening to the door and louvered window locks snapping shut.

And so with an insouciance that he had pickedup from Mungo, he took himself and his satchel to the nearest beach café, where over the next few hours and more than a few refreshing sangrias, he whiled away the remains of the day, not doing a crossword or translating *Night Train to Lisbon*, (the movie is better than the book, by the way, despite having Jeremy Irons in the main part), but listening to the crackle of gunfire from the Casa Laird.

Next day the ~~Borrfoot Herald reported~~ *The Algarve and Finisterre Eagle* reported that a splinter group calling itself the Iberian Supporters of the London Property Market (Official Wing) had turned up to open discussions on the ownership of the Casa, the whereabouts of the Krona and, most importantly that authentic Russian military satchel from the 1950s, which had sentimental value to their commander who had worked in Budapest as a defenestrator of Magyar hooligans/anti-revolutionaries. The local ~~rag~~ newspaper also quoted the police chief as saying that ordinary citizens – including Brits in this case – need fear nothing as our Russian friends always use low-calibre pistols that do not have significant ricochet velocity, nor are they dum-dum, and that anybody that claims to have suffered from fragmentation wounds should check their travel insurance provider.

From Mourinho's perspective he thought he was Krona-in because at the end of the carnage – the house was abandoned by the dead and alive alike.

---

[82] *This is no ordinary satchel, by the way: authentic Russian military satchel from the 1950s in a high quality leather. It has a detachable and adjustable strap. The satchel opens up to numerous compartments and pockets. This satchel was part of a military surplus in the city of Budapest, Hungary. It also features several authentic military number stamps. **This satchel will add that classic, robust look to any outfit and is perfect to hold your tablet and/or small laptop**; or indeed your Makarov pistol Пистолет Макарова (available atow on Etsy – the satchel, not the gun)*

He had, as if by a miracle, secured the Casa and a bag of hard cash. And what did he choose to do? Make off with it? Despite his background – Kings Lynn (nearly Essex) boy an' that, cousin of you-know-who, no, he chose to do the decent thing and as soon as he could get an Entitlement Card he hot-footed to Borrfoot of which he had heard much... but he was still willing to give it a go.

And so he set of on an epic journey the likes of yon Ranulphffff FFFFienes would not have thought about.

His passage from the Western Mediterranean (avoiding Royal Caribbean – Wolf Blass @ $35?!) was almost Hannibalian in heroism: he caught a local bus outside Faro, it took him to the airport where his entitlement card was at first viewed with suspicion by the security forces. A chat with one of the lovelies of a low-price airline that will be nameless led to him getting a jump seat with the lass doubling up on him, (which reminds us, *Catch Me If You Can*, worth a swatch, even with *both* Di Caprio *and* Hanks in the leads; could start a timber mill with them). It was worth it – even if the plane was impounded for not paying landing fees and was going nowhere.

FROM THERE, without an elephant in sight (Hannibal allusion earlier) he made his way north without further incident of note, with a perfectly pleasant channel crossing memory in a container receding as he contented himself picking up a smattering of Romanian, Serbo-Croat and a few useful phrases in Munji and Ossetic that would stand him in good stead should he ever have to take a sudden holiday to one or two remote villages in eastern Iran (he better hurry on this one: they're dying out). He assured some of his table companions that given a choice between the NHS and the hell-holes they were escaping, he would tend towards the former; and that if they should find themselves ever in need of a bed for the night they could always get a welcome at this address (Farage's constituency office in south Thanet).

In London, he was treated like a foreigner – which he was and all to the good, for everyone was kind and helpful; especially when he mentioned Borrfoot, which to many, was like Eldorado (not the wine) or Shangri-La (not the hotel chain), or Nirvana, (yes, the rock band). And so he was set on his way.

But serendipity if not simply good luck was as always at work. A louche-looking banker type, (probably ex-Paribas going by the red galluses holding up his Givenchy 'Start-and-Stripes' (£410, Harrods atow)) loitering outside Euston station claimed to 'ken Borrfit like the back o' ma haun' and offered to guide Mourinho northwards for the price 'o a cuppa tea' and a second class single plus a fourth class dining car snack (or two) plus continuous cans of Carlsberg Special.) But during the negotiations a crowd gathered, all of them agitated; all of them insisting that he take them with him, so much had they heard of this mythical Borrfoot. And at that a small group of women of the female gender, if not persuasion, approached him – there were three of them and they looked like what a captain of police would have termed, *types roumanie* – and thrust their hands into every pocked he had. And lo, when he recovered, and they had melted away in the style of *types roumanies*, and fearing the worst, M found that the little group of *types roumanies* had stuffed his *poches* with marzipan (marţipan), and sweetmeats of diverse types.[83]

Arriving at Glasgow Central, and greeted in the Taiwanese fashion by hordes (no ethnic slur intended) of train-meeters-and-greeters, Sanny (the louche banker) fully introduced himself to Mourinho as his personal customer relations bod, and asked how could he help. Having conveyed his goal to the inestimable Sanny, the young man susurrated winsomely, 'When a wiz wee, Borrfoot wis known as the shite-hole o' the world. Bested only by Nullson. Today? They're queuing up to get in. Gentrification is the name of the game. Why do you think the Merchant City east of Candleriggs is emptying? Borrfoot Mania. Worse than the Beatles variety. I've got my name down for a single-end. Nae chance.' With that he sighed and lowered himself to a bench whereupon a pair of transport police told him to move along.

---

[83] *There is no logical explanation for this behaviour; but it was probably a sort of compensatory gesture of shame for what those same three wee types roumanies did to one of the writers on a train between Antibes and Cagnes-sur-Mer. Bastairts!*

Borrfoot residents are renowned for trying to outdo Glaswegians in their pursuit of winning the Scottish accolade of *the friendliest*. And so it proved from Borrfoot rail station all the way to the bottom of the steep hill. The three Borrfooters finally resolved their argument about the quickest way, shook hands with each other then, Mourinho, simultaneously wishing him 'guid luck wi the climb, pal' and went their very separate ways.

Mourinho changed hands with the bag of Krona (and one pair of underpants and two pairs of socks – he did have delicate feet, and the constant threat of athlete's foot – in both feet) and took his first sensitive step onto the steeply upward pavement adjoining the long and winding narrow road. It was a small price to pay for reparation, to his mind a token payment for redemption of his previous sins of ambition and hubris and hopefully a major step towards regaining his speech if not his sanity.

Ethel had decided. The Algarve was better. Borrfoot of old had been a much better place for her temperament: there had been so much to legitimately complain about in those far off days: the cold, the rain, and of course the wind. The townspeople. But now? What was there to mump about? The weather was perfect – the heat of the day tempered by spring-like sunshine of an evening; the balm of the warm zephyrs from the south. But what was there to go back to – apart from those all-too-friendly small dark folk? When Mungo admitted the problem with the bookies and Bunty's bet, and that they would need to sell their place in the sun well… she had sat down with Idris and poured out her heart to her dearest (and only) friend. And at the end of it all, Idris had said the words that acted like a panacea or maybe a placebo or a P… (*Give 'Ps' a chance* we say… diversity is here to stay. Like obesity…):

'Itsnoferrsoitsno.'

And that was that – Ethel reconciled herself to not blaming Mungo. More than once he had said in the past: 'My dear Ethel, social mobility… must, needs, imply that some people will move up and some will move down.'

Later that same day – actually as soon as Idris left to feed the wolves – Ethel reverted to type and blamed and cursed… whatshisname, that little, evil Portuguese bastard… Mourinho!

She took an axe from the harness-room (all thoughts of those crazy days with Mungo set aside despite the scent of leather, the jingle of the buckles and the roar of her blood pressure in her ears) and stepped outside. And there he was.

She saw him. She must be hallucinating. No, she had had only the one Buckie that morning. The ugly conifer soughed and collapsed with her last stroke towards the utterly frightened little visage as a very grim faced Ethel hefted the axe again.

'Me next,' Mourinho thought half in Portuguese (non-Brazilian), half in Cowardese, his quick brain also reckoning that any scribbled note of explanation for his arrival to Senhora Laird would be much too slow to save him from the chop. He knew the Senhora barely tolerated him in the casa despite his very best efforts of serving her *mao e pe*. She could not have known that her asides to Senhor about the 'surly houseboy' were fully comprehended by his excellent English (for Kings Lynn). And now, she must believe that he had run away with the proceeds from the sale of the casa… That face!

Ethel was still in doubt. Maybe she was ill. Imagining things. How could Mourinho of all people be here in Borrfoot? She now walked round the conifer and looked down the steps. No sign… except a large satchel lay on the grass verge underneath the stone angel. Now that certainly wasn't there before. Surely not?

Two pairs of men's black socks, one pair of men's boxer shorts later, Ethel passed out.

The stone angel looked down and tried to smile with as much success as it had had these last hundred years in trying to fly this cowp.

Epilogue 2

Idris Redux: with one limp they were free

'Here youse out there,' Idris interjected. 'It just seemed to me that compared with the last buik, (Lallans for *Book* not Buick) ah'm no innit as much as ah was. So ah tellt thon writers that and it just goes to show, if you complain enough – tae the right people – it's worth it. So. It seems ah'm gonna get the last word – the *denouement* explained. Actually ah'm quite used to it – did it in their last book *Skelp-something-or-other...* the *Senescent* or sumthin'... anyway the reviews highlighted that *literary device* and how I had *carried it off with panache*; which makes a change from me carrying it off in an ash-pan.

Between you and me, that got right up the writers' noses – professional jealousy, if you ask me – so they wrote my part down until I created a stink. See that previous bit, aboot Mourinho and dodgy characters with accents and guns etc., that's whit the writers, and Mungo, would like you (and Ethel) to think. It's aw aboot men!

No that ah'm some sort of strident feminist, by the way, but it was the same in their previous buik – they wanted to have it that a man, actually ma man, Tim, in the last yin – came to the rescue. It's a boys' thing. The cavalry come over the brae and they're all men by the way. Well just as in the last buik, that's no' quite how it was. In fact, it's nothing like it was. And they would prefer that I said hee-haw aboot it. But too late – you create a character and sometimes it takes on a life of its own so they say. I'm going to tell how it really was. Enough ego for now...

So here's how Mungo *et fils* – that's a wee bit of French, by the way that I picked-up in yon last buik – here's how they got out of the fix whereby the owed thoosans tae wee Bunty (god-love-her) and having spent mair thoosans on doing up the shop – which by the way they borrowed from that tart Meg from the loan sharks. Okay tae be fair, she's got braw legs and she's entitled tae wear sussies with them pins, and is it her fault that old Mungo gets frisky and frothy in her presence?

ANYWAY the old yin owes money on every side and they cannae pay Bunty because neither *pere* or *fils* remembered to lay-off her line despite having instructions from Raylene – nice lassie that, by the way – and they need a solution pronto for Ethel is kicking up mair than stoor and just at that, Bunty has her *vasovagal syncope* which was timeous. And there is a long discussion about the ethical dilemma they find themselves in and Bunty is taken away to the Queen Mary or is it Queen Margaret? The Southern Effin General by any other name...

ANYWAY, Does Bunty no turn up on recovery wi' yon heid-banger nephew Richard and he's got his favourite sledgehammer – the one wi' the hickory shaft weighing in at ten pounds (*avoirdupois*, that is; don't have a price atow) – and is about to wreck the joint when, after a wee professional dispute wi' the Pole – who had the balls to call Richard an amateur and does Bunty no' get the thoosans she's owed? So how come?

Saved by the intervention of a braw specimen of the weaker sex: Raylene. On the day she was leaving her joab to go to thon poncy bookies wi' the TV screens, the biscuits, the coffee the gaming machines – *Please Gamble Responsibly:* Aye right! – does Raylene no give a wee hug of endearment and encouragement to Bunty. Whereon Bunty told her secret – that she was sure this line was going to come up. Which we know it did. And we know that Mungo and Cosmo had failed to lay it off with Benny Queen. The amount due to Bunty would wipe out Laird and Son before they even got going. AND Mungo owed money to Meg's – cracking legs – company that paid for the uber-tarting-up to make the shoap appear like Hillbrokes and that other mob. Result? Financial Disaster all round. The loan sharks, not for the first time in that old goat Mungo's life are circling.

Ethical dilemma time – Bunty collapses. Ethel has her betting-slip. After a family conclave, they decide they must do the decent thing. They will hold the money until Bunty recovers – meantime try and keep the place open. But after a week a call comes from Benny the Queen: *Mr Mungo: you trying to* *torture me? When the ph*cque are you going to collect your winnings – from the lay off bet?*

They think it's a cruel hoax. Then Benny himself appears with the loot. How come? Because the last act of Ray, knowing father and son would mess it all up, was to lay-off Bunty's line. *Enough Money* all round, plus all that money from Mourinho.

With one bound they were free. Well, in the case of Mungo, with one limp he was free. And as far as Ethel's concerned, that's The Truth and Mung's sticking tae it. An' that's how it really was. So there.

[By the way, if I was writing the thing, I'd have had Ray marry that glaikit Cosmo tae turn him intae a real man. And I'd have it that when she tossed the bouquet, it wid huv been caught by Betty the Stoker. Romantic, whit? But apparently they twa greedy writers are haudin aw that (an a lot mair) back for the Next Buik. But ah'll huv the Last Word again. So There!]

END

APPENDICES

Medical Note 1: one of the many advantages a good tonic wine has over cocaine, is that one preserves *the integrity of the nasal septum* while the other… well let's just say, the eminent consultant abdomenoplastician Mr (Doctor) Sartram (*Skelp the Aged*) would be happy to apply his skills to rebuilding that thing between the nostrils. Not that we are remotely suggesting (snigger, snigger) that those of you who have no septum due to an over-reliance on the wee white powder derived from the coca leaf (or your local supplier/dentist) in other words if you have one great cavernous nostril where there should be two – we are not suggesting that there is something queer looking about you. Just saying like, not to cause offence. We celebrate diversity. We cannot afford to be too sniffy about such matters.

Medical Note 2: Among the mental effects noted among typical Cocainites, are loss of contact with reality and an intense feeling of euphoria. In this respect it is not so much different from a good Buckie.

Medical Note 3: Speaking medicalese: it's actually quite simple this language: if things are swollen then you just give the name of the thing and add – *itis*. (Though where your 'phleb' or the 'burs' is to be precisely detected among the myriad veins and the veritable plethora of bursae (bursi?) remains a mystery to at least one of the authors) If things need cut off, then add: *ectomy*. (If you can find a surgeon who definitively kens where the *phleb* in question is and do beware of dyslexic surgical knifers who mistake a bursa for a burka or indeed a pleb for a phleb …it is no easy life being a surgeon or being dyslexic. As for both …phew.) All else is swarf (though do not add that to any part of your person other than your hands – viz: the *Journal* *of dermatological aetiology*, (vol. 3, p—123-124, 1983; apologies if this does not fit with the Harvard System of referencing – we just can't seem to get the hang o' it.)

Medical Note 4: Contrary to popular opinion and conventional wisdom,the *Sunday Post* AND the *Daily Mai,*l the vast majority of liver malaise is **not** caused by alcohol but in fact by **over-eating**. And this was indeed the case with Ethel and her liver illness...finally diagnosed (guessed) some weeks after she had been discharged (decanted/chucked oot).